Scoring Position

A Reformed Playboy Sports Romance

Nashville Songbirds
Book 3

Kat Summers

This book is a work of fiction from the author's imagination. Though inspired by the world around us, all of the characters, places, and events are fictional and not based on any one source. Any resemblance is entirely coincidental.

Scoring Position (Nashville Songbirds, Book 3)

Edited by Emma Jane of EJL Editing

Cover Illustration by Booked Forever

To all the Gigi's out there waiting to be someone's exception: I see you and it will be worth the wait.

Playlist

- Delicate - Taylor Swift
- Cowboys and Angels - Jessie Murph
- You're So Vain - Carly Simon
- Foolish One - Taylor Swift
- Are you from Tennessee? Elana Jane
- Hits Different - SZA ft. Ty Dolly Sign
- Hits Different - Taylor Swift
- Timeless - Taylor Swift

Dick-tionary

For those of you who want to spoil or avoid the spice in this book, take note of the following chapters:
- Chapter 12
- Chapter 13
- Chapter 21
- Chapter 22
- Chapter 24
- Chapter 33
- Chapter 35
- Chapter 38
- Chapter 39

Chapter One

• RAVEN •

October

"Obviously, you're the designer, but I saw a post on Joanna Gaines' Instagram the other day and..." the Brentwood soccer mom drones, but I stopped listening. I know what she wants. It's what every other one of the clients I work with wants: white kitchens, shiplap, exposed beams, blah, blah, blah. Don't get me wrong. It's a clean aesthetic, but everyone is doing it lately. Is it too much to wish for a client who wants dusty blue cabinets or emerald tiles? If I never hear the term 'farmhouse chic' again, it will be too soon.

I've worked at Green Hills Interiors since I graduated from college five and a half years ago. During that time, I have gotten great experience. But it is getting redundant. I unwittingly cornered the market for the suburban housewives, which is ironic considering I am the furthest thing from them.

Most people would consider me a hipster, a free spirit, at the very least. My East Nashville home is filled with natural woods, moon-charged crystals, and the world's most judgy cat. I spend my weekends searching for vintage finds at thrift stores and flea markets and avoiding chain restaurants at all costs. If the beautiful shade of my fiery red hair didn't tie me to the other women in my family, it would be lavender or some other pastel.

After reassuring my client I can bring her vision to life, we finally end the call. Peeking at the clock in my office, it reads 4:53 p.m. It's quitting time; it couldn't come a moment sooner. As I pack up for the weekend, I read a text from my friend Lola.

4:48 PM

LOLA

You're still coming over tonight, right?

ME

Of course! I need this girls' night.

LOLA

Tough week?

ME

You have no idea.

LOLA

Wine will be waiting!

Tucking my phone in my bag, I take a moment to thank the universe for friends like Lola. She and I were close in high school but lost touch during college. She stayed close to home and attended Mizzou while I came to Nashville to get my interior design degree from Belmont. I fell in love with the city and never left. After a nasty divorce, kismet brought Lola here earlier this year, and we reconnected.

It's not that I didn't have friends; I did. But since graduation, we've grown apart. Several of my college friends moved back to their hometowns. The rest got married right away and are in full mom mode. I love that journey for them, but it changes the dynamic since I am chronically single and nowhere near that phase in my life. One day I hope to be, but I'd have to meet a guy who doesn't suck first, and that is proving more difficult than anticipated.

Not to be conceited, but I am conventionally attractive. My long red hair and curvy 5' 7" frame turn enough heads. I may have a sassy attitude, but it comes off as flirty – usually. I'm not afraid to speak up for myself when a guy is being shady, which, in my experience, most of them are, hence my single status.

If it weren't for my brother-in-law and my friends' partners, I would think that men are incapable of meeting my admittedly low bar. Unfortunately for the rest of the male population, Brett, Miller, and Robby prove that if he wanted to, he would. And I'm not willing to accept less.

I've yet to find that 'more' I've been searching for, but I am open to it. I've been on dates with guys of all shapes, sizes, and astrological signs. But it's been crappy date after crappy date recently. This girls' night could not have come at a better time. I want to ignore my problems and live vicariously through my girls. Orbiting in the world of Major League Baseball players, their lives are far more interesting than mine.

"One of these days, you ladies are going to have to introduce me to these baseball boys.," I say. "I hear all about them, but the only time I see them is on TV and social media. And neither of those places give the impression Kent Dela Cruz is a man who cooks a woman breakfast platonically. Or at all"

"He's a smooth-talking playboy, alright," Tiffany states. "I think of him as a slightly less dumb Joey Tribiani. Out in the world, he's sowing his wild oats, but with us, he is a stand-up guy."

"'Slightly less dumb' being the operative phrase," Carina jokes. "But he is loyal and there when you need him."

Carina is married to Nashville Songbirds pitcher Robby Becker, and Lola is (was?) dating the team's first baseman, Brady Miller.

They're going through a rough patch after a media scandal, which turned out to be nothing. However, it made Lola realize she hadn't completed all the healing she needed after her divorce. They've spent the last few weeks on a break while she works on herself and the team focuses on the playoffs.

We're at Lola's condo tonight, celebrating the Cami Graham show inviting her to create a weekly self-care segment. It's a huge deal and a major step forward in her career. This announcement led to her cousin, Carina, and her roommate, Tiffany, sharing the great things happening with their jobs. Carina founded a nonprofit with her husband, and Tiffany is a makeup artist at one of the bigger music venues in town. She also does freelance work here and there.

I'm happy for all of them, but I can't help but be envious. My work is steady, and I am one of the lucky ones doing what I got a degree in, but I can't say that I love it. At least not right now. When I first started my job, it was a dream come true. Now, though, it's monotonous and boring. I want to work on more challenging projects. I want to feel as if my designs are making a difference in the world, not simply giving stodgy WASPs something to "ooh" and "ahh" over at their next dinner party.

When Lola expresses her desire to end her break with Miller, I'm happy for her. I'm glad she finally found what she needed and is back on the track she wants to be in her relationship. But I can't say I'm not envious. The second she moved here, Miller fell into her lap. She didn't have to experience the horrors of online dating.

"You bitches have no idea how hard it is out there," Tiffany laments.

"Oh please, Babs, we all know you aren't in the market for anything serious. If anything, you're the dating nightmare," Carina notes.

"Rude," the blonde gasps.

"True, though," Lola laughs. "You are the definition of a nightmare dressed like a daydream."

Tiffany flips her hair. "Whatever. How about you, Raven? Any hotties on your roster worthy of becoming first string?"

I let out a humorless laugh. "Calling it a 'roster' is being extremely generous. Tiffany is right. It is rough out there. It's all hot and cold. It's either guys trying to get in your pants or guys whose moms show up halfway through dessert."

"Wait, that happened to you?" Carina gasps, horrified.

"Oh yeah. And that isn't even the weirdest first date I've been on this month," I reply. "The pickings are slim. You're lucky you locked down Robby when you did."

"Trust me, I had some bad dates before he came back into my life. This one time, I went out with a guy who excused himself halfway through the date to take a phone call. Ten minutes later, he comes back to the table, slightly disheveled. When I asked if he was okay, he said he was fine and ran into an old friend. When I glanced behind him, said old friend was glaring daggers from across the bar with mussed hair and smeared lipstick that matched the smudge under his collar. Apparently, whenever she pissed him off, he'd take some unsuspecting girl on a date. When she'd inevitably find him, they'd hook up in the bathroom before his crazy ass would make her watch the conclusion of the date."

"Okay, wow. Maybe you do get it," I murmur before Tiffany chimes in.

"If the hookup only lasts ten minutes, she's the one who should be mad." We break out into giggles at the disgust on her face.

"In all honesty," I confess, "I think I am due for a break. Or a knight in shining armor. I'll take either at this point. Hell, he doesn't even have to be a knight. I'll take a court jester with his own horse and a cut umbilical cord. At least a jester has a job."

"Don't worry, Ray, you'll find someone when you least expect it. I have a good feeling that something great is right around the corner."

"That's what I'm manifesting," I sigh.

Carina and Lola groan. "Not you, too."

"What? Manifestation is real!" I defend.

"Don't soak in their negativity," Tiffany sympathizes. "I've been trying to get them on board for years."

With that, we shift the conversation to the universe, astrology, and other things my wannabe-hippie heart loves. As we hunker down in the living room, my mind drifts to all the ways my life isn't what I want and how I can get there.

Chapter Two

"Thank you for meeting us in person, Tabitha," my boss, Carl, says in his nasal ass-kissing tone. "It always helps to show samples face-to-face. That way you can see how they work together in real life. Your home is your sacred space, and it needs to be perfect."

"Not just perfect, extraordinary," she corrects. "I want all my friends to eat their hearts out at how beautiful and elevated my new dining room is. I want it to be a space people talk about for months, scrambling with lesser designers to recreate it without appearing too obvious."

It takes a genuine effort not to roll my eyes. Tabitha says she wants to be unique, but we all know she is going to do essentially the same as all her friends. She may upgrade to a lesser-used wallpaper pattern or pick a matte finish over gloss, but this woman is not straying far from societal norms to something remarkable.

"If you want to 'wow' your friends," I chime in, "you should consider making a splash with something out-of-the-box. Looking into the next year, rich, dark tones will be the next 'it' thing. You could paint the walls a deep magenta or even teal. Or if that is a step too far, we could switch the proposed dining chairs with something more daring. Maybe a burnt amber velvet? And match it with a walnut table instead of a painted grey."

The silence on the other side of the room has me tearing my eyes from the wall I zoned out on as I envisioned these options. I gaze up to see Carl staring daggers at me and Tabitha giving me an affronted but curious once over.

"That is certainly one direction to go," Carl grits. "I'm not sure how it would balance with the rest of the neutral palate in the home, though."

"You might be right about that," Tabitha hums. "I don't hate the thought of adding more color. I know! What if we add brass accents to the space? That would break up the grey and white."

"An excellent suggestion," Carl praises.

Gag. Adding another neutral is not at all similar to my suggestion, but his pointed glare tells me not to say anything. We spend a few more minutes discussing fabric and wall art before the mundane meeting is blessedly over.

Walking the client out, she complains about how terrible the traffic will be back to Franklin from Green Hills. "You should see it at rush hour," I lament. "Getting from here to Eastwood is awful."

"You live in Eastwood?" she questions, giving me a once-over.

"I do," I smile tightly. "I've rented a bungalow there since graduating from college."

"You don't own?" she gasps as if in shock a junior interior designer cannot afford to buy a house in the insane Nashville real estate market. Before I can respond, Carl is ushering her out of the door. When he returns, the expression on his face tells me I am not going to enjoy the ensuing conversation.

"Teal walls, Raven? In what world would she have gone for that?" he deadpans.

"She said she wanted something unique! There is nothing unique about adding gold hardware, and you know it."

"Of course, there isn't, but these women don't *really* want something out of the ordinary. They want something different enough to impress their friends while remaining safely in their comfort zone. Unless they see it in HRN magazine, these women won't touch a new trend with a ten-foot shiplap pole."

Exasperated, he continues his reprimand, "Don't suggest something that unorthodox again without first discussing it with me. And for the love of all that is holy, do not mention where you live."

"Why not?" I question indignantly.

"The people who come to GHI expect a certain level of sophistication, and they would be hard-pressed to think anyone who lives on the east side has that. While we find you adequate – if not eclectic – they will not."

With a frustrated sigh, I stomp back to my desk and flop into my chair, throwing myself into sourcing new accents for Tabitha's 'extraordinary' dining room.

When the clock strikes five, I am racing out the door. I am over this day. Hell, I am over this month. I don't know when my love for this job turned to dissatisfaction, but the sense of dread is only growing with time. I'm beyond thankful that it is a Friday, and I don't have to think about work for another sixty hours.

If the weather is nice tomorrow, I might bribe Lola with a maple pecan latte to attend my neighborhood's fall festival. But first, I'm off to splurge on fancy cheese and cheap wine to enjoy while I lose myself in my favorite TV drama and snuggle with my cat.

Of all the chain grocery stores I reluctantly visit, Trader Joe's is my favorite. While perusing the wine selection and trying to decide which red wine will pair best with Diet Coke, I accidentally bump into someone.

"I am sor—Macy?" I say to the person I ran into. I would recognize the beautiful woman anywhere. Macy Martin and I attended Belmont together. While we didn't run in the same circles, we braved Calculus together. Prerequisite math classes are ripe for trauma bonding.

"Raven, I thought that was you. I would recognize that red hair and those curves anywhere," she responds. "How have you been, girl?"

"Oh, you know, living the dream. Working at an interior design firm by day and filling up on booze and dairy by night," I retort, motioning to my basket.

"I hear that," she says, pointing to her champagne and spinach dip haul.

"Fancy," I comment.

"Yeah," she whispers with a blush. "I got a promotion today, which means indulging in my favorite treats. I'll go out with the girls tomorrow to celebrate officially."

"How are the rest of the Heron Heroines?" I ask. Macy was part of a tight-knit friend group who roomed together in Heron Hall freshman year. Ellie, Mia, and Alexis round out the group.

"They're great. Ellie and Mia graduated from grad school in the spring." She leans in conspiratorially. "Ellie is dating Mia's brother now, but that is on the DL."

"Shut up!" I squeal. "Which one?"

"Jack."

"Wow. Good for her," I mutter. "I hope it won't make Thanksgiving awkward."

"Pssh, they'll be fine. Now that I think about it, it is perfect that I ran into you today."

"It is?" I question.

"Yes! With my promotion comes an office of my own, and I am hopeless at anything that has to do with design and aesthetics. Do you think you would help me? I'd pay you, of course! My boss gave me a stipend. They're all about us personalizing our offices. They want it to 'represent me,' whatever that means."

I should say no since GHI frowns upon side projects, but they would never take on a job this small. This remodel could be the perfect cure for the creative rut I've been in.

"Sure," I say. "Do you still have my number? Let's grab coffee next week to discuss details."

She checks her phone and confirms she has my contact info before we hug and part ways. I leave the store more encouraged than I went in, excited to face a new challenge and to try Figgy Cheddar Cheese.

Chapter Three

• KENT •

November

Sitting on my back deck, I stare at the tranquil view before me. Silence surrounds me, and I can relax for the first time in a while. I bought this lakefront property two years ago after signing a new contract with the Songbirds. I didn't want to put down roots somewhere until I would be there for a while. The condo I spend the majority of the season in was something I purchased when I first moved to the city. But this place, my retreat, took longer to find.

I'm a social guy, but I also need to recharge. Whenever things get overwhelming, or I have downtime, I come here. It's the perfect place to unwind after the highs and lows of this past season.

We were close to winning the pennant and going to the team's first World Series in recent memory. Unfortunately, we let LA get the upper hand and take our championship.

As bummed as I am at how our playoffs ended, I am proud of

how I performed. My batting average, home runs, and defensive runs saved were all personal bests. I've improved every season in the league, but this year, I found my stride. I even won my first Golden Glove Award this year.

I found a good status quo in my professional and personal life, with a steady roster of women who want to have fun and go on their merry way. I'm not interested in being tied down. That hasn't stopped a few overly eager cleat chasers from trying, though. I'd feel bad about turning them down, but they know the score. I make it clear before I hook up with a woman they can and can't expect from me.

They *can* expect a fantastic night and multiple orgasms. They *can't* expect a sleepover or any claim on me. I don't do commitment. That leads to hopes for a big white dress and over-hyped cake, and I am not interested.

If we both find ourselves in a situation to have a repeat performance, I'm game. I'm not one of those assholes who will only fuck a girl once. But no matter how many times we're together, the rules don't change. It's pretty simple: keep our encounter out of the press, we always use protection, and commitment is never on the table. I'm no one's boyfriend material.

That's fine with most of the women I'm with. Most want to scream my name and then tell all their friends about it. I can live with that. I don't share anything with them that I wouldn't want to get out. The circle of people I share anything with is small. My mom, Robby, Miller, and the girls are the only people who see more than my playboy persona.

I don't mind that the media has me painted as a Casanova. They call me the Filanderer, which even I can admit is funny given my half-Filipino heritage. I may even play it up in public. Miller and Robby think I'll get tired of this lifestyle, but I don't see that happening any time soon. They may have found the perfect women for them, but that isn't in the cards for me. Maybe my mind will change after I retire, but after seeing teammates go through divorces and my parents' disastrous union, marriage holds little appeal.

If this mythical woman my boys claim will knock me on my ass and have me changing my ways shows up, I'll be sure to run the other direction.

Chapter Four

"Stupid downtown parking," I grumble as I knock on the door to Robby and Carina's penthouse.

"Ray! I am excited you could make it," the hostess greets.

"Hi, Care," I say in return. "Thank you for having this. Sorry, I'm late. Finding a parking space was a nightmare."

"Oh my gosh, I know. Make sure you have one of the guys walk you out if you parked far away."

I wave off her suggestion as I enter the open-concept kitchen and living room. God, this condo is beautiful. I would love to get my hands on it or any of the units in this building. Carina has done a great job of blending her and Robby's tastes. The unit has a lofty, masculine vibe with a homey, feminine twist.

Too busy admiring the decor, I trip over my feet and almost slam into Miller. Luckily, he grabs my forearms to steady me. "Careful."

"Sorry," I respond sheepishly as he checks me over for any obvious injuries.

"Can I take that to the kitchen for you?" Lola questions, pointing at the casserole dish of mac and cheese I prepared for this Friends-giving feast.

"I got it, thanks, though. Let me set this down, then I can hug you properly."

"Sounds good," she laughs. "I'll grab you a drink. Cranberry Apple Cider Sangria or Spiced Pear Mule?"

"Sangria, please!"

Placing my contribution down on the ginormous kitchen island, I survey the food options. Aside from the standard turkey, dressing, sweet potato casserole, and pumpkin pie, I see intriguing additions such as goat cheese and butternut squash ravioli. I assume it is a recipe from Carina and Lola's Nonna. Another dish appears to be spring rolls. They're not on-brand for the holiday, but I'm sure they're delicious.

"Those are Lumpia. But instead of ground pork, they're filled with ham," a smooth voice remarks from behind me as a tanned forearm cages me in on one side.

"Are they any go—" The words die on my tongue as I turn around and meet a pair of firm pecs. Whoever the mystery voice is attached to stands so close that I am forced to peer up at him. As my gaze travels, I see a strong, square jaw, pouty lips, and deep brown eyes that lure me in.

A knock at the door jolts me out of the trance this beautiful man has put me in. I know he can tell his effect on me when his smile turns into a smirk.

"Hi, Red. I'm Kent. I don't think we've had the pleasure of meeting before."

Right. Now that I take in his features as a whole instead of beautifully separate puzzle pieces, I recognize the right fielder for the Nashville Songbirds. I lean back to put a couple of inches of space between us. Taking the hint, he shuffles backward, grin still firmly planted on his handsome face.

"Raven," I state with a roll of my eyes.

"Huh?" He tilts his head, resembling a confused puppy. It's a level of cute that a man with this jawline shouldn't be able to achieve.

"Raven," I repeat. "That's my name. Not Red."

"You sure? I bet you could handle the big bad wolf," he croons while his thumb skims my hip. I jerk at the contact and lock into those chocolate eyes again.

"Are you going to huff and puff and blow my house down?" I flirt, matching his energy. This man is clearly an Aquarius.

"I'd do much more than that, babe." The twinkle in his eye and his teasing tone cause my core to heat up at his insinuation. I have no doubt this man could do terribly wonderful things to my neglected body.

When was the last time I let someone else touch me? Six months, at least. Has it been that long since I've had a genuine connection? Maybe it's time I bought a new toy to liven things up.

Before we can say anything else, Lola breaks the tension. "Beat it, Dela Cruz."

"I'm just talking to the nice lady," he says in mock offense.

"And I'm the Queen of England. You can't handle this one, Kenny Boy. Move it along," Lola retorts.

His smirk returns as he faces Lola. "It's a pleasure serving you, Your Majesty. You look fantastic for an elderly corpse. Reunited with Diana yet?" he quips. "And I think I know exactly how to handle this firecracker."

"You're incorrigible. Go," she says with a shooing motion.

"Later, Blossom," he whispers as he holds up his hands in surrender. With a cocky grin, he plucks a deviled egg off the table and walks over to chat with a group of his teammates.

"So that's Kent," I observe, more a statement than a question.

"The one and only," Lola replies. "He wasn't bothering you, was he? I can have Brady talk to him."

"No, he was fine. I can handle a little flirting. He is almost exactly as I expected him to be."

"Almost?"

"Yeah, there is something about him that is almost... endearing? Someone with that much sex appeal should not be able to pull off coy."

Lola scoffs. "There is nothing coy about that man. He is trouble with a capital T."

"I can see the Joey thing now."

"Mmm," she hums. "Okay, enough about him. I have more people I want to introduce you to, and I know Carina and Tiff want to have some girl time."

As she pulls me over to chat with our friends, I glance around the room and see a pair of brown eyes tracking my movements. When he sees that I caught him watching, he shoots me a wink – that coyness from earlier is nowhere in sight.

Sipping on my third glass of Sangria, I moan as I take another bite of the Lumpia dipped in cranberry sauce. However, my time savoring the dish is cut short by Lola clearing her throat. "If Raven is done having a religious experience with her dinner, I have something to run by y'all."

Carina snickers as Tiffany comes to my defense. "Don't interrupt her, Lo. It sounds like she's getting close. Not everyone enjoys being edged."

I choke on my next bite.

"Oh my God, Babs," Carina gasps. The blonde simply shrugs.

"Anyway," Lola continues, ignoring our friends and their foolishness. "What do you ladies think about going on a trip for my birthday?"

"I'm in," Tiffany states.

"I haven't even said where yet," Lola points out.

"As if she needs an excuse to travel," Carina teases.

"Damn right, Meatball."

"Where do you want to spend your birthday?" I ask.

"Not technically my birthday, but New Year's Eve. Brady and I were thinking about taking a trip to Vegas."

"Brady wants to go to Vegas? That isn't his scene at all," Carina questions.

Lola offers us an angelic smile. "He does now that I've suggested it."

"Is there anything he wouldn't do to make you happy?" Tiffany snorts.

"Not that I've found," Lola giggles with a dreamy expression. "Are you in?"

"Vegas, baby!" we all cheer together.

Chapter Five

My fanbase would be shocked to know that Kent Dela Cruz loves a potluck. Cooking is one of the ways I de-stress and is a guilty pleasure. I don't get to do it often during the season with our schedule, but I try to cook a few meals during home stands. I especially love cooking traditional Filipino dishes that my mom made growing up. They aren't as good as hers, but they hit the spot.

Mom taught me that there is no purer gesture than to feed someone; to take care of one of their most basic needs. Plus, food can bond people in ways other activities can't. It is one of the things that brought Tiffany and me close, and now I can't imagine my life with that bubbly blonde. Anytime we walk of shame at the same time – or as she calls it, run The Orgasm Trail – I ply her into my apartment with the promise of garlicky rice, eggs, and sausage.

Friends enjoying my food gives me a deep sense of accomplishment. It hits different from when I perform well on the field. Which is good as it is the off-season, and my ego needs stroking since I don't have forty-five thousand fans cheering for me several times a week.

This need for validation is why I am lingering near the buffet at Carina and Robby's Friendsgiving. I want to watch people enjoy my food. Plus, aside from the bar, it is the social hub. It is also where I find myself when a drop-dead gorgeous redhead arrives at the party. I have no idea who she is, but I am eager to find out.

After almost running into Miller, she brings her dish to the island and puts it with the other sides. I see her eyeing my contribution curiously. Deciding this is the perfect opportunity to introduce myself, I saddle up beside her, grazing the curve of her shapely hip as I place one arm on the counter.

When I go to explain my dish to her, the scent of mint and something floral surrounds me. I watch her gaze travel up my face, and her light brown eyes connect with mine; whatever she was about to say dies on her tongue. We both stand there entranced in one another until a knock sounds on the door.

The interruption allows me to regain some of my composure and slip back into the charming persona ladies love. It also gives me a second to remind my dick that no matter how soft her lips undoubtedly are, we are not on the menu. Not yet, anyway.

As we exchange flirty bars, I can't help but notice how she rolls her eyes in the cutest way. Wait, cute? That is not usually a word I use to describe women. Hot? Sure. Gorgeous? Absolutely. Sexy? You know it. But 'cute' is something I typically reserve for my friends and puppies. Somehow, it is the only description I can come up with for her action, aside from enticing.

When I call her 'Red,' her brows furrow, dislike for the nickname palpable. Duly noted. I'll find something else to call her other than the name she helpfully provided. Before I can try something new, Lola barges over, passes Raven a drink, and all but declares her friend off-limits. Nice try, but that makes me want her more.

Saying goodbye for now, I join in a conversation with two of my teammates, Robby and Crews, about our local NBA team, the Knights. As Lola drags her friend away to chat with the other girls, I watch her gaze seek me out. When her eyes meet mine again, I send a wink to let her know I caught her checking me out. I hold in my chuckle at her blush when she turns away.

The rest of the night, I steal glances at the beautiful redhead. I can't help the pride that wells in my chest when she eats my lumpia. She appears to be dipping it into the cranberry sauce, a novel idea I try myself when no one is watching. It's delicious.

It's almost as delicious as Raven herself. She's the tallest of the women here. She's not a giant by any means, but I'd put her at about 5' 7" without the boots that travel up her long legs. Displaying several inches of creamy skin, I'm curious how her suede boots would feel rubbing against my shoulders while my face was buried under her skirt. A turtleneck covers the skin on her torso, but it does nothing to hide her curves.

Both preoccupied with our friends, I don't get the chance to talk to her again before the party wraps up. Luckily, as she leaves, I hear Carina tell her she'll ask Robby to walk Raven out. This is the perfect opportunity to chat with her without any interruptions.

"I can do it," I volunteer. Raven's eyes widen, but Carina doesn't notice.

"Oh, that's perfect. Thanks, Kent. She had to park down the block, and you know how crazy it can get out there." She's not wrong. Our condos – I live a few floors below – are located off the most prominent party street in the city. It can get wild at night.

"Of course, Care. We wouldn't want her to get swept away by the masses." The girls hug a final time before Raven grabs the bag of leftovers our hosts forced on us all. Leading her to the elevator, I take it from her hands.

"Oh, thanks," she replies.

"You're welcome, ladybug."

"Ladybug?"

"What?" I laugh. "No good?"

"No good," she confirms as we exit into the lobby of the building.

"Damn, you're a hard lady to please," I respond while waving to the desk attendant and ushering Raven in front of me.

"And don't you forget it," she sasses.

"I love a challenge," I whisper against her neck, smiling when I hear her gasp.

"Which way, Annie?"

"Annie? Hard no, if anything, I am over-parented. And left."

"Hey, I was partial to ladybug. You're the one who demanded more options."

"You could call me Raven," she suggests.

"Where's the fun in that?"

"Keep workshopping. I'm no ladybug."

"You might be right about that," I muse as we stroll down Fifth Street toward her car. "You've got too much fire to be a ladybug."

"You got that right," she mutters quietly. We spend the rest of the walk in companionable silence. Typically, I'd fill it by flirting, but not having to be full-on after a night of socializing is nice. I know I won't get anywhere with her tonight, and I don't want to ruin our rapport by coming on too strong. She is close with Lola and the other girls. I'm sure I'll run into her again.

"This is me," she says when we reach a small, green SUV. "Thanks for walking me. I would have been fine, but Carina is a worrier."

"It's not a problem. Walking off that meal couldn't hurt. It will make the morning workout much easier."

"Ah, the life of an athlete," she teases.

"Being this sexy takes work, gingersnap."

"Gingersnap?"

"Yep. You're sweet, but you have a kick to you." I can't see her blush, but how she shakes her head and glances down tells me she is. "Drive safe."

"Bye, Big Shot," she singsongs as she gets in her car and shuts the door. I smile at the endearment. Watching her pull away, I wonder what other names I could get her to call me and if they would sound as sexy coming from her lips.

Chapter Six

As the bass from the club pulses through my bones, I survey the dance floor from the VIP section. This isn't my typical scene. I prefer Holler's or one of the bars on Broadway, but Derrick convinced me to come check out DJ the Kid, an up-and-comer in the city. I can't lie; the guy spins a sick set.

Derrick isn't my favorite guy on the team; he may be one of my least favorite, but he's always down to go out. With Miller and Robby wife'd up, options are limited. I spot my teammate mixed into the crowd, sandwiched between two women who are here with a bachelorette party based on their color-coordinated outfits and penis crowns. It wasn't too long ago that I would be beside him, mixed into the fray.

Now, I watch the party play out in front of me. I don't know if I'm having an off night or if my mom's visit is getting to me. When she was here last week for Thanksgiving, we spent a relaxing week together before she returned to Seattle to prepare her students for exams. We had another long discussion where I tried to convince her to retire or at least move here. My career is stable now, and I have roots in the city. The only thing missing is her. There are plenty of universities she could work at.

When I asked her why she wouldn't commit to moving here, she said, "*Nonoy*, it's too soon for me to move here. When you find a girl and settle down, then I will come to help raise my grandbabies. Until then, I am happy where I am."

If only she knew settling down is nowhere on my horizon. I enjoy my lifestyle with few commitments. I have to give so much of myself to the game that I don't want anything else placing expectations on me. Not to mention, the women I meet aren't the type you bring home to mom – or mom home to, as it were.

Before I am sucked too deeply into that line of thinking, I see a flash of red in the crowd. I lean over the railing to see if I can get a better view when my eyes land on who I am searching for. A woman with flowing ginger locks is wrapped up in the arms of some wannabe good ole boy in unmarred boots. My chest constricts until she turns around, and I see that this redhead isn't the one who's been haunting my dreams.

Ever since I met Raven at Robby and Carina's party, she has been in the back of my mind. Something about her caught my attention and hasn't let go. I rarely get hung up on a woman, but the vixen has ensnared me. She's a combination of sexy and cute you don't often see, at least not in my circles. The fact that she couldn't give two shits who I was and was openly rolling her eyes at me only adds to her appeal.

When I remember I am at a club surrounded by hundreds of beautiful women, I shake my head at myself. This is precisely why I have the rules I do. I don't have the time or desire to get involved with anyone beyond surface level, and I can tell from meeting Raven once that she isn't a casual girl. Downing the rest of my drink, I lumber down the stairs, intending to find something or someone to distract myself from the sensual girl whose honey-brown eyes plague me.

Hours later, I peel myself out of my Uber and march into the lobby of my building. I succeeded in finding a distraction, and Kelly – or Kelsey or Keiley, whatever her name was – and I had a fantastic time. After the prerequisite amount of cuddling, I hightailed it home to my bed. You don't spend as much money as I did on this mattress to sleep on a flight attendant's IKEA monstrosity.

As I run to catch the elevator, I am greeted by a familiar sight. "Hey Tiffy," I croon at one of the few women in my life I know has pure intentions.

"Hi, Kenny Boy," she replies with her bright smile and mussed appearance.

"You're getting in late, young lady. What am I going to do with you?"

"Make me waffles?" she asks hopefully.

"I think I can manage that."

When we walk into my condo, Tiffany flings herself onto the couch and snuggles into a throw blanket I know I didn't buy.

"Where did that come from?" I question.

"I left it here a couple of weeks ago. It's getting chilly, and your place isn't cozy."

"Just because I don't have seventeen throw pillows and blankets on every sitting surface doesn't mean my place isn't cozy. Besides, it's plenty cozy for one."

"Yeah, but then I come over. That one becomes two. I know you keep it sparse to discourage the rare woman you invite over for sexy time from sticking around, but I don't think I should sacrifice my comfort for your message of eternal bachelordom."

"I'm sorry to have inconvenienced you up to this point," I snark.

"Apology accepted. I take amends in the form of breakfast foods."

"Whatever man ends up with you will have his hands full," I mutter.

She smiles at me boldly. "Don't I know it. But I don't have plans to settle down anytime soon. My mother marries enough for the both of us."

"Ah yes," I muse, mixing the batter for our waffles. "How is she getting along with the new beau? Think this one will stick?"

"It's too soon to tell. He has the money and connections she's after, but he also has kids, which, as we know from my upbringing, are a mark in the con column for Rebecca. If he plays his cards right and ships the kids off, he may get to be husband number five."

"Your mother's dedication to embodying Meredith Blake is commendable," I tease. I know Tiffany is over her mom's antics, but humor and deflection are her default coping mechanisms. I support her by joining in.

"She wishes she could get her hooks in '90s Dennis Quaid," she snickers. Tiffany snuggles into the couch while I finish making our late-night breakfast. After we eat, she returns to her apartment to sleep off her night and subsequent food coma. Sleep doesn't come easy for me, though. I stay up wondering how I'm supposed to find a Tiffany in a world full of Rebeccas.

Chapter Seven

• KENT •

December

Another holiday, another party with my friends. This time, Miller and Lola are hosting. I've seen one or more of the guys almost every day the last month for workouts or to watch football, but it's more fun when the whole gang gets together. My excitement is fueled by my desire to see what Lola has planned and not at all hoping for another chance to flirt with Raven.

Since I live down the hall, I am among the first to arrive. "Hello, party people," I cheer as Miller opens the door. He scowls slightly, but I don't take it personally, especially when I spot Lola busy behind him, putting the final touches on her decor.

"Hi, Kent," she greets. Miller nods and steps back, allowing me to enter. I see Carina and Tiffany over by the gift table talking while Robby and Crews grab a drink from the bar. I wave to the girls before strolling over to my teammate.

"What's eating Papa Bear?" I ask.

"The usual," Robby says, amused. "Lola invited some guys she met through her blog, and as always, he assumes they're after his woman."

"He knows she's gone for him," I assert.

"He knows. But he hates the idea of anyone else even looking at her. I can't say I blame the guy. He needs to lock her down. The security of a ring is worth its weight in gold."

"And that says a lot based on Carina's rock," Crews jokes.

Robby punches our teammate in the arm and chuckles when he sees my pinched expression. "Relax, bro. Monogamy isn't contagious."

"Thank Christ for that. Pass me a beer, will ya?"

After grabbing my drink, Robby and I join Tiffany and Carina. The girls are discussing our upcoming group trip to Vegas. I was surprised that is where Lola wanted to celebrate her birthday, but I'm not going to complain about a week in Sin City. It will be a nice reset after Mom's next visit. I offered to come to her this time, but she wants to 'escape to a milder climate' as if Seattle is the Arctic and not the Pacific Northwest.

For the next hour, people slowly filter into the party. When I am close to losing hope the red-haired vixen will show up, the door opens, and she appears. Raven is stunning in a green sweater dress that perfectly hugs her curves. Half her beautiful hair is clipped back, showcasing her massive Christmas light earrings. She is clearly infected with the holiday spirit.

Surveying the room, I realize I'm not the only one who notices her entrance. After greeting our hosts, she flits around, talking to all the different groups. She easily navigates each group, proving what a social butterfly she is. Maybe that should be her nickname.

Before I have the chance to catch her attention, Lola announces that we're going to play games. The first game is holiday movie charades. Seeing my teammates try to act out *Home Alone* and *Elf* is funnier than I could have anticipated.

After that, we play Dirty Santa. As a natural shit disturber, this is one of my favorite traditions. I love stealing away gifts and egging on others to cause chaos. Tiffany does, too. We make a great team.

Once all the presents are opened, I'm going home with a suction cup koozie for shower beers. And Lola is the proud owner of a pair of boxers covered with pictures of me. The annoyed expression on Miller's face made the expedited shipping worth it. Raven ended up with a candle of some kind, but that isn't what has me watching her all night. What has my attention is the dark blond with a barely there beard whispering to her throughout the game. Raven's giggle lifts over the noise of the group, and my jaw ticks, knowing I'm not the one making her laugh.

As karaoke kicks off, because, of course, the girls want to sing Christmas tunes, Raven escapes to the bar for a refill. I take the opportunity to step up beside her, reaching across her body to grab a drink of my own. "What song are you performing for us tonight, Candy Cane?"

"None, and that may be your worst one yet," she admonishes, rolling her eyes. Something about the gesture has my cock thickening in my pants. Women don't usually sass me. They're typically falling over themselves to please me. That has to be why the simple act of rolling her eyes at me has me panting over Raven like a middle schooler.

"I thought you'd appreciate it was on theme," I drawl as I bring my hand to toy with her earring. "These are cute."

"Thanks," she replies with a sharp intake of air. I wait as her gaze slowly rises to mine. She flushes when she glimpses my cocky grin.

"Your eyes are pretty," I whisper. "I bet they're even prettier rolled into the back of your head." The comment makes her roll said eyes.

"That's not how I planned to make them roll," I comment with an exaggerated pout.

"Better luck next time." She smirks. I may not have made her laugh, but I relish our banter. She typically has a laid back demeanor. Drawing out her sassy side is a win in my book. Plus, I can tell by her expression she is curious about my offer, even if she thinks I am joking.

Raven doesn't realize I would enjoy nothing more than making her feel so good she loses herself. I love pleasing a woman until the only thing she can sense is me. Some might call it my specialty. Something she'll know firsthand soon if I have my way. "If you'd let me, I'll happily put my theory to the test."

Finally recovering her wits, she fires back. "You sound pretty sure of yourself, Big Shot." Hmm, that's the same nickname she called me last time. I guess she's sticking with it. I don't hate it or the smile accompanying it, as if she got away with something.

"I am more than happy to show you how 'sure' I am, Birdie. And how apt that nickname is."

"Oh my God," she chastises, slapping her hand on my chest. "You're persistent, aren't you?" I trap her hand beneath mine and relish in the heat of closeness.

"Only when I see something I want."

Raven abruptly breaks our connection when a throat clears behind me. I peer over my shoulder and glare at a scowling Miller. Discreetly flipping him off, I turn back to the beauty before me, but she is already filling her cup and preparing for her exit. "See you around," she mumbles.

After watching her retreat, I turn to face my friend. "Dude, way to cock block!"

"No," he states firmly.

"What do you mean, 'no'?"

"Raven is not for you. She is a sweetheart and does not need a ride on the Kent merry-go-round before being forced off."

"First, I don't force anyone off. They know what their ticket is for. Second, a girl like that is good for more than one spin. She's the type of girl you try on the horse, the ostrich, the lio—"

"I regret this analogy," he sighs. "You know what I mean. She wants a relationship, not a one-night stand."

"If I recall correctly, you met Lola on a one-night stand," I challenge, annoyed he thinks that low of me. And even more annoyed that he's right. I can't offer Raven anything other than a temporary situationship.

"When you're open to more than a quick fling, you'll have my blessing. Until then, don't mess with her. She's one of Lola's best friends."

"I'm your best friend," I complain. "Shouldn't you be giving her this speech?"

"Lola is my best friend," he corrects. "And I'm merely offering a friendly warning, buddy. I'd hate to have to kick your ass because you upset my woman."

"Better to be beat out by Lola than Robby," I concede.

"That's the spirit. Now, come on. We need you for our rendition of the chipmunk song."

Chapter Eight

• RAVEN •

With only a few days before I head back to Missouri for Christmas, I have been running around all afternoon getting last-minute gifts. I also picked up my entry for Lola's Dirty Santa party. I can't wait to see who ends up with a picture of my cat dressed as an astronaut – best twenty-five dollars I've ever spent.

While dropping off my bags at home, I change into a green midi sweater dress that fits like a glove. I clip half of my hair up and put on my favorite Christmas earrings. They're red light bulbs that can be turned on to illuminate, though I've learned not to do that until after I get out of the car, as they are distracting. Once Captain Wentworth's – or Cappy to his friends – portrait is wrapped, I rush out the door and head to the party.

I am one of the last to arrive, but unlike the last time I attended a gathering here, I was able to snag one of the visitor spaces. It was the furthest possible one, but a win is a win. It is almost time for the games when I arrive. Trying not to think too hard about what and where Lola and Miller do in this condo, I sit on the sectional.

"Hi," the man sitting to my right says. "I'm Marc."

"Raven," I reply. "Nice to meet you. Are you a friend of Miller's?"

"Lola's," he corrects.

"Wow, Lo invited a good-looking man over, and you're still standing? Miller must be on his best behavior tonight," I muse.

"You think I'm good-looking?" he asks as one side of his mouth rises into a sexy smile. I flush, realizing what I said. "Aww, don't be embarrassed. It's a compliment to be noticed by a woman as breathtaking as you."

"Thank you," I manage to squeak out. Blonds aren't typically my type, but this guy's confidence and cheeky attitude are. Since he's sitting, I can't say for sure, but he appears tall and well-built with tan skin, telling me he spends a lot of time outdoors. If I had to guess, I'd say he played a sport in a former life. Soccer maybe?

"Huh," he murmurs, almost to himself. "I didn't think that blush could get any deeper. Your cheeks are giving your hair a run for its money, gorgeous. I won't ask what you're thinking about. I take it you're a friend of Lola's, too?"

"Yes. We went to high school together and found our way to Nashville as adults. Are you local?"

"I was born and raised right outside of town. I attended the University of Tennessee and came home to help run the family business. I met Lola when she interviewed us for the tourism board."

"What's the business?"

"My siblings and I own the Lavigne Winery with our cousins."

"Oh my gosh," I practically shout. "I love that place!"

"Yeah?"

"Yeah! We went to a charcuterie class there a while back. I'm part of the wine club."

"We thank you for your support," he says with a blinding grin. "Which wine is your favorite?"

"Hmm," I ponder. "If I had to pick, probably the Syrah. I love to mix it with—I mean, I love it."

"Oh no, you can't stop now. What do you mix it with? You won't hurt my feelings. I'm the numbers guy, not the vintner. Juice? Ginger Beer? Club Soda?"

"Diet Coke," I confess with a grimace. "It's weird, I know."

"That's not that weird, sweetness. It's called a Kalimotxo. It's a common drink in Spain."

"It is?"

"Yep. You were worldly, and you didn't even know it."

Marc and I continue to talk as games go on around us. He initially unwraps the gift I brought, but a player for the Songbirds whose first name I have yet to learn, steals it. Something about his daughter loving cats and science. I end the evening with a candle with a label that reads, 'My Patience is in Retrograde,' and honestly, same.

When Lola announces it's time for Christmas karaoke, I sneak to the bar to refill my drink. Before I get the chance, someone comes up beside me. I am almost positive that someone had his eyes on me all night.

I groan at Kent's Christmas-themed nickname. It may be festive, but Candy Cane gives 'stripper during the holidays.' That is not exactly my vibe. As we chat, I try to hide how much he affects me when his soft touch grazes my torso, and when he directs his signature charm my way. It is impossible *not* to have a sarcastic reply to his cheesy line about making my eyes roll into the back of my head. His delivery is ridiculous, but that doesn't stop my thighs from clenching. I mentally high-five myself when I snark back without my voice shaking.

Instead of letting me pull away when I smack his chest, he captures my hand underneath his. I can sense the heat from his skin and the steady beat of his heart. Between the sensation and the determined gleam in his eyes, I get lost in him.

"Only when I see something I want," he says. I blink at him, trying to remember what we're discussing. Something about Kent has me discombobulated. It's probably his copious amount of experience in seducing women, but I'm not too proud to say I can see the appeal. His expression promises I would have the time of my life if I spent a night with him. Before I can ask him to take me home, a throat clears behind us. Jolting back, I spot Miller over his shoulder.

Turning quickly, I fill my cup with the closest cocktail and hightail it away from the situation to where Tiffany is chatting with Charlie, Lola's workout instructor and friend. I wish I could say I joined in, but I was watching a conversation unfold between Kent and Miller that I suspect was about me. It has moments of tension, but ultimately, they join a few of their teammates, queuing to perform Christmas karaoke.

I spend the rest of the party catching lingering glances from both Kent and Marc. Unfortunately for me, one is more enticing than the other, and I can't help but think I'd be better off if their places were reversed.

Chapter Nine

A contented sigh leaves my lips as I snuggle deeper into the couch of my childhood home, Cappy curled up in my lap. He didn't enjoy the trip here from Nashville, but he purrs happily in his first home as I enjoy a hot chocolate my mother made and my father spiked.

I love watching the dynamic between the two. Mom keeps Dad grounded when his head gets lost in the clouds, and Dad's playful nature ensures Mom enjoys the beautiful life she created for us. The older I get, the more in love they seem. It is a relationship to be envied.

I grew up in a regular middle-class family in Missouri. Mom stayed home with my older sister, Emily, and me. Once we flew the nest, she got a part-time job at the library, running their book club and other events. Dad still works as an electrical engineer at the same company he has for most of my life.

My household was STEM-focused. It caused some strife in my

teenage years. While Emily was the quintessential science nerd who grew up to be a chemist, I was the artistic one constantly rearranging the living room furniture. Thankfully, my parents recognized that though I was good at math, I would use it differently than they hoped. They supported and encouraged my sister and me to pursue what made us happy.

Speak of the devil, Emily plops beside me on the couch with a mug of her own. "Oh, we're almost to my favorite part," she mutters at the screen. After our annual Christmas Eve viewing of *Home Alone*, Emily and her husband, Brett, went to put their kids, Kayleigh and Courtland, to bed. As the childless, fun aunt that I am, I moved on to *Home Alone 2*.

Three years apart, Emily and I have always been close. We never went through that phase of hating each other. We had enough distance in our ages that we didn't have to share friends, but not so much that we didn't have things in common. She is the complete package: intelligent, gorgeous, and kind. She was popular in high school for playing varsity volleyball. While we share the same red hair as our mother, she is a few inches taller and has a more athletic figure – even after the twins.

I idolized her growing up. She has always carried herself with confidence and self-assurance that I envy. Plus, she's always had my back. When I was being teased in the fourth grade for being a 'ginger,' she poured a concoction she made on the little girl's hair, turning it fire engine red. When my first boyfriend broke up with me during my freshman year, she let me hang out with her friends. Clark ate his heart out when he saw me sitting with seniors at the mall.

As Kevin McAlister flees into Central Park, Emily turns her attention on me. "How are you doing, Ray Ray? We haven't had much time to catch up with the kids running around," she asks absently, reaching to pet the Tabby.

"Same old, same," I answer.

"That's a lame non-answer. Any men in your life?"

"No," I laugh. "Per usual, I haven't been having much luck in the dating department."

"What are you talking about? You dated some nice guys. What about Tommy? He was sweet," she comments in reference to my college boyfriend. Tommy was a music major at Belmont, and our relationship, though short, was fine. At least it was fine until he decided to take the starving artist thing a little too far and move into his van while traveling from unpaid gig to unpaid gig.

"That guy was a loser," Brett says, coming to sit beside Emily and stealing her mug. She swats his hand after grabbing it back as he licks his lips with no remorse.

"He was not. He was sensitive," she argues.

"Yeah, sensitive to hard work. Didn't you pay for everything when y'all came down here? And you made him a special meal for Thanksgiving because he didn't want to 'support Big Turkey?' That guy was a punk."

"Tell us what you really think," Emily deadpans. I giggle.

His assessment is funny and also not wrong. I don't need a man to pay for things, but as an equally broke college student, always footing the bill and catering to my boyfriend's eccentricities got old. Plus, you'd think as an artist, he would have been more passionate in bed. He's definitely not rock star material in that respect.

"Raven deserves better."

"Thanks, Brett," I say, pinching his cheek. "You're a real one."

Ignoring her husband, my sister continues her interrogation. "Love life is stagnant, got it. What about work? Still loving it?"

I groan

"That bad, huh?"

"It isn't bad per se; it's just boring as hell. I'm designing the same thing over and over again with slight variations. My firm's clientele is not a great fit for me stylistically."

"I'm sorry, sis. That sucks. You haven't had any interesting projects lately?"

"I ran into a girl from college the other day, and she asked me to help her design her office. I did it on the side since it's not the work GHI does. We're purely residential. I loved the challenge of doing a commercial space and the opportunity to flex my creative muscles."

"Why don't you do that, then?" Brett asks as he emerges from the kitchen with a sandwich made of the leftovers we finished not three hours ago and a refill for Emily.

"Dude, your first meal hasn't even had time to digest," I admonish.

"Don't waste your breath," Emily bemoans. "The man can eat four helpings and still want dessert. He's a bottomless pit. He's always down to eat."

"I thought my insatiable appetite was one of your favorite things about me," he teases. Emily blushes at the innuendo, and I make a gagging noise.

"Ew. Get a room. Preferably not under the same roof as me before you make me another niece or nephew." When he winks at us, I steer the conversation back to safer waters. "Why don't I do what?"

"Take on side projects that fulfill you creatively. If you get enough work, you can become a freelancer and have a job you enjoy. Working for yourself is way better than someone else."

I'd be lying if I said I hadn't thought about it. I hate having to run my ideas through senior designers before I present them to clients. They usually end up changing it entirely or dulling it down. If I have to put subway tile in one more bathroom, I will rip out my hair.

Designing for a business instead of a home was more fun than expected. I think I would get more out of doing commercial design. For one, I love supporting small businesses and helping them thrive. Two, more risks can be taken. The space is meant to be a statement and attract customers aesthetically. I don't have to consider how 'livable' something is or worry the homeowner will get tired of it since customers filter in and out.

"I've considered that, but building a client base is daunting. I don't know where to begin," I confess to Brett's suggestion.

"Let me know if you decide to stop being a chicken, and I'll be happy to help you set up the business side of things."

Instead of replying to his jab, I stick my tongue out at him and shift my focus to the hijinks on the screen. The movie doesn't hit the same, with my thoughts swirling with possibilities of making my own way in the industry I used to love.

Chapter Ten

• RAVEN •

January

When I return to work next week, all considerations of taking on side projects are out the window. Management is pushing us to start the year strong and get as many projects moving forward as we can to make up for the slower holiday season. I'm counting the days until I leave for Lola's birthday trip.

Two days before I'm supposed to depart, Carl calls me into his office. When I arrive, our office manager and de facto HR rep, Kendra, is with him. "You wanted to see me?" I ask tentatively.

"Have a seat," my boss replies emotionlessly. When I study at Kendra, she isn't giving anything away, either. I have no idea why Carl called me in here, but my gut tells me something monumental is about to happen. Sitting, I toy with my citrine bracelet, waiting for him to let me know what's going on.

"As you know, I am not one to beat around the bush. It has come to the attention of management that you have stolen at least one client from GHI. We take this seriously, and it is strictly forbidden in your contract. We're going to have to let you go."

"I haven't stolen any clients!" I croak. "I don't know what you're talking about." Kendra, the silent century, pulls a sheet of paper from a folder I didn't realize she was holding. It is a screenshot of Macy's Instagram. In the post, she is showing off her new office. I remember when she posted this because she tagged me in it. But she didn't tout my services; she simply thanked me for my help.

"Care to explain this?" Carl asks in a bored tone.

"I helped a friend design her new office. She wasn't a client, and she never would have been. We don't do commercial design," I justify.

"Ms. Wilson, your employment agreement clearly states that ANY projects taken on must go through the firm. Otherwise, it is considered poaching."

"That is ridiculous," I assert. "Are you telling me you've never helped a friend or family member design a space?"

"What I have or have not done is not the issue. But, since you brought it up, I have never designed a space for someone outside of GHI and sourced the materials for it. I have certainly never received compensation for it. Can you say the same?"

"I—" I want to deny his claim, but I can't. I told Macy she didn't need to pay me, but she insisted. She said women don't get ahead in the world by giving away free labor. I used the money to buy the citrine pendant I've had my eye on and gifted Emily and Brett tickets to a show I know they wouldn't have seen otherwise.

I slump my shoulders as the reality of the situation crashes down on me. Part of me thinks the company is using this as an excuse to fire me. I know for a fact that other staff members have design-adjacent side hustles, and I've never heard about any of them getting in trouble. I've never fit the image or style GHI wants to portray. This incident is the perfect excuse to fire me without any appearance of discrimination or snobbery.

Sensing my defeat, Kendra hands Carl the rest of the folder. He pulls out several documents and places them in front of me.

"Normally, for a contract breach, employees are terminated with no right to benefits. However, since it was just the holidays, we have decided to be lenient."

He waits for me to react – thank him most likely – but when I don't, he continues. "We are prepared to offer you two months of severance plus your end-of-year bonus and medical coverage through the end of February. We are also willing to say you resigned your position when verifying employment in the future."

"Yo—you're paying me to leave?" I ask incredulously. "What's the catch?"

My boss' features tighten as he gives me an impatient glare. "There is no catch. Consider it leftover holiday spirit."

Kendra clears her throat and chimes in. "You will need to sign an NDA, though. And agree not to contact any current or past clients." There it is. They're not paying me to leave. They're buying my silence. They know this firing is fishy and want me to go quickly and quietly. This realization turns my shock into rage. How dare they do this to me. I am the best junior designer here. Hell, I'm better than half the senior designers. I may find most of our clients tedious, but I do a damn good job.

"Six," I state, eyeing the snakes before me.

"Six?"

"Yes, I want six months' severance. I also want an estimated bonus for all the assignments I have worked on that will close Q1. And I'll agree not to contact them for residential jobs, but commercial work is fair game."

"Seriously? Do you think this is a negotiation? We're being rather generous here. You don't have a leg to stand on. You breached your contract!" Carl sneers.

"I think we both know your reason for firing me is bogus. You don't want people to know you fired one of your best designers because she doesn't fit your aesthetic. A designer who brought in several big accounts thanks to the success of the McMahan project."

The McMahans are a couple of retired California rockers who moved here to open a record label. After revamping their rental, they planned to use me to design their new build and recommended me to several friends. That relationship alone is easily worth seven hundred fifty thousand dollars to the firm. I'm asking for a fraction of that.

Carl opens his mouth to argue, but Kendra beats him to it. "Deal," she agrees with her hand outstretched.

An hour later, armed with my termination contract and a box containing a pitiful amount of personal items, I walk out of Green Hills Interiors for the last time.

Chapter Eleven

I ride a roller coaster of emotions between my firing and the Vegas trip. On one hand, I am thrilled to be out of that toxic and taxing work environment. I didn't realize how cutthroat it was until I was out and could examine my experience with distance. I am terrified of what the future might bring, but glad I have the safety net of my severance to act as a cushion while I plan my next move.

After a night filled with too many margaritas at our favorite cantina, the girls convinced me the universe is telling me now is the time to do my own thing. Tiffany may have been the only one who said it was the universe, but Carina and Lola agreed it is too good an opportunity to pass up.

As scared as I am to strike out on my own, I am also excited. I have several ideas of businesses and connections I can contact, and the girls are eager to help. Carina even offered to hire me to design the Becker Foundation. Since taking over the building, they haven't done much to the office space. The path in front of me is unknown, but full of potential. I can't wait to explore it in the new year.

Currently, I am pacing around the gate, waiting to board my plane. I'm surprised at the destination Lola chose to celebrate her birthday and New Year's, but excited. I've never been to Las Vegas before, and I know it will be a blast with this group. The only thing standing in my way is this flight. Flying has always made me nervous, no matter how often I do it.

When I hear my name called by the gate agent, I race to the desk. "I'm Raven Wilson. Is everything okay?"

"Ms. Wilson, yes, everything is fine. I wanted to let you know that you have been upgraded to first class for this flight."

"I have?"

"Yes, ma'am. It appears that a 'Ms. Franklin' purchased an upgrade for you using miles. The note says, 'Wish you could have flown with us, Ray. Drink a glass of bubbly for me!'"

I almost cry at the gesture. Tiffany may let people think she's a superficial Barbie, but she is one of the sweetest people I know. The fact that she upgraded me using her hard-earned miles warms my heart. She was the most vocal about helping me launch my business and hexing my old company if needed. I'm not sure if hexing is against the non-disparagement clause of my NDA, but better safe than sorry.

I was bummed that I had to wait an extra day to follow the group. I was initially supposed to work yesterday. Little did I know I would be unemployed instead.

I thank the airline employee for this information and board when they call out for first-class customers. Settled in my seat, I'm peering out the window when my seatmate sits beside me. Before I can turn, a familiar voice beside me says, "Fancy meeting you here, Jessica Rabbit."

"Kent," I whisper, shocked by his presence.

"Hi," he smiles. "If I had known I'd have such a pretty seatmate, I would have been the first to board." God, that smile. The man oozes charm. It's no wonder women throw themselves at him left and right.

"I didn't know you'd be on this flight," I manage to get out. "Why didn't you leave with everyone else?"

"I got back from Seattle yesterday and needed to grab different clothes. Believe it or not, the wardrobe for a PNW Christmas is different from a desert New Year's."

"You're flying two days in a row?" I ask.

"That's how the cookie crumbles sometimes."

"Sounds glamorous," I drone.

"You have no idea. They run together after a while," he sighs. "Ya know, you could help make this flight extra special."

"How could I do that?"

"I've never joined the mile-high club before. That would make up for all the boring holiday travel."

I scoff. "Are you capable of seeing me and not hitting on me, Dela Cruz?"

"I don't think I am, Merida. Any man who passes up the chance to shoot his shot with you is an idiot."

"Merida?" I ask, ignoring the way my cheeks heat at the comment.

His cocky grin returns at my teasing. "You didn't go for Jessica Rabbit. They're both sexy AF. Can't go wrong either way."

"You think Merida is sexy? Jessica Rabbit, I get. But Merida?"

"Hell yeah, I do. She's got gorgeous curves and a badass attitude. What's not to like?"

"You're a strange guy, Big Shot. Any other strong opinions on animated characters?" I ask.

"More than you know."

"No way. Absolutely not!" Kent objects. "There is no way you would fuck Dimitri and kill Prince Eric. Have you seen those muscles? Plus, Dimitri was a con artist. Eric is royalty."

"Technically, Dimitri brought the right girl to Paris. He didn't con anyone. Plus, Anastasia was a princess in her own right," I correct. "And yes, I stand firm in my decision! Fuck Dimitri, marry Shang, and kill Prince Eric."

"I need the thought process on this one, babe. Cause the math ain't mathing."

"Fine," I huff. "I marry Shang because he's courageous, honorable, and did you see those pecs and man bun?"

Kent scoffs. Ignoring him, I continue.

"I fuck Dimitri because he's got serious BDE and you know he was getting around in the St. Petersburg underworld. Plus, he wouldn't be clingy and weird afterward. I kill Prince Eric because he is arguably the worst Disney prince. He was fooled by a voice change. I don't want to fuck or marry a man with that little attention to detail."

"Those are valid points," he concedes. Kent and I have been playing Fuck, Marry, Kill cartoon character edition for the last hour. We've rarely agreed, but it has been a great distraction.

"Let's play a new game," Kent suggests.

"What game?"

"How about—"

"Excuse me, folks," the captain interrupts from the overhead speakers. "Despite our best efforts to avoid it, we will face some turbulence. Please have your seatbelts fastened. I've asked the flight attendants to suspend service until we get through it. It shouldn't be too long. Thank you."

He sounds calm, but I am immediately on alert. My fingers immediately grasp the gemstone bracelet I wear for inner strength and protection.

On an intellectual level, I know turbulence is nothing to be worried about. Still, my anxiety doesn't care about logic. Kent must notice my change in demeanor because his brow furrows when he asks, "Are you scared of flying, Raven?"

I glance down when his hand gently cups my knee. The action

causes a fluttering sensation in my stomach that quickly turns to lead as embarrassment sets in. It must seem silly to someone who travels as much as he does.

"Scared of being hurdled through the air in a metal tube, thousands of feet in the air where humans have no business being? No. I'm totally cool."

He shoots me a wry expression for the sass. I can see the snarky retort ready on his tongue, but the sudden shake of the plane draws a whimper from my lips.

"Hey, we've got nothing to worry about. These things practically fly themselves. It will get a little bumpy, and then we'll return to smooth sailing. Before you know it, we'll be back on the ground." Right on cue, the plane shakes more insistently. I've been through turbulence before, but no amount of exposure has helped me face this fear.

The hand on my forearm trails down and links with my fingers. The warmth of his rough hand in mine forces me to open my eyes. When I do, I see a concerned Kent staring back at me.

"I'm fine," I choke out.

"Of course you are," he coos. We both know I'm not, but I appreciate him keeping up the pretense. "But I needed an excuse to hold your hand. You know what the tabloids say: I'm always trying to hold hands with pretty girls."

I laugh at the comment. "Yeah, that's what they say."

"You been reading about me, Little Mermaid?" he teases.

"I see things," I muse. "I'm sure it's mostly exaggerated. *Baseball-Bulges.com* sensationalizes things. Are you sure a player doesn't run it?"

Lifting the armrest and leaning in, he brushes his lips against my ear before he whispers, "I can assure you, that site knows exactly what it's talking about."

My body flushes at his words, and he succeeds in temporarily distracting me from the rough air. Unfortunately, the plane shakes more violently. I let out a whimper that has nothing to do with arousal and everything to do with fear.

"Hey, shhh. You're okay, babe. Think of it as a bumpy road. Nothing to worry about. This isn't the worst turbulence I've been in. One time—"

"I don't think a story about how bad it can get will help right now," I say.

"Probably right," he agrees. "What's your biggest goal?"

"What?"

"What's your biggest goal? Ya know: hope, dream, aspiration."

"I know what a goal is."

"Then answer," he taunts.

"Are you seriously asking a newly fired woman who may or may not be hurdling to her impending doom what goal she's going to perish not having achieved?"

He laughs. "That's fair. I thought it would be a good question to distract you with. People love talking about that shit."

When the lights flicker, I press my body against his, and his arms wrap around me. He rubs soothing circles on my back and does his best to keep me calm.

"To buy a house," I blurt out. "That's my biggest goal."

His hand stalls momentarily before he resumes the comforting motion. "I don't want to be an ass or make assumptions about your financial situation, but that is a pretty achievable dream."

"Technically,," I say, rolling my eyes. "But I don't want any house. I want an older home that I can renovate. I want to preserve the historic charm but add all the modern conveniences. I haven't found the right one yet, and no matter what, the project will be costly."

"I always preferred new builds," he murmurs. "Fewer issues to worry about."

"And I bet your condo is a monochromatic nightmare with no personality," I quip.

"Fair, Firefly. Fair."

Calmer, thanks to our conversation, I silently soak up his comfort until the shaking lessens. When I go to pull away and back fully into my seat, Kent tightens his arms around me and maintains his movements. The circles and his steady heartbeat lull me into a drowsy state between sleep and consciousness.

Sometime later, the seatbelt sign dings, but I can't will myself to move now that the fear and adrenaline have worn off. The last thing I hear before I passed out is the murmur of the flight attendant and the rattle of the service cart.

After a couple of days in Vegas, Lola asks all the girls to meet her for brunch and a spa day. We agree because why would we say no to mimosas and massages?

Halfway through the meal, Lola fidgets nervously.

"What's up, Bunny?" Tiffany questions.

"What do you mean?" she responds with a guilty expression.

"You're hiding something," Carina chimes in. "I've known you my entire life. You're making the same face you did when you used Mom's Nair without permission and were too afraid to tell us you were having an allergic reaction."

"That was traumatic," she recalls with a grimace.

"Tell us, Lo, or so help me..." Tiffany threatens.

"Fine, fine. Geez, y'all are a tough crowd. Brady and I were talking last night, and we want to get married while we're in Vegas."

"What?!" we all shout.

"I already had my big wedding, and Brady has never been interested in having one. We're going to fly our family and remaining friends here in two days and get married at the Little White Chapel. What do you think?" she asks, watching us with rapt attention.

"Oh my God, you're getting married!" I squeal and jump up to hug her. Returning to my seat, I raise my glass. "A toast to Lola, Miller, and a kick-ass wedding weekend!"

"We have so much to do!" Carina exclaims. "We need to get you a dress and rings and flowers, and Tiffany, you can do the hair and makeup, right?"

"Of course I can. I can also hook up with an appointment for a dress. I'm guessing you don't want a big poofy wedding dress, but need something bridal-ish?" Tiffany wonders out loud.

"Yeah, nothing too bridal, but still white. Maybe with feathers or tulle if it's short."

"Leave it to me, babe," Tiffany declares.

"One of my college classmates is a photographer here," I interject. "I'll see if they are available to take pictures. Even if you're eloping, you'll want to capture the memories. It would be hard for them to pass up an MLB wedding for their portfolio."

We spend the rest of brunch and our group mani-pedis discussing the finer details of the wedding and how we can get it all done in the next forty-eight hours.

Chapter Twelve

• KENT •

Sitting at the roulette table, I signal the waitress for another Old Fashion. Call me basic, but it goes down smoothly. I've been sitting here since the guys said 'goodnight' half an hour ago. While Robby and Miller went to find their women, I'm here alone. Being the only single guy on the trip is weird. Rivera is technically single, but I don't know the man well enough to hang out alone, and he didn't arrive until a few hours ago. Instead of prowling the town for a hookup, I'm sipping high-end whiskey and dominating this roulette table while my mind plays back to the trip, including the journey here.

I've taken a lot of flights in my life, but none like the one I shared with Raven. I was surprised to see her on my flight. Though, it made Tiffany's text asking for my seat number make sense. She must have known about Raven's fear and figured a familiar face would keep her calm. Or that I would spend the flight flirting with her, keeping her mind off it. I admit that was my initial plan, but then I saw the unease in her eyes when the cabin door closed.

At first, I thought she was simply a nervous flier. No big deal, a lot of people are. Distracting her was easy enough with our silly game. I was unprepared for the sheer terror that gripped her when the turbulence hit. As someone who flies several times a month during the season, I'm used to the challenges of air travel. Raven was not.

I was taken aback when she sought out my comfort so naturally. I'm not a total Neanderthal; I have no problem being a shoulder for the women in my life. But I am not the first person they would go to. Of all our guy friends, I am low on the list of options. That's fine with me, though. Comforting isn't my top skill.

That's why I was surprised at how easy and instinctual it was to wrap Raven in my arms. The compulsion to hold her was so intense I couldn't *not* do it. More shocking than wanting to hold her was the instinct not to let go. When she fell asleep against me, I felt like the Grinch when his heart grew three sizes. I don't remember the last time that happened to me. I may sleep with a lot of women, but I don't *sleep* with them. I was almost disappointed when they told us we were landing. I don't know when I'll get that physical connection again.

Once we arrived in Vegas, I didn't see Raven much besides group outings. The girls did their thing during the day while we did ours. With Lola and Miller's wedding tomorrow, I'll finally get to see more of her.

When Miller told us the plan for them to get hitched, I thought he was crazy. The woman hasn't even been divorced for a year, but when 'you know, you know,' I was told. After everything the pair has been through this year and Miller's personality, a quickie wedding isn't that out of pocket.

I'm excited by the prospect of seeing Raven again. Touching Raven again. Not that I should be, but damn it, I am. This girl has embedded herself under my skin since the first time I saw her, even more after seeing her normally sassy demeanor vulnerable. I need to do something to get her out of my system before this becomes a problem. I swear I can smell her sweet lavender and mint scent.

"Hey stranger," the sweet voice of the woman I was trying to forget drawls nearby. I turn to see Raven sitting beside me at the table.

"Hey, Pippi. What are you doing here? Decide to take me up on my offer for strip poker?"

"Once Miller stole Lola from Wedding Central, we called it a night. Since I wasn't tired, I decided to explore the casino. And you've never asked me to play strip poker."

"An oversight on my part. Consider this your formal invitation." She doesn't comment on my blatant line, but does roll her eyes. I find I'm becoming addicted to drawing that reaction out of her.

"Are you winning?" she asks, referencing the roulette game in front of me.

Looking down at my generous pile of chips, I smile. "Of course I am. I'm a winner, born and bred, Ms. Weasley."

"Ew, no. We're not doing a Harry Potter nickname. I won't let you ruin my childhood."

I bark out a laugh at her reaction. "Fair enough, Starfire." I throw a chip down on black and order a round of drinks as Raven watches me gamble.

"Wow, you are good," she murmurs.

"I'm good at a lot of things, baby. Roulette is only one of them. I'm happy to show you the rest whenever you're game."

"I'm not sure you're ready to play with me, Big Shot. I play to win. In fact, I bet I could beat you at this," she states, leaning in until her chest brushes against me and running her delicate fingers over my forearm.

"You see how many chips I have, right? I didn't start with this many. I'm that good."

She scoffs. "Please, roulette is mostly luck, and seeing as I am due some, I think I could beat you."

"Alright, Foxy. Put your money where your mouth is," I say, handing her a chip. "We both make a bet and see who wins."

"This is your money," she points out.

"Yes, but you don't have any chips. I see your point, though. We use my money but can make a side bet."

"What did you have in mind?" she asks, biting her lip.

"If I win," I state as my hand tucks a stray lock behind her ear. "You give me the chance to put my mouth where your money is."

"What?" she sputters.

"Okay, that wasn't my best metaphor. If I win, you allow me to show you how good I am at other things."

"I am not betting sex. What kind of girl do you take me for?"

"Calm down, babe. I know you're a good girl. And I'm not suggesting sex, per se. If I win, let me prove I'm worth your time... for a night, anyway."

"You're going to have to spell this out for me word for word to make sure we're on the same page," she says breathily. She has an indifferent facade, but I can tell from her dilated pupils that she's at least considering my proposition.

Leaning in, I lightly kiss her shoulder and trail my nose up her neck until my mouth is even with her ear. "If I win, you give me five minutes to make you come. If I can, you hear me out the next time I hit on you instead of laughing off my advances."

"And if I win?" she asks, not objecting to my statement.

"If you win, you can have all my chips," I suggest. "Or anything else you want."

"When I win, you cut it out with the nicknames and pick one."

"Seriously? That's what you want? There is at least ten thousand dollars on the table."

"I don't want your money." I'd hear the annoyance in her tone if I weren't stunned by her answer. She recently lost her job, and I can't imagine she was making all that much. Ten grand is a lot to most people. Hell, it would hurt me to part with it on principle. The fact that she would choose me settling on a nickname for her over a sum that large is unfathomable. I've had women throw themselves at me for less.

"Do we have a deal?" she asks, gaze boring into me. I swear I can see sparks dancing in her honey irises. It's at this moment that I settle on a nickname for her, no matter the outcome of our bet.

"We have a deal, Ginger Spice. Ladies, first," I urge, motioning to the board.

"One hundred dollars on even," she tells the dealer.

"One hundred dollars on red," I relay with a smirk.

"You realize we both could win now, right?"

"Trust me, sweetheart. If I win, we both win regardless." I hear the roulette wheel spin, but all my focus is on Raven's. Anticipation trickles through my veins. I'm more nervous about this spin than any other I've played all night.

I don't care about losing the money. Truthfully, I don't care about losing the bet, but this could be my chance to show Raven how good I can make her feel. To entice her into my bed. And I need to get her into my bed. It's the only way to get her out of my head. One incredible night to get her out of my system.

"Lucky number seven," the dealer announces.

A smile crawls across my face as I see Raven's eyes widen. The implications of the number connecting in her mind. She turns her head to see for herself and then glances back at me as she swallows harshly. She says nothing.

Raven sits there, shocked, while the dealer exchanges my $100 chips for more-pocketable $1,000s. "Come on," I say, tipping him and grabbing her hand.

Instead of heading to the elevator, I take us to the bar.

"What are we doing?" she questions dubiously.

"Getting a drink," I reply. "I think you could use one." When her expression remains serious, I hook my finger under her chin, bringing her face to mine.

"This was just for fun. If you don't want to do this, we can enjoy a drink and go our separate ways."

"Really?"

"Of course. I won't force you to hook up with me if you don't want to. I have no interest in anything less than enthusiastic consent. Besides, I'd be your loss, not mine."

"The way I see it, Big Shot, you still have something to prove." She takes my challenge for what it is and brushes past me to a booth near the back of the bar.

"Don't worry, baby. I always live up to expectations."

Raven and I hide away in the booth, flirting and chatting over drinks. From my observations, she's usually a red wine girl, but she's been downing cosmos like they're going out of style tonight. I signaled to the waitress that this was our last drink. I'm unsure if Raven plans to let me claim my prize, but I don't want her drunk if she does.

I've been slowly increasing the amount I'm touching her. An arm behind her in the booth, a hand on her thigh, simple touches to get her used to my hands on her body. Being this close to her has my cock aching for more, not that I'm counting on relieving it. I'll be lucky if she gives me those five minutes. I am hopeful, though, based on how she's been responding to and touching me back.

Her fingers trail up my arm as I sign the check. "Whatcha doing?"

"I love your arms. They're so firm. Is that from swinging a bat?"

"Among other things," I laugh. "Are you ready to get out of here?" She nods as she pulls her bottom lip into her mouth. Unable to resist, I brush my thumb against the abused flesh. Her gaze shoots to my lips in return and then to my eyes. Thinking this is as good a moment as any, I graze her cheek before my hand wraps around the back of her head and I pull her to me.

Our lips meet in a firm yet exploratory kiss. When she nips at me, my hand tightens, and I plunge my tongue into her open mouth.

When she melts against and moans, I know it's time to go. Pulling back, I see lust swimming in her eyes. Wordlessly, I get out of the booth and offer her my hand. Taking it, she lets me guide her toward the elevator.

When the doors close and we're alone again, I am back on her. Crowding her against the padded walls, I press my hips into her and devour her mouth. This kiss is more frantic than the one we shared at the bar, more insistent. Her lips taste like cranberry and sin. The warmth of her body against mine is short-circuiting my brain. All I can think is that I need more of her. More of her taste, more of her touch, more, more, more, until I have consumed every piece.

"Tell me you'll give me a chance. Tell me I can have my five minutes," I beg.

Chest heaving, she nods.

Not a man to waste an opportunity, I ask, "What's your room number?"

As the elevator dings, she slides her keycard out of her clutch and directs me to her room. When her door closes behind us, I pick her up and pin her to it. I slow our kisses to build up the anticipation as I grind into her center. The change in pace leaves her frustrated and needy. Good. I feel the same way. When she claws at my shirt, I slide her down my body, setting her on her feet.

Her eyes widen and fill with panic as she watches me take a step away. Holding her gaze, I unhurriedly undo the buttons of my shirt. "Don't want to get it messy," I remark as I shrug it off my shoulders. Reaching into my pocket, I pull out my phone. I open the timer app and set it for five minutes.

Raven is still leaning against the door. It isn't the most practical place to make her come undone, but I've managed it in worse. Returning to the space in front of her, I flash her my screen before placing it on the console table. Brushing my lips against hers, I gauge her consent one final time.

"Ready for this?"

"Yes."

Dropping to my knees, my fingertips trail up her smooth legs until they reach the hem of her skirt. If I had time, I would undress her properly and explore every inch of her. But I don't. Not yet, anyway.

"Normally, I would draw this out and take my time worshipping you, but I have a bet to win. Start the timer."

Removing a shaky hand from the door, she taps my phone screen. The moment weighs heavily between us, both knowing that no matter the outcome, things between us will never be the same.

"Go," she whispers when she hits the countdown.

With no time to waste, I push her skirt above her hips, holding it there with one hand. The other nudges her legs further apart, giving me more room to settle between them.

"You smell like heaven. Let's see if you taste just as good," I tell her. Wetness shines against her panties even though I haven't touched her yet. I slide the lacy fabric down her legs before slinging one over my shoulder to spread her further for me and hold her skirt in place.

As I take a long, languid lick through her slit, her taste bursts on my tongue, and I moan. Based on the curse she lets loose, the vibrations must do something to her. I smile into her center as I nuzzle my face against her. Using my thumbs to open her lips, I admire the sweet cunt that has been the star of my dreams since November.

"Your pussy is so fucking pretty, Raven," I say with a bite to her thigh. The sting causes her to whimper and thrust herself further toward my mouth.

With no time to tease, I kiss the mark and kiss my way back to her spread pussy. My tongue makes slow circles around her clit, avoiding direct contact. If I am going to win this bet, I need her desperate for it.

"You taste so good, baby. I could feast on you all night," I say as I increase the pressure of my tongue. Her hands sink into my hair as she tries to move me where she craves me most. Resisting, I slide my tongue down to her entrance before flattening it to offer her clit a fraction of friction.

"Kent," she finally begs, and it is music to my fucking ears.

"You need more, sweetheart? I can give you more." I have no idea how much time is left, but no matter when the alert sounds, I am going to make this girl fall apart for me.

When my tongue flicks her clit, she jerks and lets out the sweetest moan. Done playing, I attack her pussy like a man starved. Licking and sucking her nub as she trembles above me. I can sense her muscles growing tense and know she's close.

"That's it, Raven. Are you going to come for me? Are you going to explode on my tongue like a good girl?" Her hips buck at the praise. "I want you to make a mess of me. To soak me in your release until it's dripping down my chin."

"Oh God," she moans. "I'm so close. Don't stop!"

"I'm not stopping. I'm not stopping until you give me my prize." The hands in my hair tighten to the point of pain, but nothing is going to stop me from making her come.

I plunge two fingers inside and feel her walls immediately clench around me. She's so wet they slide in easily, and she bows into me, legs trembling. I know if I weren't holding her up, she'd fall.

As she gets nearer and nearer to her peak, the keening noises from her lips grow louder and louder. Of all the times I thought about my head between her thighs, I imagined her quiet, expressive face whimpering softly. She's whimpering alright. Every graze of my tongue against her draws out the sound, but it isn't soft. It's needy and uncontrolled, and I love seeing her like this. I love making her loud.

My cock is aching in my jeans, begging to be the reason she cries out. For that to happen, I need to make her come. I should have known that one small taste wouldn't be enough. I need to completely consume Raven and let her consume me in return.

With renewed vigor, I slide my fingers back inside her and curl them against the spot I know will have her seeing stars. "Come for me, Raven. Be a good girl and come all over my tongue and fingers," I demand before sucking her clit back into my mouth.

A few more flicks of my tongue are all it takes to have her coming apart for me. As her walls flutter and head bangs back against the door, she shatters. My only regret is that I can't see her face. Licking her through the aftershocks, she turns her face down to study at me. Chest heaving, she silently observes me as her body continues to spasm. Before I can break the silence, my alarm does it for me – the shrill beeping signaling my victory.

Chapter Thirteen

Holy fuck. I knew Kent Dela Cruz would be incredible in bed, but he rocked my world on another level. I don't know what came over me when I agreed to that bet with him. I was caught up in the flirting and the attention. I am not one to have hookups, especially not with men like him. But all the crap that built up over the last few months had me wanting to do something reckless, something to make me feel good.

When the croupier announced where the spin landed, the implications of our wager crashed down on me. I should have panicked, but his reaction made me wonder if giving into the chemistry that almost suffocates would be such a terrible idea. He may be a playboy, but Kent isn't a bad guy. The cosmos lowered my inhibitions enough to settle my nerves.

What was the worst that could happen? A hot guy failed at making me come? I could live with that. In the best-case scenario, I get an orgasm and humor him at a later date. With his short attention span, I figured that day would never come, anyway.

I was not prepared for the earth-shattering pleasure that consumed my entire being. Staring down at him now, face wet with my release and cocky smirk, I thank the casino gods it landed on red.

Below me, Kent licks what is left of me off his lips. "I win."

"I think I won," I laugh. His eyes twinkle with satisfaction, and I don't miss the massive tent in his slacks.

"Trust me. I count that as a win for both of us. You coming against my tongue is going to be the star of my fantasies for a while. I don't think I will ever erase your sounds from my memory. I can't wait to do that again."

"Again?" I ask.

"The other part of our deal. If I could make you come in five minutes, which I did, you had to give me a chance the next time I hit on you. I plan to cash that in real soon."

"Hit on me now," I blurt out before my brain can catch up to my mouth.

"Hit on you now?" he questions slowly, trying to comprehend my meaning.

I nod. God, what has gotten into me? My pussy is still tingling, and I already want more. If he can create that magic in five minutes, there is no telling what he can do with an entire night. I believe he threw the word 'worship' around.

Kent rises to his feet but keeps me pressed to the door. His chocolate pupils are blown so wide they appear almost black. "You want more, baby? You want to see all the ways I can satisfy this luscious body?" Again, I nod.

"If we do this, we follow my rules. This is a onetime thing. Just tonight. One night to get it out of our systems. All pleasure, not emotions. I'm not the guy you take to brunch. I'm the guy who fucks you so well you sleep through it. Are you okay with that?" he asks, eyeing me dubiously.

"One night. My life is too complicated for more," I reply. At this point, I'd agree to anything he asked if it meant he'd go back to touching me. I know he isn't a commitment guy. I know not to expect hearts and flowers or even a call the next day. His cards are on the table, and I won't make the mistake of misreading them. We'll share this one hot night, and tomorrow, it will be as if it never happened.

After searching my eyes for some hidden agenda, Kent finally speaks. "Are you from Tennessee, Raven?"

"What?" I ask, confused by the abrupt change in subject. His head drops to kiss below my ear as his lips trail down my neck.

"Are. You. From. Tennessee?" he repeats, nipping my neck and then shoulder with each word as he grinds his hips into mine. "Because you're the only ten I see."

As soon as his cheesy pickup line registers, I am on him. I don't even care how lame it was, I need him too much to tease him about it.

My hand drifts down his chest across his abs until I reach the waistband of his pants as he takes his teeth over my shoulder. I palm his erection and shiver at the size. When he lifts his head to gauge my reaction to the Louisville Slugger in his pants, I cup his head with my free hand and pull him to me.

At first, he lets me lead the kiss, tongue dancing with mine. As the heat around us ratchets, he takes over and plunders my mouth. The hand on his neck comes down to help me unclip his belt and shuck his jeans to the floor. Using his distraction, I thrust my hips away from the door, knocking him backward. His eyes flick to mine as he lets me corral him to the King size bed that drips indulgence. When his knees hit the mattress, he sits.

Leaning onto his elbows, he watches with rapt attention as I kick off my shoes and lift my shirt over my head. That attention burns even hotter as I unhook my bra and let it slide down my arms. When my skirt falls to my ankles, I am completely bare in front of him. Instead of being self-conscious as I would with most men, I feel powerful. Kent is eyeing my curves like a bear out of hibernation, and I'm his first glimpse at food. It's heady. Stepping into the space between his legs, I place my hands on his thigh, lowering myself. He catches my wrists and stops me.

"As much as I would love your lips wrapped around my cock, I'm wound too tight not to blow my load down your pretty little throat." He shakes his head when I smirk at him.

"I want to experience your sweet little cunt strangling me. I need to feel you come apart on my cock the way you did on my fingers," he says as he pulls me onto his lap to straddle him. With both hands in my hair, he captures my mouth with patience that contradicts his previous statement.

"You want that, baby? You want me deep inside your pussy, making you feel so full? Stretching you so good that you'll feel me for days?"

"Yes, please. I want that," I say, swiveling my hips against his hardness. "Please fuck me."

Instead of responding, he flips us and positions me under him. "These tits," he mutters, hands kneading my flesh. "If I could, I would tattoo these tits to the back of my eyelids so I could enjoy them every time I close my eyes."

"That's so che—mmm." My taunt is interrupted when his lips suck my nipple into his mouth. His hand continues to palm my other breast until he switches his attention to my other hardening peak.

"Kent," I beg. He is mastering my body in a way no one has before. It's as if he had a guidebook to tell him exactly what I need. But now, I need him inside me. Letting nipple slip from his mouth, he bites around my breasts in a way that I know will leave marks tomorrow. But with how it makes me squirm underneath him, I can't find it in myself to care.

When my moans turn to cries and whimpers, he finally offers me a reprieve.

"Don't worry. I've got you," he coos. I release a sound of disappointment as he stands. He grins at my needy reaction, and he grabs his pants to fish out a condom from his wallet. I watch as he strokes his cock and slowly rolls it on.

Using my thighs, he pulls me down to the edge of the bed so my legs dangle off the side. Sliding his length through my wetness, he asks, "You ready?" With my confirmation, he pushes a few inches into me. My pussy clamps around him as I adjust to his girth. I feel myself stretching deliciously to accommodate his size.

"More," I rasp.

"You'll get more. I don't want to hurt you."

"More," I demand. Hooking my legs around his waist, I dig my heels into his ass and urge him forward. Giving in, he plunges to the hilt until his hips meet mine.

"Shit. Holy hell, you're tight," he groans as he pulls out and pushes back in. His pace quickens, making me wild and out of control. My hands, searching for purchase, land on his forearms, nails digging into him, leaving a mark.

"Goddamn, Raven." Falling onto his hands above me, I see his face twisted in concentration, and he pumps into me. The motion tilts my hips, allowing him to hit a spot that makes my vision flash white. My hips buck into his as much as they can with my legs wrapped tight around him.

"Kent, fuck. Oh my God." My pussy clenches around him as he hits it over and over again. The steady pressure causes heat to pool in my stomach as I once again surge toward my climax.

"Fuck yes, Firefly. You're gripping me so tight with your perfect pussy. You're so close, aren't you? So close to shattering on my cock?" His dirty words level up the physical sensations between us. My mind is empty of everything but him and the ecstasy threatening to take over my world at any moment. I'm overwhelmed as I fighting to stay at the precipice, scared to tumble over.

As if he can read my thoughts, he coaxes me toward the edge with him. "Give it to me. Come for me, Raven. I'm not going to last much longer in your hot cunt. I need to experience you rippling around me as you finish."

"I-I, it's too much," I cry at the power of the sensations pulsing through me. Tears prick the corners of my eyes as I writhe under his urgent thrusts.

"No, it's not. You can do it. Come again with me right now, or I swear I'm going to get hard again and fuck you until you pass out."

The threat unlocks something in my mind, allowing me to let go.

"Fuck yes, I can feel your pussy quivering on my cock. That's it. Good girl." he roars. Helpless to stop it, my body detonates into a million pieces as his cock twitches inside me.

My body shudders through my release as everything around me fades except our sharp pants and the symphony of your bodies moving as one. Eyes slammed shut, I ride out the aftershocks of my orgasm. When my muscles finally relax, the legs encircling his waist go limp.

Kent lands on his forearms over me but keeps most of his weight off my body. His lips leave a searing kiss on the middle of my chest as he catches his breath. The weight of his body settles my raging pulse.

"Fuck," he murmurs before he rolls over beside me and pulls me into his side. I nuzzle into his side and accept the connection he is offering. The steady beat of his heart and my utter exhaustion pull me toward sleep. A busy day of wedding prep and mind-blowing sex will do that to a girl.

"Thamazsogoo" I slur.

Kent laughs at my unintelligible garble. "I'll take that as a compliment."

Soft lips brush the top of my head as I sink deeper into oblivion. "Goodnight, Firefly. You were the best prize I ever won."

When I wake up the next morning, I'm alone. The sheets beside me are rumpled, but their cool temperature tells me they've been vacant for a while. Turning into the pillow, I smell Kent's fresh scent. It's faint, but it's there.

Pushing off the covers, I enter the bathroom to see it empty, as expected. A pang of disappointment seizes my chest at the realization Kent didn't stay the night. I knew he wouldn't, but a small part of me wishes he had. I would wonder if last night even happened if it wasn't for the discarded washcloth he used to clean us up and the hickeys littering my breasts and inner thighs. For someone who hates commitment, he sure enjoys leaving a mark.

While cleaning up in the shower, I contemplate my next move. I don't know the protocol for having a one-night stand with someone in your friend group. We said we'd act as if it never happened. But it will be hard to forget the way he made my earth tilt on its axis when his face was between my thighs. I push all thoughts of our encounter aside. I have many more important things to focus on today. Today, all focus is on getting Lola hitched.

Chapter Fourteen

• RAVEN •

Ignoring my mixed emotions surrounding my night with Kent, I meet up with the girls for wedding prep. It's all hands on deck, but almost everything for Lola and Miller's elopement is sorted. Tiffany handled all things fashion and beauty, while Carina booked what we needed to celebrate after the nuptials. My photographer friend was ecstatic about the opportunity and will meet us at the chapel. I also managed to get a bouquet for Lola that is both simple and unique. Robby took care of purchasing rings, and the guys all got tuxes. It may be a Vegas elopement, but that doesn't mean we can't dress to impress.

Miller arranged travel for Lola's dad, Carina's parents, and his family. The only other person who needed to fly in was her friend Georgie, who arrived last night. I am excited to meet George Rivera after hearing all about him from the girls. Tiffany was oddly quiet about his attendance. Something is happening there, but I don't have time to dive into it right now.

Unlike a traditional wedding, we all arrive together for the appointment at the chapel. I can tell by the staff's reactions that we are vastly overdressed for what they are used to, but they appear delighted by it. The chapel is run by an elderly couple who, based on appearance, have one hundred years of marriage under their belts.

After helping the photographer get set up, I head to the bathroom to touch up my makeup with the rest of the girls. Scanning myself in the mirror, I take in the form-fitting, puffy-sleeved black cocktail dress Tiffany chose for me. It's simpler than I would choose for myself, but it pairs perfectly with the vintage emerald earrings I received on my eighteenth birthday from my grandmother. They are one of my most prized possessions. I rarely have the opportunity to wear them, though. Vegas has been the perfect opportunity to bust them out. Running my fingers over the stones, I stare at them lovingly before tuning into the room's chatter.

"Alright, ladies, let's go get this Bunny hitched!" Carina tells the group. I follow our cruise director bestie out of the room and watch one of my oldest friends marry a man whose world stops and ends with her. After a few tears, heartfelt vows, and a wave to the livestream cameras, we throw petals at the happy couple. Once we finish taking photos outside the chapel, we pile into the limo to return to the hotel for dinner by the fountain and a night of dancing and debauchery.

The lights in the club are hypnotic as they pulse in time with the bass. Carina secured a private booth at the Vegas hotspot inside our hotel. She also got what must be unlimited bottle service. I've lost count of how many tequila shots and glasses of champagne I've consumed in the hours we've been here.

The love around me is palpable. Not only with Lola and Miller but between the entire group. Finding real friends as an adult is hard, and I'm thankful reconnecting with Lola brought this group into my life. Something I yell at the girls as we dance.

"I love you guys!"

"We love you too, Ray. I'm glad you could come," Carina slurs, rocking on her heels. Robby swoops in to steady her before she face-plants.

"I think it's time we head out," he states, taking in Carina's glassy-eyed appearance.

"No, I want to keep having fun!" she argues.

"We can have fun in the room, baby," he coaxes.

"Oh, can we do that thing we did on our honeymoon where you used your fingers to—"

Robby clamps his hand over Carina's mouth before she can finish. Turning her, he steers her toward the exit. "Say 'bye,' Kitten."

"Bye, Kitten," she singsongs on her way out the door.

Surveying our booth, I notice our numbers have thinned.

"Where is everyone?" I ask Tiffany.

"Those quitters all called it early," she answers.

"Is it only us?"

"No, Kent is still here, and Miller's brother and sister-in-law are making good use of their baby-free night. I won't be surprised if Chloe has a little brother or sister in nine months," she predicts.

I shift my gaze to the dance floor and see the couple in question making out while Georgie and Kent shower them with champagne.

Suppressing my giggle, I address my friend, "Georgie is still here, too."

"Yeah, I guess he is," she replies dismissively.

"Are you ever going to tell me what is going on there?"

"I don't know what you're talking about," she retorts. "Are you going to tell me why you and Kent – who usually generate enough electricity to power a small country – have been avoiding each other all day?"

"We're not-point taken," I concede, amusement dying. I haven't been avoiding Kent, per se. But I also haven't been able to look him in the eye. Neither of us is eager to discuss what happened between us last night.

"Thought so," she hums.

Wanting to prove her wrong, I grab her hand and a bottle of Veuve. "Come on, Tiff. If half the group is going to turn in early, we've got to make up for their absence."

"Ugh," I groan as light hits me directly in the face. I turn over and snuggle into the pillow wrapped around my back. The warm pillow. The warm, hard pillow. Squinting one eye open, I realize I am not snuggled against a pillow but a man. Shit. Who the hell is that, and why are they in my room?

Fully opening both my eyes, I notice the vault above me. My ceiling was not vaulted yesterday. When I sit up, I realize I am not in my room. Great. I'm in a strange place with a strange man. The breeze hitting my nipples tells me that I am also naked. What the fuck happened last night? The last thing I remember is throwing back a shot with Tiffany, Georgie, and Kent. Kent!

Braving a glance at the mystery man beside me, I realize it is not a stranger but Kent. Thank God. At least I am with someone I know and in the same hotel. I was not ready to go from no one-night stands to two on back-to-back nights. Although, I guess my record is still zero since Kent and I had a two-night stand, apparently.

I spot my clutch sitting on the table by the door and spy my dress thrown over a chair in the corner. Slowly extracting myself from his arms, I slip out of bed. Stumbling the first few steps, I regain my footing without making too much noise. I search his silhouette for signs I woke him. When I don't see any, I slip my dress over my body and locate my heels. With shoes and clutch in hand, I tiptoe out of the room.

As quietly as I left Kent's room, I sneak into my own. My room is connected to Tiffany's, and the last thing I want is for her to see me coming in wearing last night's dress. Once I'm back in my room, I sink against the door, this is a shitshow. I am too hungover to deal with any of this right now. What I need is a hot shower. I can contemplate all my poor life choices while hot water washes away my shame and alcohol sweat.

Thirty minutes later, my memory isn't any clearer, but at least I'm clean. Deciding coffee and carbs are the only things that will make me fully human again, I head into Tiffany's room to see if she wants to grab breakfast before we fly home. I enter at the same time her door closes, and she whips around guiltily.

"I hope I'm not interrupting anything," I drawl.

"Oh my God!" she gasps, clutching her chest. "You scared the shit out of me, Raven! How long have you been there?"

"The real question is, who just left here?"

"No one," she mutters.

"You sure? Because it appears to me that someone snuck out of your room. Anything you want to tell me?"

"Anything you want to tell me about where you and Kent disappeared to at 2 a.m.?"

"We disappeared together? I mean, no... Nothing to tell," I reply.

"Because nothing happened, or you don't remember it?" she asks like a dog with a bone.

"Hey. we're talking about you, not me. But I think we can both agree we don't need to talk about last night. Now go shower so we can stuff our faces with French toast before we fly home."

"Ma'am, yes, ma'am." She salutes.

Chapter Fifteen

• KENT •

March

It's been two months since Vegas, and not a day has gone by that Raven hasn't consumed my mind. Who am I kidding? She's been plaguing my thoughts since long before then. But now that I know how she tastes? It's pretty much impossible to get her out. I was an idiot for thinking one time would be enough.

Technically, it was two nights. I may not remember what happened once we left the club after the wedding, but I remember her sneaking out in the morning. I don't blame her. I told her I didn't do 'the whole sleepover thing' the day before. Truthfully, it's not often I even have repeats, but I guess my body had other plans.

Part of me regrets not letting her know I was awake as she scampered around my room gathering her things. I blame the hangover. Mostly, though, I regret that whatever we did the night before is lost in my subconscious. If it was similar to the first time, it was nothing short of spectacular.

In the weeks I was home before spring training, I only caught glimpses of Raven. With Robby and Carina visiting family in California and Lola and Miller on an extended honeymoon, there were few excuses to get together. By the time they were back, we were in typical preseason prep mode.

Typical, aside from the fact my dick had no interest in indulging in our preseason ritual of banging Broadway bunnies. Nope. The traitor was only interested in seeing a certain redhead again, which wasn't going to happen. Sure, I could have called to see if she wanted to hook up, but that would have sent the wrong message, and the lines between us are already blurry. That didn't stop me from using the memories of our time together to get through the lonely spring nights. Not even Coach's insane running drills could get me down after a night dreaming of her creamy skin and lavender scent.

Today is our last preseason game. We head back to Nashville tomorrow, and I can tell the guys are excited.

"Jesus, if I didn't know any better, I'd say Miller was giddy," I joke to Robby.

"I'm right there with him, man. If you had a girl to go home to, you'd be the same."

"Nah," I assert, "that life ain't for me. I'm good being the charming bachelor of the group. Although I guess I have to share the title with Rivera now."

Directing my attention to our newest team member, I ask, "What do you say, Rivera? Want to plan our singles cruises while these two get bogged down by PTA meetings and math homework in their old age?"

"Speak for yourself, Dela Cruz. If I don't give my mom grandchildren, she'll never let me hear the end of it. You can show me what Nashville has to offer when we get back, though," he replies with a smirk.

I was worried about how George would integrate into the team after his initial meeting with Miller, but Lola has both men whipped. If they still hate each other, they're good at faking it. Truthfully, it's great to have another single guy in the friend group. Not that I don't love my boys, but it sucks having to go out with the rookies and Derrick. The fresh blood was needed.

"It's nice to have you on board," I tell him.

"You know it," he replies with a fist bump. "But be warned, the second there's a Baby Miller in the picture, the competition for funcle is on, and I plan to take no prisoners."

"What the fuck is a funcle?" I ask.

"A fun uncle," he states as if it is the most obvious thing in the world.

"You'll have to excuse the Filanderer," Robby insists. "No one in his circle has kids yet. Whenever Miller manages to knock Lola up, he's in for a treat, considering he's afraid of pregnant women."

"I already have a leg up? Sweet," George comments. "And what do you mean he's afraid of pregnant women?"

"I am not afraid of pregnant women!" I exclaim.

"You literally ran away from Martinez's wife at family day last year after eating the last BBQ slider."

"What was I supposed to do? She was CRYING!?"

"Dude, you made a pregnant lady cry? That's messed up," George questions.

"No!" I say at the same time Robby says, "Yeah. She had been excited for BBQ all day. When catering told her they were out, she broke into sobs watching Kent take a big bite out of his sandwich. People felt so bad that someone ran down the street to grab her one."

"See? It ended up fine. How was I supposed to know she'd react that way?" I grumble as my teammates laugh.

"I know Miller is planning to get Lola pregnant the second she says 'go,'" Rivera remarks. "But what about you, Becker? Any plans to do the same?"

Robby blows out a raspberry before answering. "I don't think so, man. Some days, that idea sounds tempting, but Carina wants to wait until the foundation is fully donor-funded. I'm sure she'll get baby fever once she has a niece or nephew from Lola. In the meantime, I'm enjoying the hell out of practicing."

"I'd rather have crabs," I grumble, shivering at the thought of being a dad.

"Alright, boys," Miller shouts over the chaos of the locker room. "Let's go kick Blue Chip ass and get the hell back to Tennessee!" His announcement has us all gathering our gear and heading to the dugout.

April

A week later, I'm at MusINK City to get the final touches to my half-sleeve. I do a double take when I walk in. The waiting area has been completely revamped. Instead of a sterile, auto repair shop aesthetic, the lobby is filled with a tufted leather couch and colorful accents that match the logo. The formerly white brick wall is adorned with a mural showcasing the city skyline in those same colors. The front desk has even been upgraded.

"Hello?" I call out. Since I come in after hours, Zade is usually the only one in. I've told him he doesn't have to stay late for me, but he said he's used to it working with VIP clients. I'm not going to complain about getting my ink without fanfare. When no one responds, I walk further into the shop and hear voices in the piercing room.

"A little to the left? Right there," a familiar voice says. I must be going crazy because it sounds like Raven, but I can't imagine what she would be doing in Zade's piercing room, especially after hours.

"You sure this is where you want it?" a deeper, masculine voice drawls. "Last chance to change it before I make the hole."

"I'm sure! This is going to look amazing. It's the perfect focal point for anyone brave enough to venture down here," she replies.

'Down here?' What the hell is Raven getting pierced? Surely not—

I'm jolted out of my thoughts when I hear a loud bang. A few more taps help me recognize the sound of a hammer. Unfortunately, that only adds to my confusion.

"Hello?" I shout again, not wanting to barge in.

"One sec," Zade replies. A few seconds later, the man himself steps into the hallway. "Hey, man. You're early. Good to see you."

"I finished with the trainer sooner than expected," I confess. "Now still a good time?"

"For sure. We're putting the finishing touches on the studio."

"Yeah, I noticed things were different out there. Looks great, man. You said we?" I ask even though I know the answer.

Zade motions for me to go into the room. "Kent, this is Raven. She's the designer who helped me transform this space from cold and lifeless to chill and, what did you call it?"

"Chic," she replies.

"Right, chic. Raven, this is my buddy, Kent."

"We know each other, actually," she comments.

"Of course! You're both friends with Miller."

"Hi, Firefly," I greet. She gives me a tight smile instead of her normal, flirty one. While I'm happy to see her, she seems anything but. I notice the subtle way she curls into herself as if my presence makes her uncomfortable. It's a stark contrast to the last time we were this close, dancing the night away in Vegas.

I can understand her reaction, though. Seeing her here has thrown me for a loop, too. It's almost as if my constant thoughts of her conjured her out of thin air. We haven't been around each other since our hookup. Despite knowing this, I hate the idea that being near is causing a negative reaction.

"Thanks for your help, Zade. That was the last thing we needed to hang. I'll let you get to your appointment," she states.

Instead of trying to prolong our interaction, I allow her to retreat. After she's gone, I can regroup and figure out how to get things back to how they were before – filled with banter and those addictive eye rolls.

"Thank YOU, Raven. I'll send you the pictures from the magazine profile as soon as I have them and ensure they credit you."

With that, she exits the room. Zade turns his attention back to me.

"You ready for another torture session?" he asks.

"Do your worst," I answer.

I spend my time in his chair dreaming up ways to get back in Raven's good graces and maybe even back in her bed. Seeing her again only further proved that one time wasn't enough to sate my desire for her. I want more, and I'm going to get it.

Chapter Sixteen

Seeing Kent at MusINK City was a shock. Of all the places I thought I'd run into him, that wasn't on my bingo card. I remember noticing his tattoos during our night together, but I was too busy to admire them. That's a shame. Asking to stay and watch the session was on the tip of my tongue, which was my cue to leave.

Kent was very clear about what our night together was. A night. I don't want to give him the impression I am after more. I'm not sure what all his 'rules' are, but I'm sure they're in place to keep lines clear and clingers at bay. I don't want to make things weird in the group.

Plus, I have no interest in forming something with him. As much fun as that night was, I am a relationship girl at heart. It's why it had been so long since I was with someone. It's hard for me to enjoy the physical connection without the emotional one. The months of flirting and tension must have been why it was different with Kent. Not to mention, I never had to wonder about his intentions. It was refreshing, to be honest.

Men, including Kent Dela Cruz, are the last thing I should be thinking about right now. I don't have time to date. With my severance pay dwindling, all my focus is on building my business. I'm pleased with my progress with it up to this point.

Between Macy's post on social media and Carina's virtual tour of the updated Becker Foundation, I've gotten several requests from entrepreneurs and consultants in the area to transform their offices. Lola's feature of MusINK City in the Nashville Chronicle also led to an influx of small businesses seeking my services. I'm booked through the next three months and getting more exposure daily.

While working on a floor plan redesign for a realty company, my phone rings. Looking at the caller ID, I see it's one of my former clients from GHI, Meredith McMahan.

"Hi, you've reached Raven," I greet.

"Raven! How are you, hun," she says in reply.

"I'm great, Meredith. How about yourself?"

"I am shocked and delighted! Shocked those idiots at your snobby design firm let you go but delighted that it means you can work with me again."

"Ah, that. Unfortunately, I have shifted direction and no longer do residential projects. I am primarily focused on small businesses and commercial spaces."

"That's why I'm calling," she replies.

"Then I'm all ears. How can I help?"

"You may recall that Jimmy and I were searching for a space for our label. We found one and close on it next week. It's a cute little bungalow on Music Row, but horribly outdated. We want to create a space where artists enjoy spending time. That's where you come in. We'd love to have you revamp the entire building from the exterior to our offices and even the studio itself. You'll have to consult with the sound engineers, but with how social media is these days, the recording space needs to be as aesthetically pleasing as any other.

"We want to document the entire process and create a short film on founding a label. We've already got Declan Ryder signed on to be part of it, and we think you'd be the perfect addition. I know it's a big project, but would you be interested?"

My ears perk up at the idea. The girls have been encouraging me to pitch myself for a show on the Home Renovation Network (HRN). They have an open call for hosts in Nashville for their upcoming pilot season. This would be an excellent opportunity to get footage to send in.

"Congratulations, Meredith! That is amazing news. I need to shift some things in my schedule, but I would love to be a part of this!"

I tell her about the HRN application, and she agrees to share any content I need to help me make an audition tape. With a meeting set to tour the space, we say our goodbyes. Tossing my phone aside, I grab my laptop and research recording studio design.

The next few weeks are an absolute whirlwind of establishing my brand and learning everything there is to know about acoustics and how they are affected by design. Before I know it, Tiffany's birthday has arrived. Beloved party princess that she is, Tiffany has rented out an entire karaoke bar and filled it to the brim with her friends and clients.

Working at a music venue downtown has added some talented and hot musicians to Tiffany's circle. I am stoked to hear them sing for us. I can tell Tiffany is delighted by the attention and the attendance. Deep down, she has this innate need for external approval, even if her vibe says otherwise. I'm sure it has something to do with a mother whose love was conditional. Having this many people choose to celebrate her must soothe the little girl inside her.

While waiting at the bar for Tiffany's signature cocktail, the Malibu Barbie, I see a post from *BaseballBulges.com* updating their rankings. I'm scrolling through the pictures when a warm breath skates across my neck.

"I see I moved up a spot," a voice rasps behind me. Face heating, I quickly shut off my screen and whip around.

"It came up on my feed," I mutter, making eye contact with Kent.

"Sure it did. Is that why your cheeks almost match your hair?"

"They do not!" I declare, but even I know that's a lie. The bartender passes me my drink, but Kent tells him to put it on his tab before I can pull out my card.

"I can pay for my own drinks," I say. Grabbing his beer, Kent presses his hand on my lower back and guides me across the bar to where our friends have settled.

"Of course you can, Carrot Top. But so can I. Besides, I owe you for the page views fueling my ranking increase."

"You are so full of yourself," I reply, rolling my eyes at his gall.

As we reach our destination, he leans down, ghosting his mouth against my ear. "I liked it better when you were the one full of me." A shiver races down my traitorous body. I peer up as a knowing smirk decorates his features before watching him saunter to the other side of the room to chat with some of his teammates.

He may be a cocky son of a bitch, but I know he can back it up. Worse, he knows, I know he can back it up and the effect he has on me.

The night is a whirlwind of pink drinks, laughs, and karaoke of all varieties. Tiffany and Carina sing a duet that would make Hilary Duff proud, and the guys perform their best impression of The Backstreet Boys. Lola has spent the last fifteen minutes helping me pick a song, but most of my taste is too folksy for the vibe of the party.

"Kent found his conquest of the evening." Carina jokes as she joins us. Glancing up, I spot Kent listening intently to a debate between Robby and Georgie as a dolled-up blonde plasters herself to his side. I don't think mean thoughts about her because slut-shaming is so 2019. But I also want to claw her eyes out for the possessive way her hand lies on his arm.

Beside me, Tiffany scoffs. "No way. He wouldn't go there again after the fit Erica pitched the last time they hooked up."

I prickle at the 'again' before I casually – I hope – ask for more details. "Why did she pitch a fit?"

"She thought she had a claim on him because they hooked up on a semi-regular basis. He told her that wasn't the case, and she wasn't thrilled. She made a scene. It wasn't even a good scene either."

"Is there such a thing as a good scene?" I inquire.

"Hell yeah. You should have seen the one Lola made at Carina's bachelorette party. That was pure theater."

"Hey!" Lola protests. "It wasn't that dramatic."

"Bunny, you yelled that Miller ate people's faces to the entire room."

"I don't recall that," she replies primly, causing the three of us to laugh before she changes the subject back to my song choice. The birthday girl is requiring everyone to perform.

As we flip through the catalog, my gaze shifts to Kent and the perfectly manicured hand he still hasn't pushed away. When my eyes lock with his, I know he caught me in my moment of jealousy. He shoots me a wink before taking a pull of his beer and rejoining his conversation, blonde still attached.

Irritated at his behavior, an idea pops into my head. "I thought of the perfect song," I exclaim. Heading toward the stage, I psych myself up to put on a show.

Chapter Seventeen

Tiffany's birthday party is incredible, not that I expected anything less. The karaoke bar is decked out in pink to celebrate the birthday girl, and the crowd is vibing. I've been excited about this night for weeks. I'd be lying if I said it was only because I wanted to celebrate Tiff. It's also because it's the first chance I've had to see Raven in weeks.

She hasn't been around much lately. I heard the girls mention her revamping a recording studio and a film project, but I am not tuned into all the details. Whatever the case, sightings of the beautiful redhead have been few and far between. That's why I practically raced to the bar when I saw her earlier. Catching her scrolling through the latest Baseball Bulges rankings was the excuse I needed to tease her and earn one of her coveted eye rolls. I don't know why those are such a turn-on, but I swear every time, the action goes straight to my dick.

Glimpsing over to see her staring at me with a hint of jealousy is the only thing that kept me from telling Erica to get lost. I should probably regret letting her think anything could happen between us, but with how crazy she's been since I declined her last hookup request, I don't. She should know the score now better than anyone, but the girl can't take a hint. Her reaction will be worth seeing the fire in Raven's eyes.

After I shoot her a wink, she says something to the girls and makes her way to the stage. She hasn't performed yet tonight, and I'm interested to see what she chooses. She says something to the DJ before hopping on stage and taking her place at the mic. A familiar tune I can't place plays, and I watch enraptured as she sways her hips to the beat.

When she sings the first line, I can't help the smile that spreads across my face, knowing she picked this song especially for me. She may think she's calling me out with the '70s classic, but she'll have to try harder than that if she wants to hurt my ego. In fact, I drift closer to the stage until I'm standing front and center.

When she finishes her rendition of "You're So Vain," I stick my fingers in my mouth to whistle and cheer obnoxiously. She huffs a laugh and, with a shake of her head, dismounts in front of me.

"You're supposed to serenade the birthday day girl, Cherry, not me."

"You thought that song was for you?" she asks.

"If I say yes, I think I prove the point." Raven fights to keep her expression neutral, but I see the corners of her mouth tip before she rolls her lips together. As our gazes lock, the rest of the room slips away, and the tension around us ratchets. We stand there silently daring the other to make a move. The fire burning in her eyes tells me her mind is exactly where mine is: a hotel room in Las Vegas. As I'm about to give in, cheers filter in and break our stand-off. Tiffany is on the stage, thanking everyone for spending her birthday with her. When I peer back to Raven, she's flittered away and taken her light with her.

Chapter Eighteen

May

I smooth a hand down my jeans as I approach the main gates of the Songbirds stadium for my meeting with the team's hitting coach.

When I knock on the side door as directed, an intern ushers me through the tunnels to Zach's office. It's equally cool and unsettling being at the stadium during the day. It has an abandoned amusement park vibe minus decaying animatronics.

"Ms. Wilson," the truest definition of Zaddy I have ever seen, greets me. I don't know what I expected an MLB coach to look like, but Zach Reeves is not it. I'd estimate he's in his late forties but built better than most thirty-year-olds. His strong arms are what arm porn dreams are made of, and his grey athletic shorts? Yum. The only sign of his age is his salt and pepper beard and the crow's feet around his eyes. Both features add to his sex appeal rather than detract from it.

"Raven, please," I stutter when I realize I have been staring at him. If he thought my pause was weird, his soft expression doesn't show it.

"Of course," he replies. "Call me Zach. Thank you for coming out to the stadium. I know navigating it can be painful, but I have strategy sessions all day. It's hard to get away during the season."

"No problem at all. I understand." I sit across from him at his desk and pull out my notebook. "Miller didn't have many details about your project besides the fact that you're opening a training facility?"

"That's right. My daughter graduated from college with her business degree, and I want to create something we can do together. It will be part batting cage, part elite performance facility. She'll run the operations side, and I'll use my connections and limited free time to manage the training side."

"That sounds interesting. How can I help exactly?" I ask. Zach explains the aesthetic they are after and shows me photos of similar hybrid sports facilities that they can model. Aside from the entrance and lobby, I'll need to design a couple of offices, a physical therapy space, and a classroom for group sessions and meetings.

"Are you excited about doing this with your daughter?"

"Excited and cautious," he admits. "Our relationship has always been strained. I was away a lot, playing in the early years. Plus, her mom and I were never married, and she holds it against me. I'm hoping this venture will help us grow closer. Giving her a job is the same as attending her piano recital, right?"

I laugh at his self-deprecating joke. Before I respond, the rap of knuckles against the door frame cuts me off.

"Hey, Coach. I know I'm a few minutes early, but—" Kent stops mid-sentence eyes widening as if seeing a ghost. Maybe not a ghost, but certainly like Britney Spears at a full-length shirt store.

"Dela Cruz, give me one minute. I'm finishing up here. I'll be at the cages in five."

"Uh, okay?" he replies, still stunned and unmoving. Ignoring him,

Zach wraps up our conversation and shakes my hand. "It was a pleasure to meet you, Raven. We'll speak again soon."

"Thank you. I look forward to it." Rising from my seat, I shoot Kent an awkward smile as I brush past him. I'm halfway down the hall when I sense him creep up behind me and push me into an alcove.

"Hey!" I protest.

"What are you doing here?" Kent whisper-shouts. The irritation in his tone causes my hackles to rise.

"I was here for a meeting," I answer dryly. "What are you doing here?"

"I'm here for a meeting; seeing as I work here, that makes sense. What doesn't make sense is a girl I hooked up with being on my turf, flirting with my boss."

"First, your turf? Really?" I scoff. "I didn't realize by letting your dick inside me, I lost access to half the city. Should have pulled out a map during your pre-sex speech so I didn't encroach on your territory."

He stares at me incredulously, but I don't pause long enough for him to get a word in. "Second, I was not flirting with your boss. Zach mentioned needing help to set up the interior of his new business. Miller overheard and gave him my name. What you witnessed was strictly professional. And even if it wasn't, that's not your concern, is it?"

Kent's face scrunches in annoyance, but he doesn't have a leg to stand on in this argument. "Are you that friendly with all your clients?" he sneers. "I can see why your business has taken off so quickly."

"Wow," I gape at his audacity. "Is that what you think of me? That I use my body to get business? It can't be that I work hard and am good at what I do. It must be from batting my eyelashes and flashing my tits."

Remorse flashes across Kent's features. His hand hovers as if he wants to touch me, but he pulls back at the last second when I back up a step. "Firefly—"

"Don't," I interrupt. "I have to meet with another Joh—oops, I mean client. I'll see you around."

With those parting words, I turn on my heel and stomp out of the stadium, trying my hardest not to grab the nearest object and hurl it at him. He'd probably catch it, the bastard. By the time I return to my car, I am still fuming. I blast *Reputation* all the way across town to my next meeting.

Chapter Nineteen

Watching Raven strut away, I fight to keep my lips from tipping at her tantrum and my eyes from watching the bounce of her ass in her jeans. The second she is out of my field of vision, the gnawing sensation that I should go after her creeps in. And I hate it.

I'm usually a chill, level-headed guy. I don't lose it on people, and I am confused about why I did. She was right. There is no reason why I should care that she was here talking to my boss. I rub my hand on my chest, a foreign burning springing to life in it. Why did I have that reaction?

I need to apologize. But what would I even say? 'Sorry for being an ass; seeing you laugh with my hot boss made me want to throw him through the concrete walls of his office?' That wouldn't win me any points.

Grinding my teeth in annoyance, I leave the alcove I pulled her into – another thing I should apologize for – and meet Zach at the batting cages.

"All good?" he asks.

"Yeah, sorry. I had to take care of something."

"Seeing as you're already back, I'm not sure how good of a job you could have done taking care of anything." He smirks.

"Perv," I retort, before clearing my throat. "That wasn't that. If anything, it was the opposite."

"Pissed off your girl, huh? I'll be honest, Dela Cruz. I'm surprised you landed a girl of that caliber."

"Hey, I'm a catch!" I defend. "But she isn't my girl, just a friend."

"I bet. I had a lot of friends back in my playing days, too. None that made me scowl at my coach the way you did at me, though. I'd be jealous over her, too. Take it from me, kid. Don't let a girl like that slip through your fingers, or you'll end up a lonely old man."

"I wasn't jealous," I grumble. "And you've barely been out of the league for ten years. Old man, my ass."

Zach grins at my reply. "Okay, you got me there, but I still wouldn't be dumb enough to let her go. She's got a good head on her shoulders, and what a pretty head it is."

"Can we focus on my training, please?" I ask, not appreciating his assessment of Raven. He can lust after her on his own time or, better yet, not at all.

Lying in bed later that night, my encounter with Raven still nags at me. My brain has latched on to what Zach said. Was I jealous? That isn't something I'm used to experiencing. Usually, once I've been with someone, I couldn't care less about who or what they do. I thought sleeping with Raven would have gotten her out of my system, but I crave her more.

Seeing her friendly with Zach awoke something inside me. It wasn't only that my pride took a hit when he questioned my worthiness of being with her. The idea of her being with someone like him puts a pit in my stomach. Even if, by all appearances, they'd be a great match.

She deserves a nice guy. One who has his shit together and wants a commitment. Although he's been single as long as I've known him. Maybe commitment isn't his thing. He could want to be fuck buddies. I wonder if that's something she'd be into. My chest burns at the thought of them having that arrangement – at anyone else touching her.

If she's going to have a fuck buddy, it should be me. I know how to make her body feel good, and we already know our chemistry is off the chart. Having a regular thing may not be a bad idea. The jealousy inside me ebbs as I devise a plan to convince her that getting together again is a good idea.

Chapter Twenty

• RAVEN •

A few days later, I'm riding the elevator of the Broadway Lofts, the high-rise condo where the girls live, down to the lobby. When the doors open, I attempt to step out and meet a familiar pair of chocolate eyes.

"Hi," I greet Kent while locked in place.

Appearing equally surprised to see me, he takes a moment to respond. When the doors close between us, he juts his arm out to stop them. "Hey, Firefly, fancy meeting you here. You're turning up all over the place this week."

Shaking out my shock, I leave the elevator. "I was hanging out with Tiffany before she works a show tonight," I tell him, succumbing to the urge to defend my presence in his building.

"Who's performing?"

"Rhett Nelson. He's a newer artist," I reply. I wring my hands together as I squirm under Kent's sharp gaze. He's watching me closely, and his attention is heavy on my skin.

"I'll see you around," I state, moving toward the exit. I lucked out and only had to park down the block this time.

"Wait," he calls out, grabbing my wrist. When I turn to face him, something akin to nervousness flares across his expression.

"Yes?"

"Are you hungry?"

"What?"

"Are you hungry?" he repeats.

"A little, I guess. Why?" I question skeptically.

A wide grin shatters his tentative expression. "Come with me."

Without waiting for me to respond, he tugs me out the same doors I was heading toward.

"Where are we going?" I ask, voice drowned out by the noise on Broadway. This time of day, the crowds are thin, but the sounds of the city fill the air.

"You'll see," I barely hear.

Releasing my wrist, he places his hand on my lower back. The touch may be light, but it sears my skin like a brand. Six blocks later, we're standing outside a grilled cheese food truck.

"How do you know I'm not gluten- or dairy-free?" I tease as we wait in line.

"If you were, they have options for both. But I know you aren't because I saw you down mac and cheese balls at Friendsgiving as if you were a death row inmate with a ticking clock," he quips. I stick my tongue out at him, earning me a chuckle.

After we order and Kent pays for our meal, he leads me to a picnic table in the back corner of the makeshift patio area. It rests against a building and offers a sense of privacy.

After we finish our food, I break the silence. "What are we doing here, Kent?"

"I wanted to see you. I've been hoping to talk with you but haven't seen you around lately. That wouldn't be on purpose, would it?"

"Of course not," I scoff.

Kent takes a deep inhale. "I'm sorry we haven't had much time to talk since Vegas. With preseason and now regular season games, things have been hectic. I wasn't trying to ignore you or anything. I told you I couldn't offer anything beyond that one night we shared."

The mention of our 'one night' together has me freezing. A pang of guilt shoots through me, knowing it was two. Considering I don't remember what happened, I don't know how to tell him about it. Pretending it never happened is the best recourse I can come up with.

"Don't worry, Big Shot. I knew the score. I wasn't expecting you to roll up to my door with flowers and declarations of love. We had a fun night, and I don't expect anything else. I know you aren't boyfriend material."

He gives the tiniest flinch in response to my statement but otherwise appears unaffected, so I continue.

"I understand why you would be apprehensive about me thinking you could be more. I'm not ashamed to admit I love commitment. But I don't have the time or energy for a relationship at this phase in my life."

"What do you mean?" he asks.

"I'm starting my own design firm. Building up a client base and getting the word out takes significant effort, especially without a company's resources behind me. I don't have the capacity to give a partner what they need right now. Physically, I have a few hours to spare each week, but emotionally, I am drained.

"As nice as it would be to get an assisted orgasm, my battery-powered boyfriend is the only one I'll be spending time with for a while."

I flush when I realize what I said. Did I really just talk about my vibrator to Kent Dela Cruz, one of the hottest men I have ever met?

"Oh, God. Now would be a great time to be abducted and sent to an ice planet," I mutter under my breath.

"What?" he questions, with a mischievous smile.

"Nothing. I can't believe I mentioned my vibrator to you."

"Don't be embarrassed," he replies. "It's good to know you can take care of yourself. But what if you didn't have to?"

"What do you mean?"

"I mean," he clarifies. "What if there was another way you could get assisted orgasms without the toll of an emotional relationship?"

"Finding one-night stands is as much, if not more, work," I reason. "I have to spend time making a profile and swiping on apps. Then I have to cyber-stalk them to make sure they aren't a serial killer or a creep searching for sister wives. If the guy does check out, I have to spend time getting ready and going on a pretense date. That's a lot of work for something B.O.B. can knock out in fifteen minutes."

"B.O.B. takes fifteen, huh? Did you tell him I can do it in five?"

I roll my eyes as he continues.

"You know, you only paid in half your bet."

"Excuse me? I fulfilled my side of the bargain."

"I was left more than fulfilled, but not what I mean. You were supposed to give me a chance next time I hit on you."

"Uh, I did."

"That cheesy line doesn't count."

"You want to hit on me again?" I question.

"I have a proposal for you instead. Let me be the one who assists in your orgasms."

"I thought repeats were against your rules?"

"I don't often hook up with the same person more than once. It gives off the wrong impression, but you already said you don't think I'm 'boyfriend material.' You know I can't be your boyfriend, and I know you don't want to be my girlfriend. It's perfect. We can both meet our needs and save our mental bandwidth for the things in our life that are truly important."

My initial reaction is to reject his offer. I am not a friend with benefits girl. But when I consider what he's offering, it makes sense. We both know we don't want a relationship with each other. We're compatible in bed. There would be no awkward dinner dates for the sake of propriety. It's an ideal setup.

"What are the ground rules?" I hedge. If there is anything I know about Kent, it's that the man loves boundaries, at least when it comes to women.

"Nothing too crazy."

"Let's hear them, then."

"No sleepovers, no back-to-backs, and no strings. We call or text the other when we want to hook up; otherwise, we let them be. We avoid each other in public."

I cringe at the mention of back-to-backs. We've already broken that rule.

"Now that I'm saying it out loud, I don't think normal fuck buddy rules work."

"Why is that?"

"Considering we're in the same friend group, avoiding each other in public would be weirder than interacting. And if we're out with friends, I don't want to miss the chance to get together simply because we may have hooked up the day before."

"Sounds as if you need some friends-with-benefits rules, emphasis on the friends," I state. "How about this: no sleepovers but also no frequency limits. No strings. We interact as usual in public, but don't tell our friends about the arrangement. Neither of us needs that heat. As soon as one of us no longer sees the benefit in the arrangement, we call it off. No harm, no foul."

"That works for me," he agrees. "And if you do find that you need some guy to show up with chocolates or carnival-won stuffed animals, you can get that elsewhere. I don't care what you do in your free time, as long as I'm the only one you're fucking. It's none of my business."

"I didn't take you as the possessive type, Mr. Dela Cruz," I tease.

His eyes darken. "I'm typically not, but I find the idea of anyone else making you come when I could do it maddening."

"Great. I'll let you take care of my orgasms and get my dating fix elsewhere." I say, standing and sticking my hand out for him to shake.

"Oh, Firefly. That is not how you seal this type of deal," he says before getting to his feet, leaning across the table and pulling me into a searing kiss. After a few beats, his tongue licks against my lips. When I open my mouth, it slips inside to play with mine. Several moments later, Kent pulls back and smiles at my dazed expression.

He guides me away from the table and walks me to my car. Giving me a slightly more chaste kiss, he tells me 'goodbye' and that he'll text me in a few days. Staring at him in my rearview mirror as I drive away, I wonder if this is the best or worst decision I've ever made. Only time will tell.

Chapter Twenty-One

Despite wanting to take Raven home with me immediately, I decide it would be best to wait a few days before setting up our next meet. As much as I can't get her luscious curves off my mind and how cool she appears about the arrangement, I don't want to set a bad precedent.

After beating Jacksonville last night, today is a great day for a pregame treat. I text Raven to see if she's interested.

9:15 AM

ME

Hey, Firefly. Interested in some afternoon delight?

RAVEN

What did you have in mind?

ME

> Come over before my game? I'll gladly trade in my pregame nap for a pregame shag.

RAVEN

> As long as you never call it a shag again, I'm down.

ME

> Not feeling groovy, baby?

RAVEN

> Gross.

> I'll be there after eleven.

With two hours to wait, I plop down on the couch and de-stress by kicking ass in Call of Duty. Before I know it, I hear a light knock on the door. When I swing it open, I'm greeted by the sight of Raven in athleisure.

"Damn, and here I thought your sweater dress from Christmas would be my favorite thing I saw you in," I drawl, motioning for her to step inside my condo.

"That's funny. I would have thought my birthday suit would be your preference," she teases. "But thanks for the compliment. I was in a workout class when you texted. Mind if I use your shower?"

If I didn't know any better, I'd think she was wearing her outfit for style, not function. "Are you sure you came from a workout class? It doesn't appear you broke a sweat. Charlie must be slipping."

"Don't tell her that," she pleads. "She doesn't need an excuse to go harder on us. I was at a restorative yoga class; it was more stretching than sweating."

"In that case," I suggest. "How about you let me get you dirty and then clean again? We'll both need a shower after I've had my way with you."

Without waiting for her to reply, I grab her full hips and pull her against me for a kiss. I don't ease into it. I slant my mouth over hers, tongue demanding entrance. It only takes a moment for her to kiss me back with matching vigor.

Without disconnecting our lips, I navigate us over to my couch and pull Raven down to straddle me. I am quickly learning how much we both love this position. It puts her spectacular tits and eye – and mouth – level and perfectly lines up her core with my cock. The faces she makes when she grinds at the right angle are enough to make a lesser man bust on sight.

I rest my hands on her hips to encourage her movement, but also to slow her down when needed. "Fuck, yes. That feel good, baby? Are you going to get off rubbing your hot cunt against my cock before I even get you undressed?"

"Kent," she moans as she continues to rock. Keeping one hand on her hip, I use the other to pull her tank top over her head.

"We need to set these perfect tits free," I murmur against her lips. "Whoever invented front zip sports bras deserves a Nobel Prize."

She snorts. "I don't think they give million-dollar awards for giving you easier access to boobs."

"They should," I retort as my fingers slowly drag the zipper down. I grow exponentially harder when her breasts bounce out from their spandex prison. "Fuck, these are too pretty to cover. You should never wear a bra again."

"As much as I'm sure you would enjoy that, I don't possess the kind of breasts that can exist freely without some support."

"I'll support them. I'll hold them in my hands all day," I promise as I nuzzle my face against them. They vibrate with her laughter, but it quickly turns into a moan when I tweak her nipples and run my tongue between her cleavage. Raven's boobs genuinely are fantastic. They're full and soft. They're the type of mounds Renaissance artists would have drooled to paint.

It's only fair that I show my appreciation for the works of art in the flesh. I lick and suck one of her pretty pink nipples until it forms a hard point and switch my attention to the other side, offering it the same treatment.

Still rocking against me, she loses some of her rhythm as I play with her tits. "You like that, Firefly? Me sucking these pretty nips while you grind on top of me?"

My words cause her body to shiver and being able to get that reaction out of Raven puff my chest with pride.

"Fuck, Kent. I think—I need—oh my God," she hisses when I use my free hand to slap her ass.

"I know what you need, baby." I take over her movements and tilt her hips so her clit is dead center of my cock. It's sweet torture having her rub against me, but I'll be damned if I come anywhere aside from her hot, wet cunt.

"That's it. You're doing so well. Can you come for me? Fall apart so I can bend you over this couch and fill you up with my thick cock?"

"Yes! Yes! Yes! Yes!" she chants. I expect her eyes to be closed, but they are glazed over and boring into me with pure lust. If she keeps looking at me like that, I am never going to last. Needing a distraction, I lean down, flicking my tongue over her nipples once more.

When I sense her tensing, I offer one final command, "Then do it. Let go and come!"

As soon as the words leave my lips, I latch back onto her nipple and grab her ass so tight I might leave bruises behind. The idea of marking her creamy skin sends a thrill through me. I use my grip to pull her down harder and faster across my dick.

Moments later, her back bows, pushing her chest further into my face as her orgasm crashes over her. I slow the movement of her hips with my hands as I rock her through the aftershocks. "Holy hell, babe. That was so goddamn sexy."

I place her on her feet without giving her time to catch her breath.

"Pants off," I order through gritted teeth, smiling when she shivers once again. Whether she knows it or not, she loves when I take control. Peering up at me through glassy eyes, she shucks off her leggings and reaches for my sweatpants to do the same. Pushing them down my legs, her hand circles my cock, and she gives me firm, slow strokes.

"You want that?" I ask as her grip tightens around me. It takes every shred of my willpower to keep from thrusting into her hand.

"Yes," she pants.

"Turn around and bend over the arm of the couch." Without question, she twirls around and does as I request.

"Good girl," I praise as I step behind her, quickly rolling on the condom I brought into the living room before she came over.

When she wiggles her ass at me in invitation, I slap one cheek and then the other, causing her to let out a squeak. I revel in the pink that forms from my hand. Running a soothing hand down her spine, I yank her hips back and rub my cock through her folds, slicking it with her release.

"You're going to take every inch of this hard dick until you squeeze the cum out of me. Understand?"

"Yes. Fuck. Please," she begs. I can see the whites of her knuckles as she balls her fist into the fabric of the couch. With her body still sensitive, it won't take much for her to come for me again.

Soaked from her earlier orgasm, my cock slides easily into her tight cunt. Her walls ripple around and The intensity of her heat causes my control to slip I pull out until only the tip remains and slams back in. The muffled moan Raven rewards me with is all the motivation I need to fuck her in earnest.

"God, you feel so good," I groan. I can't hear her response since her head is pressed into the cushions, and that will not do. I crave her reactions in a way I never have before. I need to know that I'm pleasing her, that I am making her as wild as she does me.

Since we agreed to this arrangement – no, since that night in Las Vegas – I have been dying to hear her scream my name. To draw animalistic sounds out of her that tell everyone in a five-mile radius that she is satisfied. That I gave her what she needed.

Removing one hand from her hip, I fist her ponytail and pull her chest off the couch. Her elbows move to support her weight, and the new angle forces my cock impossibly deeper.

"That's it, baby. Take it. Take my cock. Your pussy is fucking heaven."

"Kent, fuck. I'm going to come again," she mewls. I can see the shake of her thighs as she nears her peak. I pound into her harder, expending more energy than I should on a game day, but I can't stop. I'm so close to exploding right along with her.

"Take me over the edge with you. I'm not going to last when you clamp down on me like a vise."

She clenches around me right as my dick swells and balls tighten. We come together in an epic eruption of moans and cries.

"Now you're dirty," I tease.

Taking a moment to gather my strength, I lean down, chest blanketing her, and kiss the back of her neck and shoulders. When I slide out of her, I immediately miss the warmth.

Scooping her up in my arms, I laugh at her squeal of protest and carry her into the bathroom. I blame it on her shaky legs, but really, I wasn't ready to lose the connection between our bodies.

Flipping on the shower, I press her back against the cold tile and tangle our tongues together as the shower heats.

"I'm addicted to your flavor," I confess. "I need a better taste." Sitting her on my shower bench, I drop to my knees and lap at her sweet pussy as steam fills the stall. The next half hour is spent getting clean and dirty and clean again.

Raven leaves my condo with a blissed-out smile on her face, and I head to the clubhouse, completely relaxed and ready to kick ass.

Chapter Twenty-Two

• RAVEN •

June

One of the things I love most about working for myself is not having to go into an office to show face. I transformed what is supposed to pass as a second bedroom nook into an office. The space is filled with aventurine, amethyst, lapis lazuli crystals, rosemary and lemon-scented candle, and soft light from my salt lamp. It's perfectly curated to optimize my creativity and sense of calm.

I love spending more time in my cute little bungalow, but it has me itching to redesign the space to fit my needs – something I can't do as a renter. One day, I'll have a genuine home office I can bring clients to, but for now, this will do.

Another perk of being my own boss is making my own hours. GHI was all about time in the office. I can understand the need for collaboration and creative brainstorming sessions. But having to come in to 'show face' on days when I worked off-site at clients' homes was a waste of time.

Now, I work when I want and relax when I want. It also gives me more time to see Kent since his schedule isn't exactly traditional. In the few weeks we've been hooking up, we've met up mostly at my place during the day or after games.

I still remember the first time he came over. He walked around my house as if it was a museum exhibit, and he could learn more about the natives by studying it. He somehow didn't notice Cappy was sleeping on the back of the couch and sat directly in front of him.

Not only did my grumpy cat hiss his displeasure, but he settled across the room and glared at Kent the rest of the time we were in the living room. He made me shut the poor guy out of the bedroom because he said the judgment was giving him 'performance anxiety.' He performed perfectly fine. Twice.

They've reached a tentative truce since then, but it is still funny to see them interact. Kent has taken it upon himself to call Cappy his formal title, Captain, to 'offer him the proper respect of his station.' It's a good thing they get along because even though I've gone to his condo a few times, the chances of getting caught are higher. Since neither of us wants this to be permanent, hiding it from our friends is imperative.

I hate lying to our friends, but they would stick their noses all up in our business and make things weird. They would never believe we can do this and not catch feelings, but they would be wrong. Kent is not boyfriend material, and while I am an excellent partner when I apply myself, that's not what either of us wants. We've avoided their suspicions, but our luck may run out soon as we're throwing Lola a surprise baby shower in a few weeks.

I'm not worried about that now, though. Now, I am zhuzhing myself up for a late-night booty call from Kent. He was out at the bar with the guys, celebrating their latest win and is on his way over now.

Not wanting to appear as if I am trying too hard, I slip on a cute silk pajama set my mother got me for Christmas. Since I am not worried about impressing the man, I do my normal bedtime routine.

My doorbell rings as soon as I finish the extensive skincare routine Tiffany got me into.

When I peer through my peephole, Kent is leaning against one of the pillars on my porch with an amused expression. "What's so funny?" I ask as I usher him inside.

"I ran into your neighbor," he answers. "When he saw me, he groaned and said, 'My noise-canceling headphones haven't arrived yet, man. Can you try to keep it down? I've never heard a girl outside of porn make those noises. It's going to give me a complex.'"

My cheeks heat in embarrassment. "I am not that loud! What did you say to him?"

His smile turns from delight to that cocky smirk he's known for. "I told him I would do my best to keep you quiet, but when you're top five on *BaseballBulges.com*, I can only control so much."

"You did not!"

"You should know by now that I'm a wildcard, babe."

"Oh my God. I can never show my face around Joe again. I will have to get my mail at 2 a.m."

Ignoring my dramatics, Kent struts toward me until my back hits the wall. He braces his hands on either side of me, caging me in. "Do you think we should be quiet for him, Firefly? Can you hold in your moans when I'm licking your pussy so good that you come all over my face? Can you swallow your cries of pleasure when I'm pounding your hot, wet cunt until you're so full you explode?"

"I-I-don't know." I swallow.

A wicked gleam flashes across his eyes. "Let's find out."

Bending down, Kent presses his shoulder into my stomach and lifts me in a fireman's carry. I will never get over the strength of this man. The last few men I've dated have been artists or musicians. Their bodies were attractive but not strong. They would never be able to manhandle me the way he does.

"Hey," I squeak, feigning protest.

"You love it," he mutters with a smack to my ass. His hungry gaze rakes over my pajamas after he deposits me on the bed.

"Unbutton your top," he commands. I don't know if it's my agreeable Libra nature or the electricity that pulses through me every time Kent is near, but I ache to obey him.

My fingers move quickly, fumbling as I rush to disrobe. He chuckles at my urgency before reminding me, "We aren't in a rush, babe."

When I throw open the silky top, his eyes darken with desire. "Every time I see them, they look better than the last. Your tits are incredible. I know I joked about tattooing them to my eyelids, but they may have done that on their own. I jerk off to the memory of them when I'm on the road, remembering how they feel and taste as I envision you bouncing on my cock."

His praise washes over me, making me more desperate for him.

"Your turn," I whine. He reaches one hand behind his head and pulls off his shirt in that sexy way only men can. My gaze eats up his taut muscles and the tattoos that litter his chest and arms.

"One day, you'll have to let me trace your ink with my tongue," I comment, mouth salivating at the idea.

"Any day, any time. For now, it's *my* tongue that's going to explore." His hands drift up my thighs, sliding under the hem of my shorts. "These need to go."

With my shorts pulled off, he pushes my legs apart, exposing my soaked core to him. Kent always gazes at my pussy as if it is his own personal treat, and I have no problem letting him think that. But right now, I need less looking and more touching.

"You're already soaked for me, Raven. That doesn't bode well for your neighbor. Maybe I should flip you over and take you from behind with your face pressed into the pillow to muffle your cries."

"Yes."

"But then I don't get to enjoy my favorite late-night snack," he states mischievously. "I guess I'll have to taste you while you're on your hands and knees. Flip over."

I roll onto my stomach and push up to my hands and knees. Kent slides his hand up my thigh before tossing my pajama top until it drapes over my head, exposing my back.

"I'm going to devour your sweet little cunt, and you're going to try your hardest to stay quiet. You make a noise, and I stop. I don't want to hear a peep until you're screaming my name through your orgasm." Without offering me the chance to reply, he dives in.

Kent does not ease me into it. He is immediately circling my clit with his tongue, and the intense contact has me crying out. When I do, he pulls his head back and tsks at me. "You're not being a respectful neighbor, Raven. The poor man wants to sleep. You have to be quiet."

Using his thumbs, Kent spreads my pussy lips, opening me up for him. He amps up his teasing as he laves my sensitive bud, softer than before but still with intense pressure. When another moan escapes me, he stops for even longer, kissing the backs of my thighs and tweaking my nipples from underneath.

By the time he goes back to licking me, I shoved my face deep into the mattress in an attempt to muffle any noises. His tongue roves over every inch of my pussy, inside and out. I can sense my orgasm floating above me, right out of reach.

That's when his thumb presses against my puckered hole. My hips freeze momentarily before relaxing back into his ministrations. "No one's ever played with your ass," he declares. I shake my head in confirmation, even though he already knows.

He brings his mouth back down to my core. His tongue travels up, teasing my entrance and then further until it reaches my puckered hole and swirls against it. I jolt away from both the sensation and the taboo of someone touching me there for the first time. Undeterred, Kent licks me from clit to ass. He continues the action until I'm a squirming, needy mess.

"Please," I whine.

"Please, what, Raven? Please keep licking your pussy while playing with your ass? Is that what you want? Is that what you need to come?" I nod, thankful he forgot the 'no making noise' rule.

His tongue slides to focus on my clit as his thumb rubs my back entrance. He deepens the pressure but never breaches it as he sucks my clit into his mouth. When my thighs fight against his hold, aching to close, he redoubles his efforts.

My orgasm is close. My chest heaves as I revel in this new experience. As I teeter on the edge, he pushes his thumb inside down to the first knuckle, and that's all it takes to push me over. I choke out my release, thighs shaking, the bed muffling my sound.

When I finally open my eyes, he's rolled me onto my side and is staring at me with a look of male satisfaction. He is very proud of himself and what he accomplished. I'd be annoyed if I wasn't the recipient of that accomplishment.

Kent pushes back, standing beside the bed. I take advantage of the situation and scoot down until my face is level with his hard cock. Precum drips from the tip, and my mouth waters. I stick my tongue out and lick it up.

"Do that again," he groans. Following his request, I do. I lick the tip before sucking it into my mouth. As I hollow my cheeks, Kent pushes in further. On my side, I don't have much leverage as he slowly fucks my mouth, never going deeper than I can handle. When I moan against his length, he pulls out. I pout.

"Fuck, Raven. You're too good at this."

Pleased with his praise, I lean forward to take more of him into my mouth. I wiggle my tongue to add a new sensation as he gently fucks my face. I can see the effort he is expending to keep from thrusting harder by the tension in his thighs. Who knew self-control could be so sexy? When I moan around his length, he pulls out abruptly.

"No more. I'm too close, and I don't want to come down your throat tonight. Roll over," he commands. I flop onto my back, watching Kent grab my extra pillows off the floor. He piles them underneath me before motioning for me to lift my ass. Once they are situated how he wants, he crawls on my bed and hovers over, dick already sleeved in a condom.

The pillows angle my hips flush with his when he is kneeling between my thighs. The angle allows the head of his cock to scrape my front wall and his pelvis to bump against my clit. Something I find out moments later when he – slowly but with no hesitation – pushes into me. The shock of the intrusion forces the air out of my lungs.

"Fuck," he grits, stilling above me, allowing me to adjust to his size. "No matter how many times I take this pussy, I forget how tight it is. You're nirvana, baby."

"You feel so good," I mewl. "Move, please."

Kent plunges back into me, pacing remains steady as he alternates between shallow and punishing thrusts. The dueling sensations keep me straddling the line of pleasure without pushing me over. I'm forced to remain supercharged by his touch and quivering beneath him.

He leans down and captures my mouth, his tongue thrusting in to mimic his cock. I turn my head to the side when the need for air overwhelms me. His lips trail down my neck, sucking love bites on my skin. I'm trembling as I near my orgasm. When he presses his teeth into my shoulder, I let out a piercing scream. Kent must follow me over the edge because both our chests are heaving as I come down from my high.

The moment is broken when we hear a shout through the wall. "If you have any tips on how I can get a girl to scream like that, leave them on my porch!"

Kent rolls his lips to stifle a smile as I die of embarrassment. Yeah, never facing Joe again.

Chapter Twenty-Three

• RAVEN •

"Will you shut up," Tiffany yells at Leo and Georgie as they chat in the corner of the rooftop pavilion we rented for Lola's surprise baby shower. Leo, the catcher who was recently called up from Memphis, throws his hands up in surrender while Georgie's eyes narrow at her.

"Excuse us for having fun, princess. Is this not a party?" he asks.

She huffs at his attitude. The two of us, along with Carina and Miller, have been planning this party for weeks, and the stress is getting to her. We shouldn't have been surprised by how involved Miller wanted to be in the process. If it wasn't for Carina, I think Tiffany may have killed him by now. Unfortunately Carina is busy distracting Lola today, which left Tiff, Miller, and I on day of prep. Watching the tiny blonde yell at the someone twice her weight over party favors has been the highlight of my week.

The cousins are on a fake scavenger hunt around town that Lola thinks Robby set up for Carina's birthday. It's partially true since Robby ended up surprising her with a real hunt, but it's also the ruse we used to get Lola out of the way. They are due to arrive at the rooftop bar any minute and it couldn't come sooner for Tiff's sanity.

"You can have fun once the woman of honor gets here. Until then, shut your pie hole so you don't give it away."

Georgie gears up for a retort, but Miller jumps in. "They're on their way up."

We take our places around the patio and prepare for their arrival. The second the elevator doors open, the girls are greeted with confetti cannons and cheers.

"Oh my God!" Lola yells. "What are you all doing here?" As she puts the pieces together, tears spring to her eyes.

"Shit," Miller curses.

Lola falls into his arms but quickly waves him off. "Sorry, this pregnancy has made me an emotional wreck. I can't believe you all are here to celebrate me and—Marilyn?!" Lola squeaks as she spots her mother-in-law. As the mama-to-be makes the rounds, hugging and crying over everyone, the rest of us return to the party.

I haven't met up with Kent in over a week. The team had an away series in New York and returned yesterday. It's why Miller couldn't help as much with the planning as he wanted.

Despite Miller's absence, the party is going off without a hitch. It's fun seeing the older players with their wives. They're softer than when on the field or in interviews.

This is the biggest event Kent and I have attended since starting our arrangement. I don't quite know how to act. I don't want to make it too obvious, but I also want to be near him. Pushing my desires aside, for now, I introduce Carina to Macy.

"Care, have you met Macy? She's an agent at G&K. We survived Professor Freitag's Calculus course together at Belmont. Mace, this is Lola's cousin and Robby Becker's better half."

"Of course, it's nice to meet you officially. I have heard great things about you from Robby."

"It's great to meet you, too. I am thrilled to celebrate Baby Miller! This is my first client to have a baby."

"Is that a good thing or a bad thing?" Carina's expression holds trepidation. I wonder if she and Robby are going to try soon.

"It's great," Macy answers. "Now that he's officially a family man, Miller's stock has only gone up." Carina smiles in relief and Macy turns her attention to me. "What's this I hear about you redoing the McMahan recording studio? I saw some footage when Eliza showed off Declan's new EP short film. It is stunning!"

"Thank you." I beam at the praise.

"Didn't she do such a good job? She redid the Becker Foundation offices, and I never want to leave now. Robby is always having to drag me away! Did she tell you her big news?"

"She did not!" Macy glances at me expectantly, and I flush.

"Go on, Miss HRN Star!" Carina prompts.

"No way!"

"Yes, way! Our little Ray is going to have her own show on HRN and become so rich and famous she'll stop returning our calls," Carina teases.

"Let's not get ahead of ourselves. All they did was green-light a pilot. If it tests well, they'll order a twelve-episode mini season. If that has good ratings, then they'll offer me a full contract."

"Still," Macy gushes. "That is such a cool opportunity. And I can say, 'I knew her when she was the girl with the cute dorm.' You're going to kill it!"

"What are we killing?" a masculine voice asks behind me. The hair on the back of my neck stands at Kent's proximity, and his familiar scent fills my lungs.

"HRN asked Raven to film a pilot of her show!" Carina shares.

The only sign he's surprised by the news is the slight widening of his eyes. Otherwise, he keeps his features neutral aside from his typical, easy smile. "That is amazing. I didn't know they announced their decision on that."

"They called me a couple of days ago," I state, chastened that I didn't tell him as soon as I heard. He knew I was working toward it, but he'd been out of town, and I hadn't told him I got it yet. I wanted to call him as soon as I heard, but that read too relationship-y. I didn't know how to causally bring it up later.

His expression softens when he takes in my demeanor. "That's incredible news. I know you're thrilled. Macy is right. You will kill it."

Carina is watching our interaction with interest but is soon distracted when Macy asks about the gala she is planning next month. Tiffany announces it's time to play some shower games. I laugh my ass off, watching Georgie dominate in the diaper-changing challenge, and Charlie and Robby battle it out in the baby food taste test.

Miller thanks everyone for coming, and Lola cries as she tells everyone they're having a girl! We all cheer and badger them for names. They announce they are naming her Leona Rose Miller after their maternal grandmothers. Marilyn and Teresa join in on Lola's crying until their husbands rush to wipe away their happy tears.

As the party winds down, Kent pulls me aside and confronts me about not sharing my news with him. Next thing I know, he's pulled me into a car and we're heading to my place so he can 'reward' me.

Chapter Twenty-Four

• KENT •

I didn't have 'attend a baby shower' on my bingo card for this summer, but Miller made it clear attendance was mandatory in case my absence made Lola cry. Which is a pretty common occurrence these days. I can't handle the pregnancy tears, so I do what I'm told and do everything I can to keep her smiling.

The fact that Raven will be there is a bonus. The team has been out of town playing an away series. We returned yesterday morning, but I didn't want to appear too eager to see her by reaching out immediately. I find myself itching to text her when I'm gone simply to see how her day is or to get updates on her crusade against single-use bags at the farmers' market.

I don't understand my strong emotions toward Raven, but I'm chalking it up to this being the most consistent FWB I've had and the only one from my friend circle. I care about what happens to my friends; she is one of them. The fact that we fuck is secondary. Although, I've never been territorial or annoyed at the idea of Tiffany hooking up with someone. I'm usually cheering her on from the sidelines. She and I are kindred spirits in that way.

My relationship with Raven is different. The idea of another man touching her sets my blood on fire. I know I should spend more time understanding those emotions but I am afraid to see where that will lead. I'd rather blame it on our friendship and fire our chemistry is. No need to delve deeper.

As I talk to George and Leo, the newest addition to our team, I track not-my-girl from my peripherals. She and Tiffany did the lion's share of party prep. I don't want to interfere with their plans. As she's chatting with Macy and Carina, that blush I love colors her cheeks, and I can't stop myself from walking toward her to find out what caused it. It's as if I'm a moth and she's a goddamn flame.

As I land behind her, I hear the girls gushing over being selected to film a pilot. Surprise rushes through me. Raven told me about her dream to be on HRN and help more small businesses, but I didn't realize it was this close to being a reality. I'm taken aback that she didn't share such big news with me. Not wanting to appear affected, I plaster on my best party smile.

Raven bites her lips and diverts her eyes away from my gaze. When she peers back up at me, her expression is sheepish when she says the news is recent. As much as I wish she would have told me, I can understand why she didn't. We're friends, naked friends even, but not 'call each other with life-changing news' friends. That would blur some lines.

The thought that I'm not one of the people she calls with good news gives me heartburn. Rubbing my chest, I congratulate her. She graces me with a smile so genuine it eases the tension in my body and has my mind working overtime.

The party continues for several more hours as we play games, open presents, and listen to Miller wax poetic about his love and their expected bundle of joy. I haven't spoken to Raven again, but my body is constantly aware of her presence, oddly in tune with where she is and who she's talking to.

When she lingers in conversation with Macy and Leo, rolling her eyes at something the blond said. The sight causes my jaw to tick, and I wonder if our catcher can still play with his jaw wired shut. Doubtful.

The whiskey I'm sipping sours in my mouth. After a few minutes, Raven makes her way over to the favors table, and I use the opportunity to get her alone. Sliding in behind her, my mind flashes back to the first time we were in this position – Friendsgiving.

When she senses me, Raven turns her head to greet me. "Hi."

"Firefly," I murmur. Surveying those left at the party, I usher her behind a large decor piece covered in the baby outfits we were forced to decorate. I inhale her lavender and mint scent, and it's a balm to my soul. Pulling her toward me by her hips, I trace the line from her shoulder to her ear with my nose, kissing as I go. "You've been keeping secrets."

"I wouldn't say it was a secret; I just hadn't gotten around to telling you yet. You've been out of town, and we haven't had much time to connect," she replies.

I hum in response. "That is true, but I'm here now with plenty of time to connect and, most importantly, reward you for your accomplishment."

"Reward?" she asks, perking up at the idea.

"Mhmm. You deserve one for achieving one of your goals. But what reward should I give you? Jewelry? Nah, too flashy for your tastes. Flowers? Maybe, but not impactful enough. Decisions, decisions." The truth is I'd give her either of those things if she wanted them, but I can think of something much better that will be rewarding for us both.

Her breath catches as I slide one hand up her body to twist a strand of her soft hair around my finger. The other coasts down to rub the creamy skin of her thigh under her dress. "What do you want, Raven?"

"You," she answers without hesitation.

"Me? Do you want me to reward your hard work by making you

come over and over until you pass out from pleasure? Is that what you want?"

"Yes, please."

"Such a polite, needy girl." I press my mouth against hers. Not in a kiss, not yet. I want to build up her anticipation. I want her to be as desperate for me as I am for her. To crave my touch, my taste, my everything the way I crave her. "You beg so sweet. I'll give you what you want. But not here. Let's go to your place." It's not a suggestion but a demand.

When she nods, I link my fingers between hers and guide us to the emergency stairwell. I called a car before approaching her, and it is waiting outside. Raven is silent beside me as the driver and I discuss the Songbirds' season. I'd think she was indifferent if her pulse wasn't fluttering under my thumb.

I thank the driver when we pull up to her house and follow her inside. The second the door closes, I am on her. I push her against the wood and plunge my tongue into her mouth as my hands roam over her curves.

"God, I missed this," I mutter into our kiss.

"Me too," she moans.

It's only been over a week since we have seen each other, but my body has been aching for her. Maybe her crystals and manifestation have bewitched me, but as long as I get to experience her pussy gripping my cock, I don't care. "I've got to take you now, baby. I'll worship you after, but I'll die if I don't get inside you now."

She nods, and I hoist her up into my arms.

Grabbing the bottom of her dress, I quickly peel it off her. As much as I enjoyed watching her in it all night, it has to go. The bra is next, but I can't rid her of her panties without putting her down, which I don't want to do. Pulling them to the side will have to do.

As I unfasten my belt, Raven clumsily works my buttons. "Shirt off. I want your skin against me," she mutters.

With my belt unbuckled, I pause to help her. Buttons undone, I shrug off my shirt and push my pants down the rest of the way. With one hand, I slide on a condom while the other swipes through her folds to make sure she's wet. I may be desperate, but I'm not a prick. She's more than ready to take me, thank Christ.

Readjusting her in my arms, I thrust into her warm heat. An immediate sense of rightness settles over me. Being inside her is like no nothing I've ever had. It leaves me both calm and frantic, content and out of control. I know I should explore it more, but its too good to question.

Making good on my earlier promise, I hammer into Raven, pressing her further into the door. It's reminiscent of our first time together. Both in location and how needy I feel. But this time, I know I can have her again and again.

"So hot. So tight," I grit when she flutters around me.

Raven throws her head back as pleasure overwhelms her. When her pussy pulsates around my cock again. I'm done. I'm coming right along with her.

I don't know how long I stand there with her wedged between me and the door, but when I glance up, her blissed-out eyes stare down at me. I kiss her gently as I tighten my arms around her thighs and carry her through the house and into her bedroom. She lets out a contented sigh when I gently lay her down.

Leaving her on the bed, I head to the kitchen to grab two glasses of water. While filling them, her cat jumps on the counter and glares at me expectantly. When I shut the water off, he meows. I turn it back on and witness him drinking straight from the faucet. Shaking my head, I wait as he gets his fill. With not so much as a 'thank you,' he returns to whatever perch he came from.

Back in the bedroom, Raven is curled up on her side. She graciously accepts the water, placing it on the nightstand after she's done. When I settle in beside her, she eyes me quizzically.

"What are you doing?" she asks.

"Laying down. What does it look like?"

"I don't know. You don't normally stick around for long." Her tone holds no malice, but I still have to hold in a grimace at her observation. She's right. I usually provide the requisite aftercare and then dip. The idea of doing that right now feels wrong, though. After being apart over a week, I crave connection with her. I don't tell her that, though.

"I told you I planned to worship you, Firefly. I just need a few minutes to recoup my strength, and then I'm not stopping until you forget your own name."

"Why do you call me that?"

"Call you what?"

"Firefly," she repeats the main endearment I have used for her since Vegas.

"I've called you lots of nicknames."

"I know, but that one stuck. Why?"

"I guess I found one that finally fit," I answer.

"What makes it better than the others? It doesn't have anything to do with having red hair."

"It doesn't directly, but it does have fire in it."

"Why does it fit?"

I take a moment to think about why I chose it and whether I want to tell her the truth. Seeing no reason to lie, I tell her. "Because you have a spark, I can't help but be drawn to, and you shine even in the darkness."

I expect her to have a sassy retort. Instead, she pulls my face into hers and fuses our lips together. Licking the seam of my mouth, she coaxes her tongue into it. When mine fights for the lead, she submits beautifully. We lay there making out for so long I feel like a high schooler.

I can tell the moment Raven registers my thickening cock against her leg. She removes the hand on my chest and lightly grazes it down my body until she wraps it around my length and pumps lazily. I buck into her hand.

"I'm supposed to be worshipping you," I argue. Now that my initial need is satiated, I want to show her how proud I am of her accomplishment. I don't know how to do that with words, but my body knows exactly what to do. I've become a Raven expert the last several weeks and I'm ready to pull out all my tricks.

"No one is stopping you," she teases. That's all the invitation I need to spend the next several hours making her come on my fingers, tongue, cock. She's so oversensitive by the end that she may have come from a puff of air against her clit. We'll have to try that again another time to be sure.

Raven passes out in my arms after using a washcloth to clean up as much of our mess as possible. She'll probably wish she took a shower in the morning, but there's nothing I can do about it now.

Laying there with her wrapped in my arms, I know I should get up and leave. For whatever reason, I can't muster up the mental or physical strength to go. I am overcome with a sense of peace and calm that I don't want to disturb. I tell myself I'll close my eyes for a moment. Contentment washes over me. I don't know why, but I think I'd do almost anything to keep it.

Chapter Twenty-Five

• KENT •

Rousing from the best night of sleep I've had in, I don't know how long, I stretch out in my bed. Only, I'm not in my bed. I'm in Raven's. Her red hair is splayed across my chest, and her shallow breaths ghosts my skin. I didn't intend to fall asleep here last night, but the peace that washed over me with Raven in my arms was too much to fight. Now, I don't know what to do with myself, uncomfortable that I broke my rules.

I've taken power naps at girls' houses before but never stayed until morning. I usually leave before the sun rises. I don't know how to do the morning after. The last time this happened was in Vegas when I pretended to be asleep as Raven snuck out of my hotel room. I may not remember our night together, but I remember the peace that thrummed under my hangover the next day.

Unable to ruminate any longer, I slip out of bed and freshen up as best I can in her bathroom. Her rental is charming, but I'll take my modern shower over her plaster tub any day. I smile when I see the cute note on her mirror: 'You can do hard things.' I'll have to tease her about the innuendo later.

Usually, after a night like last night, I cook myself a traditional Filipino breakfast. Cooking helps me center. I know I won't get the full impact at Raven's, but I'm sure I can conjure up something. Searching through her kitchen, I find eggs, bacon, and grits. It's not the silog I am craving, but it will do.

Humming to myself while I cook, I get lost in thoughts about last night. When something fluffy unexpectedly rubs against my leg, I barely hold in a high-pitched squeal. I can't keep hold of the spatula, though, and it flies through the air. Once I regain my composure, I spot Cappy licking my discarded utensil. Shooing him away, I toss it in the sink and pull a new one out of a jar I'd put money on Raven found at a flea market. It is just eclectic enough to be vintage and matches the hodgepodge vibe of everything else in her kitchen.

Returning to the stove, I peer into the living room to be met by a judgy feline stare. "Listen," I say, "I don't think cats are supposed to have bacon, my dude. I'm thinking of you here." I swear he rolls his eyes at me before jumping down to settle at his perch in the window. I smile to myself. If anyone's cat could roll its eyes, it would be hers. Like mother, like son.

As I resume my cooking, Raven finally stumbles into the kitchen, adorably ruffled from a hard night of fucking and sleep. "Morning, Firefly."

"Oh my God," she gasps. "You're still here."

"I am," I state. "What were you reading so hard that you didn't hear me banging around in here?"

"My horoscope. Gotta see how my day is going to go? I'll read you yours, too."

"You let pseudo-science determine how your day is going to go?" I ask, smirking when she scrunches her nose at me.

"It's not pseudo-science, people have trusted astrology for millenniums. And I don't let it 'determine my day,' but it doesn't hurt to know what I'm up against. That's such an Aquarius opinion to have which doesn't surprise me at all. You're so—"

Before she has the chance to tell me what fictional traits I share with other February babies, the doorbell rings.

"Expecting someone?"

"At eight o'clock in the morning? Not a chance." Raven drifts to the door and peers through the peephole. She's paler when she turns back to me. "I'm so sorry about this."

"About what? You don't have a secret husband coming home from deployment who's going to kick my ass, do you?" I joke. The idea brings back the burning in my chest.

"Worse. It's my sister. She won't beat you up, but she will interrogate the shit out of me."

"I can hear you talking," a feminine voice shouts through the door. "You might as well let me in."

Pushing out a raspberry, Raven's gaze locks into mine. I don't know if she's gauging me for permission but we don't have any options at this point. "I'll make more eggs," is my only response.

"Hi, Em," Raven says, letting her sister inside.

"Hey, Ray Ray. If you left me out there much longer, I was going to chat up your neighbor. He seems interesting. Giving major Mr. Robutusen vibes. Could have been highly informative."

While the sisters bicker back and forth about the resemblance of Joe to someone from a 'oos teen movie, I take in Emily. If I hadn't known she was Raven's sister already, the red hair and tall stature would have given it away. Their faces and mannerisms mirror each other, but their bodies do not. Where Raven is all soft curves, her sister is lithe muscle. While I can appreciate her form, I've become partial to Raven's hourglass shape.

"What are you doing here?" Raven asks as I tune back into the conversation.

"I'm in town for that half-marathon, remember? It's this weekend."

"Oh my God. I forgot about that! I've been preoccupied."

"I bet," her sister smirks, scanning over my bare chest. I feel oddly exposed under her perusal. I'm normally beyond confident, but the idea that an important person in Raven's life might find me lacking taps into my vulnerabilities.

"Kent? Your water is boiling over," Raven informs me.

"What? Oh shit," I say when her words register.

Emily waltzes into the kitchen and plants herself on a barstool, picking up Cappy, who swarmed her when she came in. "Are you going to make introductions, Raven, or should I pretend one of the best hitters in the MLB and top-ranked baseball bulge owner isn't shirtless in your kitchen."

"Jesus," Raven groans. "Have you ever heard of subtlety? Kent, this is my sister, Emily. Emily, this is my, this is Kent. My friend."

"Friend, huh? Do your other friends spend a lot of time topless around you?"

"You'd be surprised how comfortable Tiffany is with her body," Raven deadpans.

The sisters chat among themselves while I finish making our breakfast. I chime in occasionally, especially when the topic of Raven's childhood horse obsession comes up.

"I can't picture you as a horse girl," I murmur, seeing Raven in a new light after some of the stories her sister regaled me with.

"That's because she wasn't. The first time she was around a horse in person, she panicked and never talked about them again. She's afraid of them."

"I'm not *afraid* of them," she huffs. "I simply respect the majestic creatures that they are. Besides, have you ever been around a horse before? They're massive!"

"They sure are," I cajole, earning me an eye roll. I grimace when I glance at the time. "Shit, I've gotta get going. First pitch is at six today."

"I'll walk you out," Raven says. I hurry back into her bedroom and grab my stuff. I threw my shirt on before we ate.

"Sorry about this morning," Raven apologizes when we're on the porch. "I forgot she was coming, and even if I remembered, I wouldn't have expected her to be over this early."

"It's fine, Firefly. It was cool meeting your sister. Her stories were great. Now I know never to try to impress you by showing up on a trusty steed."

"You don't have to do anything to impress me. You do that by being you."

"I do?" The question slips out before I can stop it.

"Of course. You're ranked in the top ten on *BaseballBulges.com*. Who needs a horse when I can ride you?" Her eyes twinkle with delight as she moves in closer.

I bark out a laugh when a wink follows her statement. "You're too much. I'll talk to you later, babe."

"Bye," she whispers against my lips. Not one to pass up an opportunity, I turn the kiss dirtier than warranted for a morning goodbye. I swear I can taste her on my tongue for the rest of the day.

Chapter Twenty-Six

When I woke up alone the night after Lola's baby shower, I wasn't surprised. Imagine my shock when I walked into the kitchen and was greeted by the sight of Kent cooking me breakfast. I figured he would be long gone by then. Spending the night wasn't something we had done before unless you count that night in Vegas. Seeing as we've never brought it up, he either doesn't recall or we're pretending it didn't happen.

Unfortunately, we didn't have the chance to talk about it because my sister decided to show up early for her race. I was caught off guard by the two of them together in my home. I don't recall much of the conversation. My brain may have also been fried from the night before when Kent orgasmed it into mush.

After he left, Emily dialed up her interrogation to one hundred. I gave her the quick version of how we are FWBs, and neither of us wants more. She didn't appear convinced. "That man has it bad for you, Ray Ray," she declared after my debrief. "He wouldn't have hung around all morning if he didn't."

"He does not. He was being polite."

"Please," she scoffs. "Polite would be offering to leave, not making extra food, and listening to stories of how you petitioned to get unlimited ketchup packets at lunch in the third grade. Funny now that you're an anti-single-use plastic queen."

"Two isn't enough!" I argued.

"Yeah, yeah. I know. What I'm saying is that he stuck around because he wanted to. He wanted to learn about you and make an impression on me. You don't do that if you're just being polite – especially with a woman you're only screwing. That boy is catching feelings whether either of you realizes it or not."

With no clue how to respond to her assessment, I change the subject. "Do you want to see the design for my friend's gym? I could use the critical eye of someone whose idea of working out is more than having to park six blocks away."

We spend the rest of the day chatting about my upcoming pilot and her race and plans for the weekend. Brett and the twins will be flying in tomorrow to cheer her on. We thankfully avoid the topic of Kent for the rest of her visit.

July

For the first time in club history, the MLB All-Star Week is taking place in Nashville. Since the guys skipped out on the festivities for Robby and Carina's wedding last year, they're excited to enjoy it at home. It's an exciting week for everyone.

Earlier this week, Georgie played in the celebrity softball tournament, where I met Xavier Jackson, one of Macy's clients and shooting guard for Los Angeles Condors. My dad practically fainted when I sent him a selfie of us together. As a Midwestern girl, a love for basketball is in my blood. It doesn't hurt that Xavier has pythons for arms.

We also watched Ryan, a friend from Nashville's minor league team, play in the All-Star Futures game. And last night, Miller narrowly lost the Homerun Derby to a player from Miami. We're all hanging out in the team's suite tonight as we cheer on Kent and Robby in the All-Star Game.

I am both excited and nervous about watching Kent play. Things have been going great between us lately, but we are still on the DL. Every time I cheer for him, I can't shake the feeling that people are wondering why. But that's my paranoia talking.

As Kent's team returns to the dugout, a small Asian woman settles beside me. "He's good, isn't he?" she asks, nodding to Kent, taking practice swings while he is on deck.

"He is." When I take her in, I notice she shares Kent's warm chocolate eyes and bright smile. "Are you his mother?"

"I am," she beams. "Are you a friend of his?" The once-over she gives makes me squirm inside, but I try to maintain my composure.

"Yes! I went to high school with Lola, who is Miller's wife," I explain, pointing to my friend, who is currently covering a hotdog with questionable toppings. "I didn't know you'd be in town for this."

"Of course. I couldn't let my boy play in such a big game without someone cheering for him from the stands. I know many people are wishing him well, but it isn't the same when they are a fan." I nod in understanding.

Her gaze once again rakes over me and my generic Songbirds shirt tied at in a knot above my red midi skirt. "A pretty girl like you must have your eye on a certain player, no?"

"Oh, no, ma'am. I'm just here to support my friends."

"That's a shame," she chides. "My son is single, you know. He may be a little wild, but a knockout like you would have no trouble taming him. Ariel was always his favorite princess. "

I choke on my drink at her admission. My mind quickly flashes back to our Fuck, Marry, Kill game on the way to Vegas. He always chose to marry the Little Mermaid. A hand on my back pulls me out of the memory.

"Clara, you're here!" Tiffany says to my conversation partner.

"Hello, my dear," Clara replies. "If only this one could have fallen for my son. They would make such cute babies."

"You know he's more of a brother to me, Mama C. You'll have to get grandchildren elsewhere. I'm in my fun aunt era."

"*Sayang naman!* Tell me dear, how are you? Any new gossip from those celebrities you work with?"

My chest burns with an unfamiliar sensation at the ease at which the women in front of me have with one another. I know Tiffany isn't interested in Kent, but I envy her rapport with his mother. "I didn't realize you two were close," I murmur during a lull in their conversation.

"I accidentally crashed one of Kenny Boy's weekly video calls a few months after I moved here, and we've been besties ever since. The ube cookies she sends him are half the reason I put up with him." Clara and Tiffany laugh over their inside joke, increasing my jealousy.

Not wanting to make a poor impression, I continue to chat with Clara even after Tiffany heads to grab another drink. Out of the corner of my eye, I see her squaring off with Georgie, and a small part of me smiles that not everyone loves the vivacious blonde.

Hours later, our group has migrated to Holler's to celebrate the boys' winning the All-Star Game. Robby struck out several batters, and Kent caught the game-winning pop fly. Going to dinner with his mom, Kent still hasn't arrived yet.

Despite our arrangement being a secret and keeping our public contact to a minimum, I feel adrift without him here. His presence has always been an anchor in the room.

I'm wandering the VIP section when I spot Macy in the corner. "Hey, lady!" I call out in greeting. I do a double take when I notice the arm around her waist is attached to Leo. "This is new." I motion between the two of them. The catcher sports a sly grin as he peers down at my friend. Macy appears less comfortable but shrugs. "We haven't been seeing each other long."

"We met at the baby shower," Leo interjects. "The moment I spotted her across the room, I knew she was meant to be mine. It took some convincing, but she finally agreed to give me a shot." He seems genuinely infatuated, and I love that for her.

"I'm happy for you guys," I gush! "You've got a good one, Davis. Don't mess it up. I've met her family. They don't mess around."

Something dark crosses Leo's features before he returns to his cinnamon roll demeanor. Meanwhile, Macy leans further into him. "He's a good boy," she says with a pat on his chest. "Besides, you know I can hold my own. It's you we need to match up with someone special."

"I think she's got that covered," I swear I hear Leo whisper to himself. I catch Macy up on my latest career news: my pilot was picked up for a mini season. Sometime later, Leo spots Ryan and drags Macy off to meet him, but not before she demands I let her take me to lunch next week to celebrate.

Scanning the room for someone new to talk to, my vision is blocked by a broad set of shoulders in a too tight shirt. "Hi, you look like you could use some company."

Bleh. Derrick Jones, least likable guy on the Songbirds and maybe all of baseball. I'd rather not spend the next several minutes turning him down, but with no other familiar faces nearby, I am stuck.

As he speaks, his gaze roams up and down my body, lingering on my breasts for longer than appropriate. When he finally reaches my face, his eyes spark with recognition. "I know you. You're friends with Miller's girl. Robin?"

"Raven," I supply. "And you're Derrick."

"Yep," he confirms, seemingly pleased I knew who he was. Barf.

"You guys are having a good season," I say, to break the silence surrounding us. I immediately regret it.

"Yeah, we are. It's nice to be on a winning team. I mean, they didn't have a chance at the playoffs until I joined the team, but it's a group effort." I may not be the most versed in baseball, but I've heard enough from Carina and Lola to know that Derrick is not as good as he thinks.

"What does a sexy lady like you do for a living? Let me guess: pharmaceutical sales? No, dental hygienist?"

"I'm an interior designer."

"You know," he states, inching into my personal space. "My place could use some sprucing up. Maybe you can come over sometime to check it out. I have a spare room. I've been dying to turn into something more... fun, if you catch my drift."

Of course, I catch his drift. This man wouldn't know subtlety if it smacked him with a crop from his imaginary sex room. I offer a stilted laugh in response. "That isn't my area of expertise. You might want to ask Miller about that."

"Solid point. Miller is a kinky motherfucker, but he isn't nearly as nice to look at," he retorts in what he must think is a sexy croon but is more creepy than anything.

"Can I buy you a drink, Red?"

I cringe. I found it cute, if not funny, when Kent called me all those nicknames before he landed on Firefly.

When Derrick does it, it gives me the heebie-jeebies. I open my mouth to turn him down when Kent spots me over Derrick's shoulder. For once, being on the taller side has its perks. He momentarily stalls when he sees who I am chatting with, but eventually swaggers over to us.

"Jones. Raven," he greets in an icy tone. It stands slightly in front of me, cutting off Derrick's access.

"Don't tell me this one is claimed, too?" the creeper laments. "You guys can't go claiming all the choice pussy."

I gasp, affronted. Kent's jaw ticks. "We're just friends," he replies, stepping away slightly. "And if Miller hears you call Lola 'choice pussy' he'll kick your ass."

If I was offended before, I am even more so now. I can understand why Kent isn't claiming me publicly. I did the same thing with his mother earlier. But this thing between us has felt like more since the baby shower. He's stayed at my place several times, and we've even spent time together outside of bed. Granted, we haven't discussed any change in status, but hearing him call me 'just' a friend stings.

Even more maddening than that, though, is that he didn't defend me at all. He pointed out that Miller wouldn't want Lola to be discussed derogatorily but didn't say anything about me. When I peer up at him, his face is twisted in annoyance, as if this encounter is all my fault.

"In that case," Derrick drawls, moving into my personal space. "Maybe all three of us could have some fun together. I'm down if you are, Dela Cruz." I step toward Kent on instinct. He is stock still beside me. I once again shoot an expectant glare his way, thinking he will say something to defuse the situation. When he doesn't, my heart sinks.

"Pass," I declare, taking matters into my own hands.

"Aw, don't be that way, sweetheart. We'll make it worth your while. This guy is legendary with the ladies. I've heard—"

"Raven," a deep voice interrupts. Turning to my left, I see Miller watching our interaction with an assessing gaze. "Lola was searching for you. She wanted your opinion on something for the nursery. She's talking to Big Ron right now if you want to talk to her."

"Great idea," I stammer. As expected, Derrick takes a few steps back, allowing me to leave. I don't glance Kent's way as I hightail it away from the men. Guessing Miller was giving me an out and Lola isn't expecting me, I leave the bar and head home to take the hottest shower my ancient water heater can provide.

Chapter Twenty-Seven

Today will go down as one of the highlights of my career. It's not my first All-Star Game, but it was my best. I was on fire tonight. Not only did I hit a grand slam, but I also caught the game-ending ball. Getting to enjoy it with Robby was the icing on the cake. That and knowing I had people here for me.

I was so focused on getting to this point, I never allowed myself the chance to have a girl cheering for me in the stands. Not that Raven is my girl or cheering solely for me, but knowing she's here and excited for me pumped me up. Plus, my mom is here to watch me play. She only took off a few days, but since I haven't seen her since the season started, I'll take whatever I can.

I quickly shower off the game and meet Mom in the tunnel. She stays at my house when she comes into town. We grab dinner together before she returns to the lake. It is pleasant enough until the topic of Lola's pregnancy comes up.

"Is Miller as excited to be a dad soon?"

"Yeah," I murmur. "He's pretty pumped. They still have a couple months to go, though."

"I wouldn't be sure. I get the sense that the baby is coming sooner rather than later. Call it doctor's intuition."

"You're a doctor of rocks, Mom."

"Still more of a doctor than you," she scoffs. "No luck getting Tiffany to fall in love with you, *Nonoy*?"

"Jesus!"

"What? I like that girl. She's plucky. I get it, though. She'd run circles around you," she muses. "I met a pretty redhead in the suite. Have you tried getting her to fall in love with you?"

Mom met Raven? I knew they would both be in the box, but I didn't consider that they might interact. It was full of my teammates and their families. Did Raven seek her out? Did Tiffany introduce them? She's been acting weird lately. I think she may have a fuck buddy of her own. Or she knows about me and Raven. We've been doing this for almost four months now. I'd be shocked if no one was suspicious. Miller has definitely been giving me some suspicious scowls.

"I haven't tried to get anyone to fall in love with me. You know I don't have time for that right now. I'm focused on my game."

"Nonsense. If Miller and Robby have time, you do, too," she tsks. "You're at the pinnacle of your career. You need someone to share your success with. Not to mention, I'm not getting any younger. I want grandbabies. Hop to it."

"I'll take that under advisement." She nods at my response and thankfully changes the subject to all the 'rich people shit' she saw in the suite and on the flight here.

Seeing Mom off to the lake house, I take my car to the condo and walk to Holler's. My excitement for the evening has dulled from the conversation at dinner. I know she's ready for me to settle down, but I enjoy how things are now. Raven and I may not be a couple, but we have something steady and uncomplicated. If it ain't broke, don't fix it.

Have I muddied the water by occasionally spending the night at her place? Maybe. Did I buy a candle that smells like her that I sometimes light when she hasn't been over in a while? Not that I'd admit to under oath. But if I did, it would be comforting and homey. Has my interest in any other woman dwindled to zero? That is true. I've got a funny, chill bombshell in my bed several nights a week. Why search for anything else?

When I get to the VIP section, my gaze immediately seeks out that bombshell. Even though we try to limit our interactions in public, I can't help but track her in any room we're in. Her presence is a lighthouse in stormy seas. A firefly flickering on a moonless night. I may not need it at the moment, but I enjoy knowing it's there.

When I finally spot Raven, the heartburn I thought I'd gotten rid of returns. She is standing off to the side with Derrick. I'm too far away to hear what they're saying, but they're standing very close. I have to count to ten to stop myself from storming over there and pulling her away. I don't have a claim to this girl, no matter how much it feels like it during those nights I pretend to be too tired to go home.

She can talk to whomever she wants. At least, that is what I tell myself until I see her laughing at something Derrick said. She almost appears relieved when she spots me over his shoulder, but her gaze snaps back to his as I make my way over.

My expression must be possessive or predatory because Derrick groans and complains about all the 'choice pussy' being taken. Damn. I'm not the classiest guy, but even I would never say something that crass out loud. He's lucky I'm the only one who heard him say it. Some of the other guys wouldn't be as forgiving.

The territorial urge that overwhelms me is not something I am used to. I don't know what to do about it, but I want this conversation to be over and for Derrick to get away from us. When Raven doesn't say anything to him, I do.

When I tell him we're just friends and to watch how he talks about Lola, Raven stiffens. It's true, though. Miller could rock his shit for talking about his wife, and we all know he is. He's still salty about Miller staking his claim when he tried to shoot his shot with her.

When I glance down at Raven, she is glaring at me. Is she mad I interrupted their conversation? Surely, she isn't interested in Derrick. My lips curl in disgust at the thought of her wanting to be with him over me. Not happening, sweetheart.

Oblivious to the tension brewing in front of him, Derrick makes a truly insane proposition about a threesome between us. I am too shocked by Derrick's audacity to do anything but stare at my idiotic teammate.

When Raven declines, he tries to entice her by talking about my sexual prowess, which is a weird move all on its own. He hasn't even asked me if I would be down, and no, I would not be down to share Raven with him or anyone. Before he can piss me off further, Miller intervenes, and Raven walks away. I don't see her for the rest of the night, which agitates me even more. Somehow, this day that was such a high point ended low.

Chapter Twenty-Eight

• RAVEN •

"I think that is everything," I announce as I place the oversized mirror in the corner of the Lavigne Vineyards upgraded bridal suite. "What do you think?"

"This is beyond! You are a goddess," Emerly gushes. "Let's go to the office. The Money Man has to sign your final check."

"Who?"

"Marc. He won't let me on the account, even though my events bring in a third of our income. If he wants to handle all the finances, he gets to be 'Money Man.' I considered calling him Daddy Winebucks, but since he's my brother, I decided against it. You should, though! I'd love to see his reaction." Her eyes gleam with mischief at the idea.

"I don't think I'm going to call my client Daddy. I'm sure you can find someone else to do it," I laugh.

"Fine. Be professional about it."

As we walk through the building, I admire my handiwork. I worked with the Lavignes to redo most of their indoor public-facing areas, which included the groom and bridal suites, tasting room, and banquet hall for smaller events. We also created a multipurpose space which can be used for their art classes and exercise offerings when the weather outside isn't tenable.

I follow a bouncing Emerly up the stairs into the winery's main offices. The space is open with a few desks and a door at the end of a hall with a makeshift sign that says 'Boss Man.'

"Your doing?" I ask. She gives me a halfhearted shrug, but the smile she's trying to hold back confirms.

Emerly opens the door without knocking and traipses right in. "Money Man, it's time to pay the nice lady for making our vineyard all pretty."

Marc glances up from his desk and gives his sister an exasperated glare. "Hey, Raven. Have a seat while I find your check."

"Do you need me for anything else? I told Penny I'd meet her for lunch."

"I'm good, Bubbles. Tell Penny I still need her status report."

"Yeah, yeah. I will. See ya later, bro," she sasses. "Bye, Raven. Thank you for everything you did. I can't wait to see our guests enjoy the new spaces. You better come back for our end-of-harvest festival."

"You're welcome, and I will."

"I hope working with my sister hasn't been too challenging," Marc states. "Of the five of us, she has the best taste for design. I shudder to think how the rooms would have turned out if you'd worked with Josh or Payton. Penny and I are a little better, but Emerly has an artist's eye."

"I'm sure it would have been lovely no matter what, but Emerly was a delight to work with."

"That's one word for her," he mumbles, pulling out a black ledger.

"Thank you," I say, taking the check from his hand. "I'll be back with the film crew on Tuesday to shoot your reactions for the show. Act surprised."

"Hey, I'll have you know I was St. Gabriel's Joseph in my senior year Christmas nativity play."

"My apologies; I didn't realize I was in the presence of a professional actor."

"Don't you forget it," he taunts. "I'll accept your apology in exchange for dinner after the reveal."

"Dinner? Like as a date?" I question.

"I was hoping. I've wanted to ask you out since the Christmas party, but didn't want to make a move while we were a client in case it crossed any professional boundaries. Now that the renovation is complete, there is nothing to hold me back. We can celebrate wrapping the project and get to know each other better."

"Wow. I-I didn't see this coming," I awkwardly laugh. "Can I think about it? I'm not sure if there are any rules on HRN's part I need to follow."

"Of course," he says reassuringly. "And if Tuesday doesn't work, we can try another time. I'd be lucky to enjoy your company any night of the week." I blush at the comment. Marc and I flirted at the Christmas party, but he has been strictly professional ever since. I wouldn't have thought he was interested in me.

"Let me walk you out," Marc suggests. He guides me out of the office and down to the gravel parking lot with a hand on my lower back.

"I hope you'll consider my dinner offer. I'd be a fool for not shooting my shot with a woman as talented and gorgeous as you."

"I will," I reply. "Thank you for asking and for letting me film your renovation."

"The pleasure was all mine," he says with a smile. Marc opens the door to my car and taps on the roof after he closes it. As I pull away, I think about his proposal. I haven't thought much about dating since my arrangement with Kent began. After the other night, I wonder if I should.

Marc is a great guy. He's got a good job. He is sweet to his sister and obviously family-oriented. I wonder what he think about cats. He screams 'dog guy.' This is a lot to think through on my own. I need some outside perspective.

Deciding I need to talk out everything, I head downtown instead of home. This isn't a text conversation. I hope Lola isn't too busy. She said she was going to be nesting all day. I walk to her apartment as stealthily as possible, hoping to avoid Kent. When I knock, Miller is there to greet me. "Hey."

"Hi. Sorry, I didn't call first. Is Lo around?"

"She's in the kitchen," he directs. "I didn't get to check on you the other night. You good?"

"Yeah," I answer honestly. "Thank you for stepping in. I wasn't sure how to exit the situation gracefully."

His expression hardens as he levels me with his stare. "You don't owe grace to people making you uncomfortable. The only person you owe geniality to is yourself. Don't let anyone force you into a situation you don't want to be in because of social niceties. If they have a problem with that, they can take it up with me."

Damn. That is heavy advice for a Thursday afternoon.

"Let me know if Derrick bothers you again. I'll take care of it."

Offering him a soft smile, I pat him on the arm. "You got it, big guy."

When I shift past him and step into the open kitchen area, Lola peeks up from the Nutella she's dipping into. The sight stops me in my tracks.

"What in the hell are you eating?" I ask.

Ignoring my disgust, she continues swirling her pickle in the hazelnut spread. "When you're in your third trimester, you can judge my cravings. Until then, shut it. Care to explain why you barged into my condo and disrupted my pre-dinner snack?"

Walking across her kitchen, I grab a spoon and dip it in the jar before shoving it in my mouth. "Ack, pickle juice," I spit. "I'm going to need something strong to wash that down."

Several minutes later with glasses in hand – mine with red wine and hers with a virgin bellini – we sink onto her living room couch.

"What's wrong, Ray?" she questions, expression tight with concern.

"I have confusing feelings and don't know what to do about them."

"Alright, what spurred them?"

"Right now, a creepy encounter I had with Derrick at Holler's. But it is mainly Kent that is causing my turmoil."

"Fucking Derrick," she mutters. "What does Kent have to do with Derrick being a perv?"

I tell Lola all about my encounter with Derrick, and Kent's – lack of – response. She nods, but I can tell that not all the dots are connecting.

"There is something I should mention that will help the details I add up," I confess.

"Okay..."

"Kent and I have kinda, sorta have had a friends-with-benefits thing going for the last several months..."

"What?!" she shrieks. Pulling out her phone, she types furiously. "Oh, no. You are going to give me more than that. Hold, please."

"What are you doing?"

"Texting Carina and Tiffany. They need to be here for this."

"I don't think that's necessary."

"Too late and you're wrong. Drink your wine."

1:50 PM

LOLA

DEFCON-5. Please report to the Miller residence ASAP for an important discussion.

CARINA

Is everything okay with the baby?? I'm on my way down now. Do you need help? Should I bring Robby?

TIFF

I thought we weren't using the DEFCON
scale anymore since we couldn't figure it
out. Do I have time to finish this episode?

LOLA

No to Robby and no to the episode.

I'll help you out. The BAU solves the crime
and catches the murderer. Now leave!

TIFF

Geez. Spoiler alert.

CARINA

Every episode ends the same way, Babs.
I'm on the way, but Robby will want the tea
☕. Is Raven coming?

LOLA

She's already here.

"This is a little much, don't you think?" I state with a glare.

"Not when you've been hiding things from us, missy."

I pour another glass of wine while Lola catches the other girls up on my drama.

"I knew something was going on between you two!" Tiffany exclaims.

"Whatever, you so did not."

"Yes, I did. I could tell something was different with Kent. The man bought a lavender candle. And USED it. Plus, you had the chillness only consistent dicking down can give. You should have seen how frazzled this one was before Robby came back into the picture."

"I was doing fine by myself, thank you very much," Carina remarks. "How did this happen?"

I tell the girls about Vegas and everything that has happened between us since. I also get into the Zach incident and what I've been thinking about since the Derrick altercation.

"I hate to say it, babe, but I think your situationship may have run its course. Even if he doesn't want to commit, he can't let some other guy perv on you in front of him," Lola says.

"Before Robby and I even got back together, he was punching men for touching me," Carina notes. "I can't believe he let Derrick creep on you, FWBs or not."

"Maybe he was jealous," Tiffany suggests in Kent's defense.

"Of someone making me uncomfortable? He was standing right beside me. No one with half a brain and any self-respect would hook up with Derrick."

"I don't know. Maybe he thought you were into it and wanted to try being a double-stuffed Oreo."

"Ew. Don't say it that way. And pass." I state.

"You don't know what you're missing," Tiffany sighs.

"What I miss is having a guy who will defend me and be proud I'm his," I admit. "I miss having a guy who wants me – all of me. I know it was my idea, but keeping it from y'all has sucked. Then I thought the vibe changed, but clearly, it did not. It's getting complicated now."

"Nothing is hotter than a man who stakes his claim. Sounds as if you want a boyfriend," Carina surmises.

"Kent is not boyfriend material," I argue.

"No, he's not," she quickly agrees. "But, in general, I think you're missing that emotional side of a relationship, the security and commitment. Have you dated at all since this y'all hooked up?"

"No, at first, I didn't have time with building my business. And then we had a comfortable routine going. We even had a few sleepovers in the last month. Those were nice. Ugh, I think you may be right. I want more of that. The simple things: eating breakfast together, holding hands, going out on dates."

"Kent could do all those things," Tiffany interjects.

"But he doesn't want to," I say. "He's made that clear."

"Has anyone caught your eye lately?" Carina asks.

"A cute guy asked me out this morning, actually. It's what made me question this thing with Kent."

"Who?"

"Marc Lavigne. I redid a few rooms at the winery for the show."

"Oooooh, a workplace romance." Carina tilts her head as if she is already writing our happily ever after.

"Not quite. I finished the job today, and that's when he asked me out. I told him I'd think about it."

"You have to go!" Lola exclaims. "Marc is a great guy. He is kind, good-looking, and successful."

"Kent is all those things," Tiffany points out.

"Marc is also ready for commitment and has unlimited access to wine." Lola glares at our friend, who is clearly hung up on the idea of Kent and I.

"Kent's rich. He can buy all the wine he wants. So what if he doesn't want to lie around and cuddle? Cuddling is overrated," she grouses.

"Cuddling is the best," Lola sniffs. Opening her mouth to argue, Tiffany stops when she sees Lola's face.

"Oh my God. Are you crying?"

"No. Yes. I don't know! Pregnancy hormones are a bitch!" Lola laments.

As if his Loladar went off, Miller exits their bedroom. Seeing his wife wiping her cheeks, he scoops her up from the couch. They whisper back and forth, and then he glances back at us.

"I'm going to grab this one food from the taco truck. Anyone want anything?"

We all decline, telling him we'll be gone when he returns. The girls and I say our goodbyes and head our separate ways. As I go about the rest of my day, I can't help but wonder if the girls are right and my arrangement with Kent has run its course. He is unable or at least unwilling to meet my needs. I'm changing the game. It's on me to make the call.

Giving him one last chance to prove himself, I message him.

3:52 PM

149

That's it. That is all he said. We usually text every few days, if not every day. I haven't heard from him since the All-Star Game, and all he says is, 'Can't?' Absolutely not.

4:01 PM

Chapter Twenty-Nine

I never thought I had a petty streak, but I proved myself wrong. It's been two days since the All-Star Game, and I haven't contacted Raven. The longer she waits to talk to me, the more I think she may be annoyed I twatblocked her with Derrick. I can't believe she would be interested in that guy. Our arrangement is exclusive, sexually. She's going to have to tell me to my face if she wants to fuck him. I don't want to have that conversation right now.

That's why I tell her I can't meet up when she texts me the day before we leave for an away series. I need some space to get over these emotions before I see her again and do something stupid like tell her I was jealous.

I'm sitting in the Steelman's locker room after winning 4-1 when Leo plops down beside me. "Hey man, you have plans tonight? I think I'm going to hit up this bar that a buddy of mine from college works at."

"Thanks for the invite, but I think I'm going to call it a night. I'm not in the mood to deal with a bunch of cleat chasers I can't hook up with," I reply.

"Why can't you hook up wi—This wouldn't have something to do with a certain redhead, would it? I thought you didn't date."

Damn. He's an astute bastard. "I don't know what you're talking about. Nothing is going on between me and Raven." Beside me, Miller snorts.

"You good?" I ask.

"Yep," is his only response.

"And you can't hook up because?" Leo inquires. I run my hand down my face, trying to concoct an excuse that will satisfy his curiosity but not lead to more questions.

"I've got an exclusive friends-with-benefits thing going on, and we agreed not to sleep with other people."

"So you have a girlfriend." Leo states.

"It's not like that," I argue. "We aren't dating. It's a respect thing."

At that, Miller lets out a full-blown scoff.

"You sure you don't have something to say?" I question Miller. "It sounds as if you have an opinion."

My captain eyes me dubiously before he responds. "I was thinking that it's a good thing you don't want to date her, considering she's going on one tomorrow."

"What did you just say?" I demand.

"Raven. Your not-girlfriend is going on a date tomorrow."

"What the fuck?! With who? We're supposed to be exclusive!"

"Exclusively screwing. As I understand it, she's allowed to go out with other people. It's a first date, and unlike you, she doesn't sleep with every person who sends a flirty smile her way."

Okay, ouch. That assessment, while not 100 percent inaccurate, hurt. I have some standards, but it's not my fault plenty of women meet them. I haven't given anyone a second glance since we first hooked up months ago. Why would I need to when I've got a saucy little Firefly?

Any retort I can think of sounds weak, but I give one anyway. "I guess I shouldn't be surprised she's out trying to find another guy to add to her roster after flirting with Derrick the other night."

"Were we even at the same party, man? Your girl had no interest in Derrick-fucking-Jones. She couldn't get away from him fast enough. Your response to that situation is probably why she's going out with another guy." Miller's raised voice has the players left in the locker room glancing around nervously, but he continues his verbal lashing.

"In fact, all the girls think he is creepy. I have no idea why you think she'd be interested in him. Everything about her body language screamed, 'Get me out of here.' And don't think I don't know that he called her and my girl 'choice pussy' and you only defended Lola. Raven was looking to you for help to defuse the situation. Instead, I had to step in and do it for you."

"You want to know what I saw flash through her eyes when I rolled up? Relief that I was there to get her out of it. Hurt that you let him perve on her and didn't say anything in her defense. And shame that she got caught in the situation. I know you wouldn't let him proposition Tiffany the way he did Raven. I'm not sure where the 'friend' part of friends-with-benefits was, but you failed."

I bristle at his rebuke, knowing he isn't wrong. "Tiffany would have put Derrick in his place all on her own," I respond weakly.

"I'm sure. And I'd love to see it," Miller notes. "But that doesn't excuse your behavior. You had an obligation to her, and you didn't meet it. I bet that isn't the only area where she wishes you'd step up. Is it any surprise she's seeking for someone who will?"

"We agreed that this was casual. I don't owe her girlfriend privileges," I defend.

"That may be true. But that doesn't mean she doesn't want more now. She's not asking you for it. She has another candidate in mind, and Marc is a great guy."

"Marc?" I ask. "The wino?"

"Wino?" Leo interjects. I guess he didn't leave me to suffer my tongue-lashing in private.

"He runs his family winery," Miller supplies.

"Damnnn," Leo whistles. "You can't compete with unlimited wine, bro."

"I am not competing with him," I sneer.

"That's true. He can give her free wine and takes her out to show her off."

"I could do that if I wanted to," I bit out petulantly. I don't mean to, but did it have to be the guy who owns a vineyard? I saw the way they hit it off at the Christmas party. Even I can admit he's a good-looking dude. He was handsome in a Hallmark movie way that chicks love.

"But you don't. Right?" Miller goads.

"Right. As long as she doesn't fuck him, I don't care what she does."

"Whatever you say, man." He pats me on the shoulder. "Also, if I ever hear you let someone talk about my girl that way again, and you don't do something about it, I will. To both of you."

"Well, that was fun. Are you sure you don't want to come out with me? The bar has a golf simulator. You can pretend the ball is Marc's head," Leo offers.

"What the hell. I could use a drink about now."

Getting drunk with Leo last night barely distracted me from the fact that Raven *still* hasn't texted me. I want to reach out to her, but I don't have a reason. We used to text regularly, even on days we didn't link up. The urge to ask if Cappy healed from the bump he got jumping into the glass door after trying to catch a bird weighs on me as much as the desire to ask about her latest project.

Not to mention that I can't stop thinking about the date she's going on tonight. The rules of our arrangement allow her to go on as many dates as she wants as long as she doesn't sleep with them. But I'm realizing how much wiggle room that gives. How many dates has she been on? Has she kissed them? I don't think she'd do more than that without telling me, but who knows? Am I simply a stopgap to meet her needs until she finds a man she wants to be with long-term? She could end our arrangement at any minute and will the second a guy worth her time comes along.

The thought of her kissing, let alone being with anyone else, makes my skin crawl. The whole point of our friends-with-benefits situation is to enjoy the physical benefits of a relationship without the emotional ramifications. How is it only now hitting me that when we end this, I will have to see her, and whatever loser doesn't deserve her out? Will they know she has to charge her crystals every full moon? Is the wino going to judge her for sneaking Diet Coke in her glass when she thinks no one is watching?

Do I care about Raven? I want to know how her day is. I want to know if Cappy is being a judgy asshole again and if she picked a wallpaper texture. Caring about another person, let alone their cat, is foreign to me. I care about my friends and Mom, but not in the same way I do about Raven. Not in a way that has me wanting to be the reason her day is good or cheer her up when it's bad.

Fuck. Have I caught feelings for this girl? Do I want to be more than to be the guy who makes her come so hard she sleeps through brunch? Do I want to go with her, too?

Chapter Thirty

Since the restaurant Marc and I were dining at was halfway between the winery and my house, we decided it would make more sense for us to meet there. As I park outside the WeHo restaurant, I realize it is a trendy speakeasy.

Marc meets me at the front and performs a special knock. A bouncer opens and asks us a riddle. When the door shuts, I think we may have given the wrong answer, but a moment later, a side door slides open, and we enter a moody lounge. After being seated and placing our orders we fall into easy conversation.

"This place is awesome. How did I not know it existed?" I ask.

"It's only been open a few months. I wish I had an exciting story about how I know the owner, but truthfully, we're one of their wine vendors. As cool as it is here, I would be just as happy at a Chili's. I'm a simple guy."

I hold in the eye roll at his mention of a chain restaurant. He's a small business owner, for goodness' sake. Surely, he understands the importance of supporting local. Instead, I reply, "You must know the most fascinating people. Who doesn't want to be friends with the wine guy?"

"I don't know about that," he laughs, "But I have met a diverse group of people in the city. I hear you've worked with some interesting people for the show. Declan Ryder? That's impressive."

I blush at his compliment. "He recorded his EP at the recording studio I redesigned for my pilot episode. I have met an eclectic mix of people for the show. We tried to showcase a variety of businesses." I spend the next several minutes detailing all the businesses I have filmed with for *Music City Revitalized*. Marc is attentive and appears interested as he asks about my work.

I laugh out loud when he tells me a story about a prank Josh and Payton, his cousin, played on him on his twenty-first birthday. "It's not as funny when you fall asleep in the bed of a truck during the middle of the winter. This may be the south, but it can still get cold."

"You're a winter baby?" I inquire.

"Yes, ma'am. My birthday was earlier this month."

A Capricorn. I can see that. He has to be serious and straightforward as the head of his family and business. That doesn't pair well with my conflict-avoidant Libra.

Once the food arrives, we move on to discuss families. He gushes about his siblings and cousins and how they've banded together to grow their grandparents' legacy. I tell him about my sister and her family.

"It must be hard not having any family here. I only went to college a few hours away and missed everyone like crazy." I smile at his confession. His love for his family is a major green flag, even if the rest of our conversations tonight have been generic and dull.

"I do miss them, but Emily and I had enough of an age gap that we had our own lives. I brought Cappy with me once I graduated from college, so I have at least one person from home."

"Cappy?"

"Oh, my cat. Captain Wentworth. He was a present for my thirteenth birthday. Some people think he can be a little shit, but he's been by my side for most of my life, minus my time in the dorms."

Marc nods, but a veil of apprehension shades his face. "Not a cat person?" I question.

"Allergic," he responds. "Not deathly or anything. It's more of an annoyance. My sister used to hate me for it, though. When she was ten, she found a cute little calico in our neighborhood and begged my parents to let her keep it. I had recently gotten my license and kept having red, watery eyes. My parents almost took my car away until my cousin's friend, guessed it was a pet allergy and not me getting high with my new freedom. I think a small part of Emerly has never forgiven me."

"What happened to the kitten?" I ask.

"We brought him out to the winery. He's a barn cat. One of the few that isn't too feral, at least not to Emerly."

I smile at that. I imagine how sad I would have been if Emily had an allergy. "I'm glad she was still able to have a relationship with him."

"Oh yeah, I'm sure you saw Finnick lurking around without even knowing it."

"Finnick?"

"Emerly went through a big Hunger Games phase."

"I was more of a Twilight girl myself."

He eyes me skeptically. "Don't tell me you were one of those girls with a Taylor Lautner poster on her wall."

"Of course not, Team Edward all the way."

"I never got the hype of all that," he confesses. "Girls swooning over guys who weren't even that attractive." Okay, not loving the Robert Pattinson slander.

"What were you into then? Harry Potter? Lord of the Rings?"

He takes a smooth sip of wine before responding. "Girls, mostly. And soccer. David Beckham graced the posters on my wall."

"Just David Beckham?"

"And Jessica Alba," he replies with mock innocence.

"I gotta say, if we met in high school, I'm not sure we would have been friends."

"That's not true!"

"Did you have a lot of friends who spent their free periods in the art room and weekends thrifting to make their own clothes?"

"I did not," he confirms.

I pat his hand. "It's okay, Marky Mark. I won't hold it against you."

"That's gracious of you," he responds teasingly. "Do you want another drink?"

Peering down, I realize we both finished our meal, and the waiter removed our plates. I'm torn on what to say. On the one hand, this has been a perfectly lovely evening.

On the other hand, there is no spark. There should have been a spark. Marc was engaging, funny, and a gentleman. Not to mention, he has the tan skin I've always been jealous of and thick hair I wouldn't mind running my hands through. Unfortunately, there hasn't been a single tingle or thigh clench tonight. The only person who gets my body going these days is the one guy who doesn't do anything serious or long-term.

Noticing my internal struggle, Marc speaks up. "I am happy to call it a night if you want. I'm sure you're tired from filming all afternoon."

"I am a little. Getting twelve projects done in a few months has been tough."

"Forgive me if I am off base," he hedges. "But I get the vibe that this isn't the next great romance. I enjoy spending time with you, but we can agree that this is more comfortable than explosive."

I let out a breath I didn't know I was holding and nod.

"I'd love to be friends if that is something you're interested in," Marc suggests. "I'd never want to cut your connection to the wine guy."

"I'd hate to lose that," I tease.

I'm relieved he agreed that while we had a nice evening and good conversation, this isn't meant to go further than friendship. Marc pays the check even though I insist we split it. He's a gentleman till the end. "You're good people, Marc Lavigne."

"Mind writing that on the bathroom stall?" he jokes as he walks me to my car.

Even though we aren't each other's cup of tea, he's the guy you'd love your friend to date. He genuinely wants a relationship, which is rare in the Nashville dating market. I should know. I've been struggling to find a date for Carina's gala. I can't take Kent because we aren't dating, and people might talk. If this date went well, I would have asked Marc.

Maybe I still will. There is no reason we can't go as friends. It's better than going with someone who will embarrass me by fanboying over the guys or try to get in my pants. Plus, it would be a great place for Marc to meet someone.

"How about I do you one better?" I state as he opens my door. "I have a plus one open for a charity gala this weekend. There will be plenty of eligible ladies there. Fancy being my non-date date?"

"I have been meaning to dust off my tux," he replies.

"Perfect. I'll text you the info tomorrow!"

Chapter Thirty-One

When I waltz into the ballroom of the Nashville country club where the Becker Foundation's summer gala is being held, my jaw hits the floor. The room is filled with gorgeous blue and yellow accents to match the Amalfi Coast theme. Waitstaff pass by carrying charcuterie cones and lemon cocktails, and at the center of the room, there is a striking fountain with a rustic and coastal vibe.

"Dammmmmmmmn," Marc whistles from beside me. "This party is next level. Are you sure we're still in Nashville?"

"I wouldn't be surprised if we were transported to Italy when we walked in the door," I agree. "Carina's party planning skills are unmatched."

Pulling out his phone, Marc snaps a few pictures. "My sister is going to die when she sees this. She's been bugging us to purchase some Italian-inspired decor pieces for weddings. This may have convinced me."

"Tell Emerly she can send me a bottle of Malbec in thanks. Let's go grab some food and find our seats."

We take glasses of champagne from the decorative wall and locate our table. When we arrive, I spot Tiffany and her date, a player of Nashville's NBA team, the Knights. Marc is starstruck at first but mostly keeps his cool. While the men talk, I chat with Tiffany.

"I didn't realize you branched outside of baseball," I tease. "I hope the boys don't get territorial and think they're going to lose you to basketball."

She laughs. "Oh, please. You know I don't discriminate. Hot is hot. Tre was free, and I needed a date. Besides, I am excited to see if he lives up to his 6' 8" frame everywhere."

"Let me know your findings."

"You know I will, babe. What about you? Two dates in one week with the same man? I guess things went well. Cutting Kenny Boy loose?"

A server comes by and replaces my champagne with a new glass while she awaits my answer. "Marc is nice, but it wasn't the connection either of us was hoping for. He is a great guy, though, and a perfect date for a fancy night out. Who knows, maybe his lucky lady is here somewhere.

"As for Kent, I'm not sure where we stand. We haven't talked in over a week, which is unusual for us but not shocking. I guess I should tell him we don't have to hide our arrangement now that everyone knows. But I don't know how much longer it will last, anyway. I'm ready for more than a physical connection."

"Kent could give you that," she states, reiterating her stance from the other night.

"But he doesn't want to." I sigh. "And frankly, I'm not sure he even knows how."

"That's fair. At least wait to tell him it's over another day. You look way too good tonight. It would rub salt in his wound."

Tiffany scans over my hair and outfit. "I'm surprised you don't have on your emerald earrings. They would match your gauzy lilac dress."

"I know," I pout. "I lost one somewhere. I wore them in Vegas, but when I searched through my jewelry box, I could only find one. Surely, I would have noticed if I lost it."

"You were busy having your brains fucked out."

"Tiffany!" I whisper-shout.

"What? It's true. You said you don't 100 percent remember everything after the reception. Maybe you left it in Kent's room? Can't hurt to ask."

She makes a valid point. The last time I remember having the earrings, I was with Kent. And with that lost night, there is no telling where they could have ended up. Part of me is afraid to mention it, though. We've never talked about that night. From what I can tell, he remembers even less than me. The chance of finding my earring is worth the awkwardness.

Those earrings were one of the last gifts my grandmother gave me. She received them from my grandfather on her eighteenth birthday as a 'courting' gift, which was old-fashioned even at that time. But Papa Warner knew what he wanted and figured fancy jewels might help him get Hermann, Missouri's most eligible bachelorette. They were married six months later, so he must have done something right. I'll be devastated if I can't find it.

"You're right, that is a good idea. Have you seen him?" I ask. Glancing around the room, we spot him at the silent auction table.

"Check on the Taylor Swift sunglasses for me? It's exactly what I need to complete my Halloween costume. Plus, I could own a piece of Taylor history! Up my bid to five hundred dollars if you have to," Tiffany calls after me as I head in that direction.

After increasing Tiffany's bid to four hundred twenty-five dollars, I stop beside Kent, who is bidding on a personalized whiskey barrel.

"I'm pretty sure you make enough money to invest in your own whiskey brand, let alone buy a single barrel."

"Are you trying to dissuade me from spending money at a charity auction, Firefly? Not very charitable of you," he states. When he turns to face me, I revel in the way his eyes eat up my appearance. His gaze shifts up the flowy skirt of my dress and stalls momentarily at the boned corset top before landing on my face. He's unrepentant at having been caught checking me out.

"Anything else good to bid on?" I ask to break the tension.

"There is a nice wine basket over there, but considering who you brought as your date, I imagine you're set in that department." His tone is sharp and sardonic.

"Do you have a problem with me bringing a date to a charity function? Not very charitable," I throw back at him. "We both know you and I couldn't have come together without breaking any of your precious rules, and I didn't want to come alone. I figured you would bring someone, too."

"Why would I bring someone to this? She'd expect to go home with me after, and that *would* be breaking the rules. Unless there is something you want to tell me."

"If you're asking if I've slept with Marc yet, the answer is no."

"Yet," he repeats.

"Why are you mad about this? You're the one who told me to get my 'chocolates and carnival-won stuffed animals elsewhere.' Now you're upset that I am?"

"I am not upset. I just didn't expect to have your dates shoved in my face," he sneers.

"How am I shoving it in your face? You know when we end things, you're going to see me and whoever I'm dating out, right? That is how it works when we share friends."

Kent's jaw is clenched tight, and his hand grips the pen he was using to write in his bid. I'm surprised it hasn't snapped. "I know that."

Blowing out a raspberry, I take the opposite of Tiffany's advice. "I think maybe we should call this."

"What?" he asks, jerking back at my statement. "Call what?"

"Us. This arrangement. It was fun while it lasted, but it's getting complicated. Now that I'm more settled, I want more than pregame hookups and booty calls."

"I can't give you more," he replies. Frustration is evident on his face. "We talked about this on day one. You said you were fine with it."

"I was," I agree. "I was on board. But now that my life is less up in the air, I am ready for something deeper. I want to find someone who can be a partner. Someone who will take me to carnivals and peruse flea markets and out on the town. A relationship where we cook dinner together and then fall asleep watching some dumb movie we put on. I want the little things that come with an emotional connection.

"I know that isn't what you want. I don't harbor any resentment or ill will toward you for it. What we had was exactly what I wanted and needed at the time, but now I want more. I may not get that more with Marc, but I think in order to find it, I need to put myself fully out there. I can't do that if we're still hooking up. That wouldn't be fair to the new guy, and it wouldn't be fair to you to be waiting around for me to end it whenever. A clean break is best. Don't you think?"

"I *think* I need a drink," he mutters. "Yeah, sure. Let's call it. It's been real."

At that declaration, he storms past me and goes straight for the bar. I'm surprised at how abruptly that conversation ended. I figured he would be pleased that I wasn't pining for him to fill a role he doesn't want. It stings that he doesn't want me in that way, but he told me what he could give me from day one. Daydreaming about more from him would be foolish.

Chapter Thirty-Two

I am seething as I stomp away from Raven and over to the bar. "Whiskey, neat," I request. As soon as the bartender hands me my glass, I shoot it back in one gulp.

I can't believe Raven ended this. In theory, I knew our time together would run its course, but I didn't think it would happen this soon. And I didn't think it would be over a schmuck like Marc. What does she even see in that guy? He's good-looking enough in an all-American, preppy way. That isn't Raven's style. She hates everything standard and cookie-cutter.

"I think it's safe to say don't have eye lasers," a voice notes.

"Huh?" I direct to my blonde bestie, who has saddled up beside me.

"You're glaring at Marc as if you want to melt him with your stare. I think if it was going to happen, it would have already."

"I don't know what you're talking about," I retort dryly, signaling for another drink.

"You're oozing broody vibes over here, Kenny Boy," she observes. "It's freaking people out since they usually only see your puppy side."

"My puppy side?"

"Yeah. You're Mr. Happy-Go-Lucky Nothing in the World Bothers Me. You're scaring the children with that scowl."

I scoff, but my expression softens a minuscule amount.

"That's better," Tiffany beams. "What's got you grumpy?"

I weigh whether to tell her about this. The only person I can talk to about it is Miller, and based on the reprimand he gave me the other day, I don't think it would be especially helpful. He'd tell me I got what I deserved. Tiff is Raven's friend, too, but she's also loyal as hell. I know she wouldn't tell anyone. Before I can spill my guts to her, she puts up her hand to stop me.

"If this is about you blowing it with our resident redhead, I already know."

"You do?" I ask incredulously. "We weren't supposed to tell people."

"Did you truly think one of the girls could manage this long without talking to the others about her situationship? She fessed up after the All-Star Game. I can't believe you were such an ass, by the way. I raise you better. Even if she hadn't spilled the beans, I already knew. Y'all are as subtle as a tornado."

"You didn't raise me," I grumble.

"I know your mom raised you better than that. I don't want any of the blame to land on sweet Mama C. She's an angel," she quips. "Tell me what's wrong."

"Raven ended things," I confess. Her face pinches.

"I'm sorry, boo. I was afraid that might happen after I saw her arrive with Marc."

"Wow, thanks. You knew she'd leave me for Wine Guy Ken? Could've warned a guy."

"First off," she chastises with a hand on her hip and finger wagging in my face. "I didn't know she was bringing a date. I thought you would both come solo. But when she came with one, I knew that meant she wasn't planning to do anything with you tonight. Platonic date or not, she wouldn't disappear on the man."

"Wait, did you say platonic?"

"Yeah, they decided they were better off as friends. The real kind, not whatever it was you two were doing. Marc wants to settle down, and Raven thought he could meet a nice girl here. Plus, she didn't want to show up alone in case you brought someone."

"Why does everyone keep thinking I'd bring someone to this?"

"Maybe because that's a normal thing to do? I'm sure there are a dozen girls you could call right now who'd show up as your plus one."

"Bringing a girl to a fancy event with my friends sends the wrong message."

Tiffany gives me a sad smile. "You know I love you. And I get your need for no strings attached better than anyone. But we both knew our carefree approach to dating was going to bite us in the ass, eventually. Today is that day."

I eye her skeptically. Is she saying today is that day for her, too? She hadn't mentioned seeing anyone to me, but maybe she was keeping it on the DL the same way Raven and I were. I want to probe further, but she speaks again.

"I'm saying this as your friend, not Raven's: you're going to regret letting her go. I've never seen you look at anyone the way you do her, and I've never known you to get upset over something ending. You like her. And you should, she's a catch. And perfect for you. Don't let your fear of commitment and self-doubt keep you from missing out on something that could be great."

"I'm not letting fear do anything," I state with annoyance. "*She* ended things with *me*. You should be having this talk with her. She doesn't want a future with me."

"Don't be dumb. She ended things because she wants something with a future. She doesn't know she can have that with you because you haven't told her. She's respecting your boundaries. If you're open to more, you need to tell her. Otherwise, she's going to find someone willing to give her what she wants without knowing she could have had that with you."

As she grabs her drink and moves to return to her date, Tiffany kisses me on the cheek. "Don't think about it too hard, Kenny Boy. Give someone the opportunity to love you the way you deserve. At least one of us should be able to."

That comment is something I should press on, but before I can, she's gone. I mull over her words as I finish my new glass of whiskey. Is she right? Should I give this thing between Raven and me a chance?

From my peripheral, I see the woman who has plagued my dreams since I met her dancing with her date. Raven tosses her head back, laughing at something he says. Her creamy skin glows in the light as her hair floats around her. Fuck. I'm going to need more than a couple of glasses of whiskey if I'm going to make it through an evening of seeing another man's hands on her.

"Rivera!" I shout as our pitcher passes by, his cloudy demeanor matching mine. "Wanna get shit-faced and spend too much money at the silent auction?"

"I knew I liked you," he replies. "Let's get this party started."

Hours later, I am hopping out of my rideshare in a quaint East Nashville neighborhood. It's much quieter here than the downtown streets I arrived from. George and I snuck away with a bottle of tequila and lamented our mutual woman problems. As best we could anyway, without naming names or stating specifics. It may have been more mutters of "women" than anything else.

The conversation with Tiffany showed me I do want to give this thing with Raven a chance. Getting sloshed and hyped up by my teammate after I made that realization was the encouragement I needed to take my drunk ass to tell her. Tonight.

As I amble up to the front door, I send a salute to my rideshare driver. Luckily, the middle-aged woman didn't seem to know who I was. Which is good because I'm plastered enough to have agreed to video call her entire family.

I knock as if it's broad daylight and not the middle of the night. It takes a few minutes, but a sleepy-faced Raven opens the door. She levels me with a glare that should make me wither but makes me think of how cute she is when she's mad instead. I didn't realize how badly I needed to see she was home alone.

"Kent!" she whisper-shouts. "What are you doing here? It's two o'clock in the morning."

"I know," I say as I stroll past her. "I wanted to see you, and this is where you were, so it's where I am."

She shuts the door as I flop onto her couch and immediately spot Cappy. He appears about as happy at my intrusion as his owner. I rub under his chin until he nuzzles into my hand. "Think I can get your mom to melt for me, too, if I rub under her chin?"

"No," Raven answers, having heard me.

"What if I rub somewhere else?" I suggest with a raised brow.

"Why are you here, Kent? You made it pretty clear at the gala that you didn't want anything to do with me."

"Me? You're the one who broke up with me!" I snap. My good mood at seeing my girl dampened by the reminder that she ended things with me earlier.

"I didn't 'break up with you,'" she states, using air quotes. "We weren't together. We both knew this was going to end sometime. Is your manhood hurt that I'm the one who cut it off and not you? I didn't take you to have such a fragile ego."

"That isn't it," I grit.

"Then what is it? Mad I took away your toy before you were done playing with it? Newsflash, buddy, the game changed. I need more now, and I'm not one of those dumb girls that thinks she can change a guy into wanting to commit."

"But what if you are?" I stand from my spot on the couch and watch her from across the room. She remained close to the door as if she needs a way to escape this conversation.

"What if I'm what?"

"One of those girls who gets a guy to commit."

"Please," she snorts. "If I learned anything from all the 'oos rom-coms Lola has made me watch, it's that I am the rule, not the exception. And you, my friend, are no Justin Long."

"What does the kid from *Jeepers Creepers* have to do with us?"

"*Jeepers Creepers* is not what he is most known for," she responds incredulously. "He was in *Clerks, Dodgeball, New Girl,* and most importantly, *He's Just Not That Into You.*"

"But he is into you," I reply.

"Justin Long? I've never met the man. How could he be—"

"Raven," I interrupt as I move in her direction. When I'm inches away, I reach out to touch her because I think I'll die if I go another second without her under my fingertips. With my hands on her hips, I continue.

"Can we stop talking about Drew Barrymore's ex-boyfriend and focus on what I came here to say?"

"I guess," she mumbles. I bite my lip to fight the grin that shoots across my face at her attitude.

"I'm the 'he' who is into you. I want to commit to you."

Eyes widening, she meets my gaze with a confused expression. "You want to commit to being friends-with-benefits?"

I shake my head.

"I don't understand."

I tuck a red curl behind her ear. "If I would have known how hard it would be to ask you to my girlfriend, I would have waited until I was sober."

"Girlfriend?" she questions.

"Girlfriend." I repeat. "Since the day we met, I have been drawn to you. I thought it was purely physical, but it's so much more than that. Don't get me wrong, I still want to wake your neighbor by making you scream all night, but I also want to do relationship shit. I want to be the one you take to fancy galas and who takes you out to dinner. The idea of any other man getting to hear you ramble on about the difference between slate grey and artic blue or hear you blame your bad day on whatever planet is retrograde makes me feral. I want to have you. To claim you. I want to be your boyfriend, your partner, your man."

I mentally pat myself on the back for such a coherent speech, despite the copious amount of tequila rushing through my body. That fuels my shock when her response to my declaration is a simple, "You can't be my boyfriend."

"Excuse me?" I challenge. "Why not?"

"Because you told me on day one that you can't be my boyfriend. You don't want to be anyone's boyfriend. You don't want commitment. Nothing has changed. You're only saying it now because you don't want to lose easy access to ass."

"First," I say, in a tone harsher than I intent. "Never call yourself 'ass.' You are much more than that. If that was all I was after, I wouldn't have kept coming back. This stopped being easy the second we had to hide it from our friends. If history is any indicator, 'ass' is not something I have a problem getting." Jealousy flashes across her features at the mention of my not-so-wholesome past, but I'm on a roll, so I keep going.

"Second, if I say I want to be your boyfriend, I want to be your boyfriend. I may not be any good at it, but I'll try my damndest to be the man who deserves you.

"I probably won't be saying this much now that we're official if sitcoms and Robby are an example, but you should know you're wrong."

"Wrong about what?" she asks in a daze.

I run my thumbs along her cheekbones. "Wrong about nothing changing. My entire world changed the second you sassed me on that first night. My universe has been shifting ever since to revolve around you."

"Are you sure you want this? Sleepovers, seeing my flea market hauls, dealing with me reading your horoscope to you every day? Are you sure you can handle that?"

"I get paid to catch for a living. I can handle anything you throw my way, Firefly," I whisper, before pressing my mouth to hers in a firm but chaste kiss. Before I can deepen it further, she interrupts.

"You're sure you want me?" she asks against my lips.

"There is no one else I've ever wanted more," I answer honestly. When she sighs, I take the opportunity to run my tongue along her lips and kiss her the way I've been dying to all night. I never want to go this long without kissing her again. It's addicting. When she trembles, I reach my arms below her ass, hauling her up my body and carrying her back to bed.

Chapter Thirty-Three

I was more than surprised to find Kent knocking on my door last night. After the way he stormed off at the gala, I assumed that was it for us. I hated that we ended on a bad note, but I wasn't going to fall over myself trying to appease him. It rankled the Libra in me that strives for harmony, but I was doing what was best for us both.

He laid out terms. I wanted new ones. Logically, I need to find someone whose expectations match with mine. I don't harbor any ill will toward him. Our arrangement served its purpose, and it was time to pull the plug before either of us got resentful.

I know myself, and I am not good at being involved with multiple people, even if one is only physical. If I had a backup plan, I'd never be able to put myself fully out there. I've gotten this far without a safety net. No use stopping now.

Kent had other plans, though. If I want to stick to the analogy, he basically said 'fuck it' and jumped off a cliff with me in his arms. Not terrifying at all. I am still trying to wrap my head around why Mr. Anti-Relationship wants to be my boyfriend.

In my heart of hearts, I wanted him to want me in this way, but I couldn't even bring myself to think it, let alone voice it. Manifestation may be powerful, but hope is a dangerous thing. I didn't want to fall into the trap that so many other girls have, thinking they would be the ones to change the playboy.

I indulged a hormonal Lola last week and watched *He's Just Not That Into You.* For a happily married woman, she sure loves her rom-coms. In the should-be-required-watching-for-all-women master-piece, the female lead is reminded that, more often than not, we are the rule, not the expectation. She may end up as the expectation because it's a movie, but I took that point to heart. Hotter, more on-his-level women than me had tried to tame Kent. I didn't need to let their lessons be in vain.

But as he tends to do, he surprised me. Smelling like Jose Cuervo himself, Kent declared his desire to commit to me and carried me off to bed. I expected him to be on me the second my back hit the bed, but he snuggled me into his chest while tracing patterns on my back instead. He fell asleep quickly, thanks to the liquor, but I was up contemplating everything he said and my own thoughts on the matter.

Eventually, I must have fallen asleep because I wake up with my head on a rising chest and fingers tangled in my hair. I tip my head up and meet Kent's gaze.

"Morning, Firefly," he rasps. His voice is pure sex in the morning. It is totally unfair. We need to have a serious conversation, but now all I want is to hear him tell me how wet I am for him and how well I take him.

"Morning," I manage to force out. "How did you sleep?"

"Any man would be hard-pressed not to sleep amazingly with your warm body and lavender scent wrapped around them. Not that any other man will have the chance now."

"We should talk about that," I hedge.

"What's there to talk about?"

"Do you remember everything from last night?"

"Of course, I remember. I'd be a jackass to forget the first time I claim a girl as mine."

"Is that what happened last night? You claimed me?" I laugh, thinking about his drunken declaration and the way he gently snuggled me until I fell asleep. Don't get me wrong, I loved seeing that side of him, but I wouldn't exactly call it a claiming.

As if he read my thoughts, he narrows his eyes in my direction and huffs. "I obviously didn't do a good enough job, if you have to ask."

Faster than his hungover reflexes should allow, Kent flips us until he hovers over me. "Do I need to show you who you belong to, baby? Show you who owns this mouth? This body? This delicious pink pussy?"

He licks down my jaw and neck as he speaks. "Tell me, Raven. When my tongue finds its way between your legs after licking every inch of you, what will I find? Is your pussy going to be dripping for me? Aching for me to make you the best breakfast I've ever had?"

Yes, to all of that. A part of me thought he would change his mind when he woke up this morning. That last night was a reaction to seeing someone else play with his favorite toy. I never let myself dream that Kent Dela Cruz would want to claim me. And now that he has, I am anxious for him to do so in every meaning of the word.

"Fuck," I moan as his tongue glides across my sternum and down between my breasts. I wiggle underneath him as he stretches my cami to its limit. Switching tactics, he pushes it up and over my head. I lift my arms in assistance. Instead of pulling it completely off, he stops at my wrists and winds the cami around them until they're secured above my head. He plants another searing kiss on my lips before returning to his journey.

When he reaches my hips, he toys with the matching sleep shorts and stares into my eyes. "I can hear the doubt in your voice this morning. I know you can be an overthinker. I don't want you to doubt how much I want you – how much I want us. I will happily feast on this pussy every single day to prove my devotion to you."

"You don't have to," I murmur.

"Don't have to what?"

"You don't have to eat me out to prove to me how much you want me. You prove that just as well with your fingers and cock."

Kent stills as he stares up at me from between my legs. "Do you not like when I enjoy your pussy? Because from what I can tell, you really, really love it."

I flush at his emphasis. Of course, I love it. The man is a master with his tongue. I know we need some foreplay to help fit him inside of me, but I don't want him to think he has to.

"I do enjoy it..." I say tentatively. "But I don't want you to feel obligated to do it. Your fingers are just as good at getting me ready for you."

"Do you think I lick your pretty little pussy just for you?"

"Um, yes?" I answer. "Who else would it be for?"

"Me," he replies seriously. "Getting you off is a bonus, but I love licking your pussy. When I am on the road, I crave the taste of you and have literal dreams where I spend so much time between your legs you pass out on me."

I shiver at his words and the earnest tone he delivers them in. His eyes take on a predatory gleam as he returns his mouth down to nip at my thighs. "If there is one thing you should know about me, Firefly, it's that I will happily make a meal out of you any damn time you let me. Are we clear?"

"Yes," I whimper as he pushes my legs wide and settles between them.

"Good girl. Now, let's test out Joe's noise-canceling headphones."

Kent wastes no time licking between my folds, humming noises of approval at how wet I am for him. While he is usually a fan of teasing, he draws nothing out this morning. If he is trying to prove a point, he is succeeding.

He directs his attention to my clit, sucking it into his mouth and flicking his tongue over it. I buck into his face as his hands hold me down with a firmer grip to keep my legs from closing on him.

It doesn't take long for his efforts to pay off. My hands fist into the bedsheets and my hips fight to rise despite the weight of him pushing down on them. My toes curl and muscles tense as I am hurdled toward a powerful orgasm. I come hard against his tongue. He slowly pulls back and licks up the mess on my thighs, chocolate orbs never breaking contact with mine. The pure hunger in them makes me want to turn away, but the sincerity begs me not to.

When I think he'd done or at least ready to fuck me, he rolls us again so that he's on his back, and I'm straddling his chest.

"Move up," he commands. Shifting to my knees, I push myself higher, resting my bound wrist on top of the headboard.

"Not like that," he says, amusement lacing his handsome – and glistening – face.

"How else?" I question.

"Move toward the headboard and sit on my face."

"What?"

"I didn't stutter. Sit on my face," he repeats slowly, swatting my ass as if it will hurry me along. He sighs. "Put those juicy thighs on either side of my head and sink this pretty cunt down on my mouth so you can ride my tongue."

"I-what?"

He tilts his head at my hesitancy. "Have you never ridden on anyone's face, Firefly?"

I shake my head. Hunger returns to his eyes, along with smug satisfaction. "That pleases me more than it should. My only regret is that I didn't do this sooner," he admits. "Tick-tock, baby."

Hesitantly, I scoot forward and lower myself onto his waiting lips. When I'm in position, he grips my hips and pulls me further into him. Kent convinces me of the position's merits until I beg him to claim me.

By the time Kent reluctantly leaves for today's game, I am thoroughly claimed. So claimed, that I planned to take it easy for the rest of the day. At least I was until Kent asked me to come to today's game. It wasn't a hard sell considering his face was still between my thighs. He even offered to leave a jersey with Tiffany for me to wear to the game since she and Carina are going, too.

By the time the three of us are in our seats, the first inning is halfway through.

"I told you we'd be late if we grabbed all this food," Carina grumbles.

"Would you relax, Meatball? You've seen Robby pitch a hundred times by now," Tiffany retorts. "Besides, you're the one who wanted a soft pretzel and nachos. You sure Lola is the only pregnant one?"

Carina takes a big sip of her marg and gives Tiffany the finger.

Once we settle in our seats, we dig into the food. As soon as the Songbirds leave the field, I sense the girls' eyes on me.

"Yes?" I question, mouth full of hotdog. I don't care how good the other food is. You can't go to a baseball game and not get a hotdog. Coming from a long line of Huskers fans, I think my dad would disown me if I got anything else.

"Did you think Kent could drop a jersey off for you at my place after the blowup you two had last night, and we wouldn't talk about it?" Tiff counters.

"Oh, that."

"Yes, that. Don't you dare hold anything back," Carina adds.

Seeing as I am stuck beside the besties for the next two-plus hours, I have no choice but to recount everything that happened since last night. I leave out the side-eye Cappy gave me when Kent finally let me out of bed and some of the other finer details. My grumpy old man of a cat doesn't appreciate his breakfast being delayed, no matter how mind-blowing the orgasms.

By the time I am done, they are both grinning ear-to-ear.

"I knew he had it in him to step up," Carina gushes. "He just needed to find the right girl."

"What do you think, Tiff?" I ask hesitantly. I know how close she and Kent are. She's spoken up for him in the past, but now that we are giving this a real go, I hope she is still on board.

"I am half pumped you're both happy and half nervous about how he's going to screw it up."

"What makes you think he'll screw it up?"

"For one, he's a man. Even practically perfect men like Robby and Miller mess up from time to time. And since Kenny Boy has never had a girlfriend before, the learning curve is steep. Thank God you're one of the most patient people we know. He's going to need that."

My cheeks heat at the compliment. Kent praised me all morning, but hearing your girlfriends say nice things hits different.

"I'm sure he'll be fine. He's a smart guy."

"That's true. He did already text us asking for advice," Carina comments.

I whip my attention away from the game. The Songbirds are at bat, and Leo hit a double that sent Clapp to third. Kent is the clean-up batter, and as long as either Jones or Crews can get on base, he'll be up this inning. "What do you mean? He needed help already?"

"I wouldn't call it help," she states, pursing her lip as if she is searching for the right word.

"He's nervous about the whole being a boyfriend thing. He asked us how he could be a good one," Tiffany explains.

"What did you tell him?"

"Read for yourself." she says, thrusting her phone in my hand. While Clapp was able to score, a double play means Kent won't be up until the next inning. That gives me plenty of time to read the text thread entitled 'Goddesses of Broadway Lofts.' I chuff at the name.

11:12 AM

KENNY BOY NAMED GROUP, "VAGINA WHISPERERS"

180

TIFFANY

WTF is this group??

KENNY BOY

I need lady help.

TIFFANY

I am not pretending to be your wife again to scare off some chick.

KENNY BOY

Not necessary, but your unwillingness to help a guy out is noted.

I asked Raven to be my girlfriend last night.

MEATBALL

Yay!

But also, this group name makes it sound like we're here to help you get laid.

KENNY BOY

Like I'd ever need help with that.

TIFFANY

Seeing as you need girlfriend advice, I think you do. But change the group name for the love of God.

MEATBALL

Change it to something fitting for our station. Otherwise, we won't help you!

KENNY BOY

Fine.

KENNY BOY CHANGED THE GROUP NAME,
GODDESSES OF BROADWAY LOFTS

KENNY BOY

Now, will you help me?

TIFFANY

First, details?? Last I saw, she left with Marc, and you left with a bottle of Jose's finest with Rambo.

181

KENNY BOY

One, it was Casamigos. Don't insult my taste in liquor. Two, I went to her place last night and put it all on the line.

MEATBALL

You got wasted at my gala? Is that why you and Georgie bought so much shit?

KENNY BOY

No comment.

MEATBALL

Whatever. I'll happily take your money for the kids. So you two got in a fight and then you showed up drunk but somehow you woke up in a couple?

KENNY BOY

That is how it unfolded, yes.

TIFFANY

And what do you need from us exactly? Seems like things went your way.

KENNY BOY

So far. But we all know I'm bound to screw it up.

I've never been in a relationship before. What do I need to do to be a good boyfriend?

MEATBALL

Aw this is the cutest request ever! I can tell you what Robby did to get me back and the sweet things Miller does for Lola. She probably would have been better to ask than commitment-phobe Barbie.

TIFFANY

Hey! I resent that. Just because I don't want a boyfriend doesn't mean I don't know what a guy would need to do to bag me.

MEATBALL

Woof. I'd love to see that list.

KENNY BOY

Can we focus on me first? Kinda freaking
out here.

MEATBALL

Of course we can sweetie.

The most important thing is communication.
When issues come up, talk about them
directly. It will help you avoid a lot of pain
and almost heartbreak. Being honest is
crucial in building trust. Without trust, your
relationship will be doomed.

TIFFANY

Regular date nights are a must. You're both
super busy and it can be tempting to veg
out at home, but make sure you take her
out, too. Even if it's only a coffee date or out
with the group. Show her off.

MEATBALL

Pay attention to her. I know it sounds silly,
but she isn't talking to talk. She wants to
connect and engage with you. Pay attention
to her wants, needs, likes, and dislikes, that
way you can meet them.

TIFFANY

Get her presents.

MEATBALL

Seriously? That's your advice?

TIFFANY

Not extravagant ones. But going along with
what Carina said. It will show you pay
attention. Have her favorite snack and
drinks at your place. Give her a knickknack
that reminds you of her. We love
considerate men.

MEATBALL

Ooooh yeah, do that!

TIFFANY

Also, intimacy is important.

No, he certainly does not. Handing Tiffany back her phone, I can't help but grin at the idea that Kent asked our friends to help him be a good boyfriend. I know it will be rocky navigating the switch from secret friends-with-benefits to real-life couple, but I am confident we'll find our footing. With the physical side down, we're halfway there already.

Chapter Thirty-Four

• KENT •

August

It's been a couple of weeks since Raven and I made things official. There has been a learning curve, but nothing too bad. It helps that when I'm not playing or training, I want to be with her. I was always afraid that having a girlfriend would be annoying, and I'd be craving alone time, but if anything, I am the clingy one.

Raven has been busy filming her show and running various design projects at once. I don't fully understand what that entails but I nod along when she talks about it, regardless. All I know is that when she gets worked up talking about tile patterns and wallpaper, I reap the benefits. I swear we're having more sex now than when we were only fuck buddies.

Wrapping my towel around my waist, I sit at my locker in the clubhouse and scroll through my phone. Based on the selfie she sent me with Big Ron, Raven and the girls are already at Holler's having a grand time. I don't miss the earrings she's wearing in the photo either.

She brought up the one she lost the other night when we were lying in bed. She seemed apprehensive because she didn't think I remembered anything. Which to be fair I don't – about the night before at least. But I do remember her sneaking out the next morning. Her crestfallen face was too much for me to bear when I told her I never saw an earring. I know the ones I got her won't replace the sentiment behind the others, but I had to do something. Her wearing them is a good sign.

"You heading to the bar?" I ask Leo when he settles beside me.

"I don't think so. Mace worked late tonight, and even though she hasn't asked, I think she wants me to come by. At least I hope she does."

"I forgot you're dating her! How is that going?"

"Good, I think," he responds sheepishly. "She can be standoffish, but she's sweet and playful when you get through her walls. Her ex did a number on her and forced her to live with her guard up. I'm slowly wearing her down."

"I'd expect nothing less. You've got golden retriever energy rolling off you in spades."

"Thanks, I think."

"Good luck surprising your girl."

"Thanks, man. Have fun." I give him a salute before hitching a ride to Holler's with Robby.

Holler's is busier than normal tonight. Ron said there is a big concert tomorrow which brought a lot of people into town. As long as we have our spot in the VIP, it doesn't matter to me. I pat the bouncer on his shoulder as I scoot past him on a mission to find my girl.

I spy her chatting with Carina in a back booth. As I walk in that direction, a manicured hand lands on my biceps and stops me.

"Hey, stranger," Erica purrs in what I assume she thinks is a seductive voice. Did I really used to fall for that shit or did I simply not care? It's blatant how fake it is now.

"Sup, Erica?" I reply without emotion.

"I haven't seen you in ages. Have you been avoiding me?"

"Nope, just been busy. I haven't been going out as much this season."

"I miss seeing you around," she pouts. "What do you say we make up for lost time?"

"Jesus, Erica. I haven't even gotten a drink yet, and you're already trying to get me to take you home? Not happening, sweetheart. I'm off the market."

"You're celibate?"

"What? No, I'm in a relationship."

"You're what?!" she screeches, drawing attention from those around us, including Raven. I clock the moment she sees Erica's hand on my arm and cringe at the uncertainty that flashes through them. Our relationship is solid, but it also hasn't been tested yet. I guess that is about to change.

She's watching me closely as I shrug Erica off. "I have a girlfriend now. I'm not interested in hooking up."

"You have a girlfriend?" she asks almost as if she doesn't believe me.

"I do. And she's waiting for me right now. Have a good night."

Leaving her behind, I make a beeline for the booth and plop a kiss on Raven's head before slipping in beside her.

"Who was that?" she asks as nonchalantly as she can manage which isn't very. Fiddling with her crystal bracelet is a dead giveaway as is her disinterested tone. She's always interested in everything. I think my Firefly might be jealous. I usually hate when women act that way over me but Raven's envy turns me on.

"Who, Erica? She's some girl I used to know."

"Used to?" she parrots skeptically.

"Yep, we lost touch last season and all my time has been taken up by a fiery redhead lately."

She bites her lip when she meets my teasing gaze. "Okay," she whispers.

"Okay?" She nods. I give her one of my panty-melting smiles, dropping a hand to her thigh and squeezing. "Good. Now, what have I missed?"

I spend the rest of the night talking to the girls and the few teammates that wander over. Luckily, no other chasers come my way. Either they can tell I'm with Raven or Erica put the word out. I don't care which, to be honest as long as they leave me alone.

The girls leave to go to the bathroom, and when they return Carina is rushing nervously behind Raven who stares at me as if I fed Cappy people food – which only happened once!

"Everything okay?" I ask tentatively.

Instead of replying, Raven grabs her purse off the table and storms away. I sit there stunned for a second before jumping up to follow after her. I catch up to her when she is outside, calling a car to pick her up.

"Baby," I call. "Wait up. Where are you going?"

She ignores me.

"Raven, talk to me. What happened?" Nothing.

Grabbing her arm to spin her around, I cup her face with my hands and drink in the insecurity swimming in her eyes.

"Firefly," I swallow over the lump that has formed in my throat. I hate seeing her sad. All I want to do is fix it.

"Is it true?" she asks.

"Is what true?"

"That you don't actually live here. That your condo is a fuck pad and you have a *real* house only people that matter – like that girl you apparently 'used to know' – have seen?"

Oh shit. I never told Raven about my house. I don't spend much time there during the season, so it slipped my mind. Erica has been there before, but only because she worked for my realtor. It's how I met her in the first place.

"Your face tells me it is," she observes, mouth set in a harsh line.

"It's not what you think." She laughs humorlessly at the declaration.

"Come home with me, please. Let's talk this out. It isn't as bad as it sounds."

"Which house?" she sneers. "The real one or the fuck pad." Ouch. I deserved that but ouch, nonetheless. Taking her hand, I guide her down Broadway back to the condos. I'm surprisingly thankful for her chilly silence as I try to run through what to tell her to make up for this colossal omission. Hopefully, whatever I come up with is enough.

Chapter Thirty-Five

When I woke up this morning, I was greeted by a grumpy cat and a pretty box with a purple bow. Opened the box, I almost cried at the beautiful emerald earrings I found inside. I finally fessed up to Kent the other night about our second rendezvous in Vegas. Imagine my surprise when he told me he saw me sneaking out that morning!

After a good laugh, he told me he hadn't seen any earrings in his suite. He called the hotel to double-check, but it either was never there, or someone else took it.

The note he left with his present says that he knows these earrings can't replace the pair I lost. But he hopes being the first piece of jewelry he's given any woman aside from his mother will make them a fraction as special. I may or may not have shed a tear at the sweetness. And planned my entire outfit tonight around them.

Since the guys took forever to get here, Carina and I are a couple of drinks in by the time they stroll in. The commotion of the crowd is always a tip-off. Despite weeks of being together, my stomach still flutters when I lock eyes with Kent across the room. Before he makes it through the VIP, a familiar woman has latched on to his arm and is whispering something in his ear.

My gaze is locked on their connection as jealousy pulses through me. I know Kent has a long history of women from before me, but this is the first time we have had to face it. I watch as he shrugs her off and says something that causes her face to recoil in distaste. Her eyes land on me over his shoulder as he continues on his path and settles beside me in the booth.

Old fling forgotten, we have a great night hanging out with friends and Songbirds. Kent subtly touches me all night as if he needs reassurance that I'm not going to float away. It's cute. He's been a much needier boyfriend than I anticipated, but I don't mind. I love knowing that he is always seeking me out. I have no problem validating him as he does the same right back to me.

As all good things do, the awesomeness of the night comes crashing down when I exit the bathroom stall. Carina hasn't emerged yet, but there is someone else at the sink. Someone I hoped I wouldn't see again.

Studying me in the mirror, the woman who approached Kent earlier has an expression that tells me she is not impressed. I guess my boho chic aesthetic doesn't jive with her southern belle vibe.

I offer her a curt nod in greeting as I wash my hands. Her scrutiny ends when she sneers in my direction, "You aren't special, you know? He'll throw you out the same way he did the rest of us."

Her comment shocks me into silence. Luckily, my sassy Italian bestie is emerging from her stall and witnesses the encounter.

"Green isn't a good color on you, Erica." Glancing down at her red outfit, she flushes at having not caught on to Carina's meaning right away.

"I'm simply stating the obvious, Kent Dela Cruz isn't made for long-term. The red hair and fat ass may be alluring to him now, but he'll be back to his old ways soon."

Carina laughs. "Oh honey, don't let it hurt your feelings. There are plenty of men still out there you can sink your hooks in. Don't insult Raven because Kent didn't give you what you wanted. They're the real deal."

"So real he's still bringing her to the party bar and taking her up to his fuck pad? If she truly meant something, she'd be at the home he actually lives in."

With raised brows, turns her attention to me. "I've been to his house. Have you?"

Confusion must show on my face because triumph takes over hers. "That's what I thought. Enjoy it while it lasts. Soon you'll be out on our ass with the rest of us."

"Ignore her," Carina says as she links arms with me to leave. "She's mad Kent didn't want more with her. He's seriously into you, Ray."

"What did she mean by 'his real home?'"

"The one by the lake," she replies absently, only realizing something is wrong when I stop in the hallway.

"He has another house?" I question.

"Uh, technically, yes. But he doesn't stay there most of the season or most weekends. He's at his condo because it's closer to the facilities and—"

"And the bars where he picks up women," I finish.

"I guess."

"Because he doesn't take hookups to his home. Now it makes sense why his place is so bare. And why he says he prefers the 'coziness' of mine. I can't believe this."

"I'm sure there is an explanation for why he didn't tell you. Don't let Erica get into your head."

"Too late," I mutter as I storm back to the booth to grab my stuff and leave.

Kent says something to me when I reach the table, but I am too angry to listen. I stomp outside to call a ride home. We argue when he catches up to me, but I begrudgingly agree to let him explain back at his condo.

Like the walk over, the ride up to his floor is silent. I'm fuming, and he appears introspective. Once inside, I cross my arms defensively and motion for him to start speaking.

Kent runs his hands over his hair as if a genie might pop out and grant his wish to end this uncomfortable confrontation if he rubs hard enough. "I'm not sure where to begin," he notes sheepishly.

"How about you tell me why you have a condo specifically for hooking up and some 'real' house that I am apparently not good enough to know about, let alone visit. I thought this relationship was something special to you, but obviously, I was stupid to assume that."

"Baby, no," he urges. "That isn't it at all. One, I don't have this condo just to hook up. My house is forty-five minutes out of town. It's further than I want to drive during the season when I have back-to-back game days. It's more of a vacation house than anything. I stay there in the off-season sometimes and when Mom visits. Two, it's not a place I take people. There has never been a reason to."

"So no one has seen it? Because Erica sure made it clear she'd been."

He blows out a raspberry. "I mean, the guys have been out once or twice for a BBQ, but it isn't a regular thing. Erica has only been there because she worked for my realtor. I hadn't even closed on the house when she was there. She has never been an invited guest."

My puff of disbelief spurs him on. With a glint of determination, he cages me against the island as he loves to do. "Firefly. This is special. This is everything. You have to know how much you mean to me."

Sincerity shines through his pained expression. "Why didn't you tell me?" I whisper.

"It honestly never crossed my mind. I was wrapped up in the season and then you. I haven't thought much about it. Aside from All-Star Weekend when Mom came to visit, I haven't spent a night in the house.

"I can see how that sounds as if I was hiding it from you, but I wasn't, I swear. If you want, I will take you there right now. I will do whatever it takes for you to believe that you are so much more than Erica or any other woman I've been with could ever dream to be."

Checking his face for deception. I don't spot any, only hope and anguish.

"Okay," I finally reply.

"Okay? Does that mean you want to go? I can grab my keys right now."

"No, I don't want to go. I mean, I do. But not right now. I believe you."

The relief in his posture is evident. "Thank Christ. I thought you were going to leave me."

"I'm not going to leave you," I say. "This did get me thinking, though."

"What about?" he questions.

"The physical side of our relationship is strong. We need to spend more time cultivating the other parts. I know all your favorite sex positions, but I don't know the name of your childhood best friend or your favorite movie."

"Eugene."

"What?"

"The name of my childhood best friend was Eugene. Eugene Samuels. And my all-time favorite movie is *A League of Their Own*."

"*A League of Their Own*? Seriously?"

"Yes," he replies defensively. "Is it such a surprise my favorite movie is about baseball?"

"Is that about baseball, though? I thought it was a chick flick."

"How dare you!" he gasps. "Tom Hanks and Gina Davis do not deserve your disrespect, nor do any of the members of the All-American League."

That response earns him an eye roll, but we are both smiling. My smile grows even wider when he bends down and throws me over his shoulder. "Hey! What are you doing? Put me down."

"No can do, baby. We've got a cinematic masterpiece to watch."

Since neither of us is ready for bed when the movie ends, we put on my all-time favorite film, *Elizabethtown*. It may be an acquired taste, but teenage Raven spent many nights watching this film. The sound-track was the most played album on my iTunes.

Fully consumed in nostalgia, I don't immediately notice that the hand slung over my shoulder has slipped behind my ribs to graze the side of my breast.

"What do you think you're doing?" I question, shifting my attention to the shirtless hunk beside me. It isn't fair that he is this hot dressed down. Kent in a baseball uniform? Hot. Kent wearing a suit? Sexy. Kent relaxing in loungewear without his mask of smug indifference? Panty-melting.

"Nothing," he replies innocently, but he can't hide the mischief in his gaze. "Watching Orlando Bloom hang out with his wacky family."

"You sure? Because it your hand has other ideas."

"Can't help what my hand does, baby. It has a mind of its own. My mind has a mind of its own, too."

"Does it? What is your mind thinking?" I ask, amused.

"It thinks we should ditch the movie, and I should fuck you into the mattress until the only thing you're able to watch is the back of your eyelids." He wiggles his eyebrows at me suggestively. No one this hot should pull off playful the way he does.

"No way. I watched your movie. Now you have to watch mine!"

He pretends to consider this for a second before saying, "Counter proposal: we find out if you can keep yourself from coming on my hand before the credits. If you lose, you ride me on this couch like you're going for the Triple Crown."

"And if I win?"

"If you win, I'll eat that sweet little pussy until you soak my face.

Then I'll clean us both off in the shower before getting you dirty all over again. How does that sound?"

He smirks when he notices me squeezing my thighs together as his tongue darts out to lick his bottom lip. "Looks like we got a deal."

"Deal, but you can't use your mouth during the movie. That would be cheating," I agree.

Kent ghosts his nose down the side of my face and licks my pulse point. "I don't need my mouth to make you see stars, baby," he says, shifting his head to the side until his breath tickles my ear. The promise in his voice causes my body to shudder.

With the wager made, we return our attention to the move. I think he's bluffing when he remains still for several minutes. Then I notice it: his hand discreetly under the blanket. His warm palm lands on my thigh as he traces patterns. He isn't close to my center yet, but the thought that he's heading there has my traitorous pussy getting wet.

Not wanting him to know how affected I am by his ministrations, I keep my gaze locked on the screen. I've seen this movie enough times to quote it in my sleep, but with the amount of focus I give, you would think it was the first time. The rest of the night will be pure bliss no matter which of us wins the bet. But he believes he has the upper hand here, and I can't have that.

His fingers inch up until they are pressed against the hem of my shorts. Like Kent, I changed into something more comfortable. In my case, it's a cute pajama set, not grey sweatpants.

I sense the moment he realizes I'm not wearing panties. His body freezes but quickly relaxes. The discovery encouraged him to keep going, and I shift against him in anticipation. The action move sets my shorts askew and exposes me further. His easy access doesn't bode well for my chances of winning our bet, but I am close to not caring.

Kent runs his hand down one of my legs and pulls it over his lap, fully opening me up to him, even if the blanket obstructs his view. I can tell by his body language he is trying to play it cool. Sneaking a peak at him in my peripherals, I see that he, too, has his eyes on the screen. The only thing giving him away is his smirk. With full access to me, he slides his fingers to the edge of my pussy where he lightly rubs.

Continuing his teasing touches, I hear a soft chuckle when I push my body further into his hand. Looking silently at the screen, he slides one finger between my lips and toys with my wetness.

My swallow hard when his touch ghosts my clit. He repeats the motion. My body is begging him to touch it the way he knows I want. I bite down hard on my lip to keep from saying those exact words and I almost draw blood. When finally, he flicks my clit, I'm so riled up that the action makes me cry out.

Now he's laughing loudly. My increasing desperation is somehow funny to him. "How are you doing over there, baby? Going to make it these last ten minutes?"

"Yes," I rasp, though when he slips one finger inside me, I'm not so sure. He leisurely fingers me as if he has all the time in the world, and we aren't at the movie's climax with time ticking down. Minutes remain before the credits, and he hasn't cracked me yet.

Sensing my resolve, he adds another finger to join the first, pumping in and out of me and adding a twist that has fireworks sizzling across my skin. The motion has me writhing. When his thumb presses into my clit, the juxtaposition between the steady action and the increasingly fast fingering causes me to pant in exertion. I'm not even the one doing anything, and I'm practically sweating.

The skill at which he plays my body makes it clear I am out of my depth. He toys with my body as if he was made to do it. No match for his talented fingers. I give up and grind against his hand.

"Yeah, that's it. Ride my fingers." Throwing my head against his shoulder, I moan. Movie forgotten.

"Kent," I mewl.

"I know, baby. It feels good. You're getting so close. Your tight little cunt is strangling my fingers. Your movie is almost over. You can win the bet if you hold off a few more minutes. All you have to do is keep yourself from coming."

"Noooo," I whine. "Come now."

"You want to come now, Raven? You can come now," he coaxes as I ride his hand and chase my release.

He switches from twisting to come hither motion that allows him to rub directly against my G-spot. The change is all I need to trigger the orgasm that was waiting at the surface. I scream my release as he works me through it, never stilling his fingers.

"That's it, baby. You come so pretty for me," he croons. When my pleasure is wrung out, all the tension in my body bleeds out. Rolling my head, I gaze up at Kent and watch him draw his fingers into his mouth to suck off my release.

The image captivates me and despite coming moments before, my pussy pulses. Something he must know based on the glimmer in his eyes.

"Your orgasm hit before the credits," he notes. "That means I win. Saddle up, cowgirl."

I snort out a laugh. "Saddle up? You're so lame."

"Is that any way to talk to the man who made you come so hard you practically passed out?"

"You are so full of yourself," I retort.

"Do I need to repeat the performance?" he challenges.

"Give me a second, geez. Can't a girl bask in post-orgasm bliss without a guy trying to give her another one?"

He chuckles. "Sure, bask away. I'll find us a better setting for the rodeo."

Chapter Thirty-Six

• KENT •

The image of her falling apart against my hand is going to live rent free in my head for a while. It will definitely be the star of my spank bank during the next road trip. It's only rival for top spot is the way she rode me afterward. She has officially been crowned the winner of the Kent's Wood Derby.

After we've showered off the evening's activities, Raven is lying with her head on my chest, tracing lazy circles over my abs. "What are you thinking about?" she asks abruptly.

I'm thinking about the fact that since dating Raven, I've barely visited my other property. That sense of calm I had when I was there isn't something I've needed because being around her gives me that. She's more of a home than any place I've ever lived. The sentiment should scare me, but instead it settles something inside me.

"How bland my condo is," is what I say instead.

"It does lack personality," she hums. "Does your house have more?"

"Some. I bought it furnished. It mostly matches the old owners, but Mom helped me add some personal touches."

"You wanna know a secret?"

"Is it that you snore? Because I already know that, baby."

"No!" she exclaims, swatting my chest.

"I can't wait to have a house of my own. I've been saving up to buy a rundown Victorian in Historic Edgefield. There is this block of Eastlake-style homes that hasn't been fixed up yet and I want to be one of the people who does."

"Why there?" I ask, curious. I assumed she'd want to stay in her current area since she's been there for years already.

"The architecture of the homes, for one. That style is hard to come by, especially one that hasn't already been gutted of all its charm by investors. But it has a great proximity to downtown and other districts I love. Plus, it's a good place to live with a family. Not that I have one, but one day." As she finishes her statement, her voice trails sleepily.

I want to ask her more about this dream. Like if she's married in it; if family means kids. The future isn't something we've discussed. I've barely got the hang of this boyfriend thing. Thinking about more makes my chest seize. Unfortunately, she is already lightly snoring in my arms. I make a mental note to bring it up soon and join her in slumber.

Chapter Thirty-Seven

"You can put that in the corner," I yell to the delivery guys. "To the right of the mirror!"

I peer back down into the box I am sorting. I jerk up when I sense a presence beside me. "Hey, Charlie!" I greet. "What do you think?"

"Raven, this is incredible. I can't believe how much you've gotten done."

I smile as I wipe the sweat from my brow and angle my body toward the camera the way the cinematographer taught me.

"I'm glad you think so. I only have a few more things to go over with you before you are kicked out until reveal day."

"Let's get to it, then!" she says.

For the next few hours, Charlie and I discuss the different areas of her gym renovation. The producers make us go through it a few times until they have enough options for what snippets to use. Once we're done, Charlie and I take a break on one of her new workout benches.

"Thank you for agreeing to be on the show. Having a gym is such a fun project and balanced out some of the others. Plus, designing around workout equipment was a fun challenge."

"Thank you for letting me! I am excited to open up my own space finally. Having you help me has been a godsend. It would be bland without your guidance. I can't wait to see the finished product and get people in the doors. You're almost done, right? Lola told me the pilot airs next month."

I have been working hard at my show all summer. HRN signed on for a mini season, which is twelve episodes. Twelve projects that I had to film from start to finish in two months. It was technically eleven, but we went back to the McMahan recording studio project to film some additional content that fit into the sequence and style of the show. The first episode airs the Wednesday after Labor Day and the last right before Thanksgiving. To say I'm nervous is an understatement.

"Yeah," I reply. "We're in the final stages for half the projects. The first six are done and with the editors. I'm also filming promos for the network to use on TV and social media next week."

"Wow. You're going to be on TV, Ray!"

"I know. I have to pinch myself sometimes it doesn't feel real."

"I want to hear about the other projects!" Charlie demands.

I tell her about the pediatric dentist's office I redesigned – complete with a movie room – and the doggy daycare where pups swarmed me. I also share the work I am doing with Zach's training facility, since I figure it will interest her. The clientele at a batting cage won't be the same as a trampoline-pilates-yoga studio, but both projects required me to keep athletic performance in mind.

"Oh! Right now I'm working on this adorable indie bookstore set to open in Hillsboro. It's run by a woman in Charlotte who is trying to expand into other cities in the south. She's a total sweetheart. And her nephew plays for the Knights, will be there."

"No way!" Charlie exclaims. "I had a poster of the Knight's championship team in my room as a kid. My mom used it as an example of how she didn't believe I was gay."

"You're kidding!"

"Nope."

"Her face when I explained to her it was mostly for the cheer-leaders and that I had my lesbian awakening at thirteen thanks to Megan Fox in *Jennifer's Body* was priceless."

"Megan Fox always gave off a mean vibe to me. Maybe because she played the villain in that Mary-Kate and Ashley movie."

"I don't mind. I like 'em a little mean. Makes putting them in their place all the more fun."

I burst out laughing. "Honestly, that doesn't surprise me at all."

"I wouldn't have pictured you with Mr. Good Time," she comments.

"No?"

"Obviously, you're perfect for him. But I didn't think he'd be good enough for you. For someone who never had a girlfriend, he sure had some baggage."

"I was nervous, too," I sigh. "He's cagey about the show. He read a text over my shoulder where the producers mentioned having him appear and freaked out until he saw I shut them down."

"That's dramatic." I shrug.

"I've never had to worry about people wanting to be in my life for clout. I can't blame him."

"That's about to change soon, you fancy reality star," she teases. "But seriously, I'm happy for you. I'm glad he stepped up."

"Me, too," I beam.

"Speaking of budding romances, don't think I didn't notice the tension between you and Kristie the other day."

"I don't know what you're talking about," she responds. The blush forming on her cheeks tells me she's lying. Instead of pressing for details, we chat about Lola's impending due date and how excited we are to meet Baby Miller. When our break is over, I film a few more shots while unpacking boxes and call it a day. I left my team with instructions on what to do and I'll return later this week to put the final touches on the gym before we film the big reveal.

Chapter Thirty-Eight

I high-five my teammates as I rush off the plane. We just landed after a successful away series where we kept our win streak alive against Miami and Carolina. There were some nail biters, and we had to come back from a three-run deficit, twice, but we ended up victorious.

Not only is the team winning, but I am on fire. My batting average is up, I'm faster than ever, and mentally stronger. I'm sure partying less helps, but I think it's mostly due to Raven, or at least my relationship. I thought having a girlfriend would be a distraction, but turns out it has settled something inside me and allowed me to level up my game.

Not to toot my own horn, but I've been killing the boyfriend thing, too. Aside from the house issue, we haven't had a single fight. My place is stocked with all her goodies. I text her first and last thing every day, and I'm giving her as many orgasms as she can handle and then an extra for good measure.

Did I mention I take her on the best dates because I do? Tonight we're headed to the state fair. A VIP fair package is one of the things I bid on and won at Carina's gala last month. After a quick nap at the condo, I'll pick up Raven. Then we'll spend the evening stuffing our faces with unnecessarily fried foods and try not to throw them up on the rides we have unlimited access to.

"I feel bad that we're skipping all those people," Raven says as we are ushered through a special line at the fair entrance.

"They could have gotten VIP tickets," I reply.

"Not everyone has ten grand to throw around on fair tickets, Big Shot."

"Whoa there, the VIP tickets are only two hundred fifty dollars. I threw my ten grand at a charity to help feed underprivileged kids and give them sports supplies. Thank you very much."

"My apologies," she mutters with an eye roll. And dammit, that action is just as sexy to me now as it was the day we met.

"Careful with those eye rolls, Firefly, or I'll give you a reason to roll them," I tease.

"By making even more dumb comments?"

My girl is saucy tonight. Too bad for her that I have no problem giving it back. I bend down until my mouth is next to her ear. "No, by fucking you so good in the fun house they roll to the back of your skull."

She flushes and swats at my chest. "Behave! There are kids every-where. You've used that line before."

"That's because it's not a line, it's a guarantee. And I think you're the one who needs to behave, or else I'll make good on my threat."

"You mean promise?"

"No, baby. It's a threat to rock your world so hard I have to carry you out of here."

My words make her skin heat even further, and I can't help the satisfied grin that takes over my face. "Come on, shortcake. Let's go get you some fried corn on the cob. They serve that in Missouri, right?"

"We'll eat just about anything fried in Missouri, but we do love corn. Haven't you seen all the cornfields when you've played the Huskers?"

"Only from the plane. Maybe we can visit after the season and you can show me."

"We could go to the haunted corn maze! Wait, you want to go to Missouri?"

"Of course, how else would I meet your family? I figured we could take a trip out there and a trip to Seattle to see Mom."

I'm yanked backward by our linked hands when Raven stops in the middle of the crowd. Her eyes are shining with unshed tears and I think I've said something wrong. Before I can apologize, she stands on her tiptoes and uses her free hand to drag my face down to hers, where she kisses the life out of me.

We break apart when we hear someone whistle. "That sounds nice," she says, resting her forehead against mine.

"Good. Now feed me, woman!"

Too much food later, we find ourselves wandering through the games. "You know, you've only fulfilled half of your boyfriend duties," Raven asserts.

"How so?"

"You brought me chocolate cheesecake last time I was on my period, but you have yet to win me a carnival stuffed animal. I'm not sure we can consider this a relationship without one."

"That's a valid point," I consider with mock seriousness. "I supposed we should rectify that."

She giggles when I drag her toward the bottle-throwing game. "Come on, that one is cheating. You play baseball!"

"I'm not a pitcher!" I defend. "Fine, fine. I'll pick something else. How about ring toss?"

She wrinkles her nose. "That is satisfactory."

"I'm glad it passed the test," I deadpan. Pulling out the game tickets we got with the wristbands, I hand them to the operator. My first two rings are right on the money. The third and fourth ping off.

"Uh ohhhh," Raven taunts beside me. "Only one left. Are you going to be able to do it?"

"You're writing checks your ass can't cash," I tell her as I let the final ring go. It lands dead center on a bottle and the lights above the game tell me I'm a winner.

"What prize do you want?" The operator asks with as much enthusiasm as I would expect from someone who travels from state to state working at fairs.

Surveying the options, I'm disappointed when I don't see a cat. "We'll take that one."

I take my prize and present it to Raven with a flourish. "Why on earth did you choose an octopus?" she asks, voice full of amusement.

"Looked cool." I shrug. "Alright, I think our food has settled enough. Let's try a ride."

As silly as I found these wristbands, getting to skip all the lines has been sweet. Raven refused to go on the rickety roller coaster – calling it suspect at best – but did agree to ride the tea cups and pendulum swing. Now, we are settling into our carriage on the Ferris wheel, and she looks happy.

"Having fun?" I ask as we ascend.

"I am. You?"

"Fuck yeah."

"You're about to have even more."

"What do you me—" Before I can even finish my sentence, she's dropped to her knees in front of me and undoing the button on my shorts.

"Babe, you can't do that here," I argue.

"Who's going to stop me? No one can see anything below your chest. Relax. Let me show you how much I loved this date."

Because there is no world where I stop her from putting her mouth on me, I comply with her request. Leaning back in my seat, I watch her pull out my cock as we climb higher.

Even if I prefer to give more than receive, the sight of Raven on her knees, wanting to suck my cock is not something I would ever turn down. This isn't the first time Raven has blown me, but it's never been from this position. With all my blood surging toward my cock, I don't know how long I'll be able to last.

When my length is free, she bites her lip and locks her light brown irises with mine. Slowly leaning forward, she licks me from root to tip as I rapidly harden against her tongue. She pulls my sensitive head in between her lips and sucks softly. God damn, it feels good. My entire body is one charged nerve.

I'm no stranger to public hookups. The bathroom at Holler's has seen my bare ass more than a few times. But something about the height, the exposure, and the girl kneeling at my feet takes the exhibitionism to the extreme. It's a heady combination. As with every other time we've been together, I don't think I have ever been this turned on.

Raven pulls a groan out of me as she works me deeper into her mouth. "Fuck, your mouth is so hot." my cock twitches when it grazes the inside of her cheek. "You can take more."

Her nostrils flare in challenge, and she sucks me deeper, gagging when I hit the back of her throat. She swirls her tongue around me as she pulls back. She brings one hand up to rest on my stomach for balance while the other works my base, so it feels like she's sucking me deeper.

I am getting there embarrassingly quickly, but that is good based on how much closer the ground is since the last time I checked. This Ferris wheel ride is simultaneously the fastest and slowest I've ever been on. Raven slows her bobs and reduces the pressure as if she can read my mind. Fucking temptress.

After my orgasm ebbs away, she teases me with light touches

until the hand on my shaft slips down to toy with my balls, and she sucks with renewed vigor. Hell yeah. "You're such a dirty girl, Firefly," I say as my hand runs through her hair. I move to grip it around my fist, but she slaps it away.

"No touching," she warns as my cock slips from her lips with a satisfying plopping noise. "You touch, I stop."

"Please," I groan. She shakes her head and lowers back down to lap at my tip. When she's waited long enough to be sure I'll follow her rule, she takes me back between her heavenly lips.

"Have I told you how perfect you are today?" I feel more than hear her snort at my shameless compliment. I'm not above using flattery to get on her good side. I hold my breath when I buck up into her, praying she won't stop. She shoots me a playful glare but keeps working my cock in and out of her skilled mouth.

Her ministrations are so good I don't even realize I closed my eyes until the noise from the fair below gets louder. "Fuck. We're getting close to the bottom. Please don't stop," I say.

As heat pools at the base of my spine and my balls tingle, I realize too late I made the mistake of bracing a hand on her shoulder. The whine of protest that comes out of me when she pulls back is one I've never heard from a human before.

"Tsk, tsk, Kenny. Don't you know how to follow the rules?" she taunts.

My mouth gapes in dismay. Is she seriously about to leave me like this? We're close enough to the bottom I don't think she'd have time to finish, but I am crazed at the disruption. "Raven, I swear to God. Don't make me carry you through this fair with a massive boner in my pants. People will think I'm kidnapping you."

The top of the other rides is almost level now, and I know I am not getting relief until we're alone again. Pushing myself back into my pants, I place the stuffed octopus over my crotch so no one can see the wood I'm sporting.

Raven giggles. "Is this funny to you?" I grit.

"I thought octopuses only have eight legs."

"Hilarious. You're a real Taylor Tomlinson," I deadpan. She lifts a shoulder in response and settles on the bench across from me. We're three carriages from the bottom now. "You're in so much trouble, baby."

Chapter Thirty-Nine

There are women out there who will tell you giving oral is one of their favorite things. I am not one of those women. Still, I can't deny that blowing Kent while the Ferris wheel spun was exhilarating. Normally, the ride makes me nervous, but all I could focus on was turned on while I had Kent in my mouth.

The sensation of his strong muscles under my hands was powerful. Having this man at my mercy is heady. I'm almost as amused by his pouting as I am horny. The expression on his face when I pulled off the second time was priceless. One glimpse of the scene behind me, and I knew he wouldn't finish by the time we hit the ground. His begging was cute, though.

His disillusionment has been replaced with determination and vengeance. I may have laughed at him using Octavius (yes, that's what I named my octopus) to shield his boner, but it wasn't the worst idea. Especially since it left one hand free for him to drag me alongside him. I'm practically running to keep up with his strides when I realize he's taking us to the parking lot. I've unleashed a facet of Kent I've never seen before. I fucked around and I'm about to find out.

When we get to his SUV, he pulls open the door to the back and tosses Octavius onto the seat. "Get. In," he practically growls.

Eyes wide, I follow his instructions. He is radiating with so much need and lust, I now understand how we made it all the way to the car without being stopped by a fan. He looks practically feral.

Once inside, I'm surprised when he follows behind. All thoughts of a tense ride home, until he could take me against the front door, fly out the window when he yanks me onto his lap. His steel length presses against the apex of my thighs as he holds me against him. "Is this what you wanted? To get me all hot and bothered? Was this your end game?"

"I-I-I didn't think that far ahead," I whimper as he rubs directly against my sweet spot.

"You made two mistakes, Firefly. That was your first. Don't play games with people who play better." His hands are holding my ass in a punishing grip that is sure to leave bruises. He takes my mouth in a savage kiss, and I get lost in the moment as I grind back and forth against him.

"No more teasing. You are going to come on my cock, not my lap," he grits.

When I lift onto my knees, Kent rips the side of my panties until they are nothing but a scrap hanging on me. When I glance down at him, he stares back with a smug grin. "They were in our way. Are you ready to finish what you started?"

"Yes," I pant. Without warning, he pushes two fingers inside. We both moan. Me at the intrusion and him at how wet I am for him. "You're soaked, baby. Did sucking my dick above everyone's head turn you on? You miss our secret rendezvous; you had to recreate one?"

I mewl as he thrust his fingers in and out, my legs spread wide across his thighs. When I don't respond to him, his hand pulls away, only to come back down and lightly slap my pussy. "Answer me. Did toying with me in public excite you?"

"Yes," I hiss in reply to his question and at the sensation of his fingers back inside me. It doesn't take long to get close. Right as my pleasure is about to crest, his fingers slip free again.

"Nooooo," I whine.

"Isn't as fun being on this side, is it?" he taunts. "Here is what's going to happen, my beautiful tease. You're going to ride my cock until you come, and then I am going to flip you over and pound this tight pussy until I explode inside you."

I nod in response. He squeezes my hard buds between his fingers and leans forward to nibble the spot on my neck he knows drives me wild. "I'm glad you agree, but it was more of a command than a question," he laughs.

Rolling my eyes, I reach between us and slide his zipper down to release the hard length I am dying to have him inside me. Lining him up to my entrance, I glide down inch by inch. For all his barely contained frustration, Kent allows me to go at my pace as I work him in. We exhale matching groans when I am fully seated.

I rock back and forth tentatively, finding a pattern that sends warmth through my entire body every time he rubs that spot inside me. I set a steady tempo, alternating between bouncing up and down on him and swiveling my hips. Despite the semi-public location, I struggle to contain my whimpers.

"Fuck yes, baby. You feel so good. Tell me how much you love having my cock inside you?"

"Yes. I love it. So good. So deep."

Kent toys with my nipples through my shirt, giving them enough attention to make me a trembling mess. When I lose my rhythm, he takes over.

"I will never get over how sexy you are riding me. Your wetness dripping down my shaft is incredible. Fuck, keep going. I need you to shatter on my cock. Make yourself come."

His dirty words cause me to ride harder and faster. When my

motion falters, he places a hand on my hips and lifts me up and down his shaft. His other hand snakes between us and swipes circles against my clit. The rush of my orgasm overtakes me as I clamp tightly around him. Kent thrusts from underneath me to prolong my high.

I wince when he pulls out of me. Stilling when I hear him curse. "Fuck, we didn't use a condom," he mutters. Shit, he's right. Both focused on quelling the ache, we didn't think about protection.

"I'm on birth control," I blurt out as he fishes a foil packet out of his wallet. "And you haven't come. I think we're good."

"I'm clean," he admits. "I always use a condom. No one else has ever gotten me worked up enough to forget." Even though it isn't really a compliment, I still preen at the thought that I drive him as crazy as he drives me. No one has ever made me ache the way that Kent does. His attention and affection are only matched by the immense pleasure I experience every time he touches me.

"Ask what your second mistake was."

"Second mistake?" I repeat.

In a swift move, he maneuvers until I'm kneeling with my hands on the seat and he's behind me. He flips my skirt over my ass and pushes his knee in between mine, spreading my legs. "I told you that you made two mistakes. The first was playing games with someone who could play them better."

Sitting on his heels, I hear the telltale sign of foil ripping. It's the only sound aside from our ragged breaths. I can't see what he's doing as I consider what my other miscalculation may have been.

"Your second mistake," he drawls, "was thinking I was above payback."

Before I can ask what he means, a loud crack echoes as heat blooms on my ass. It takes a moment for my brain to process that he spanked me! Kent spanked me while I am ass up in the back of his car. A smack hits my other cheek, and I jolt forward before his hands smooth over the smarted skin. "Fuck, your ass is pretty with my hand prints on it. This is going to be quick and dirty, baby. I'm not stopping until I come. Got it?"

I lose my ability to answer coherently when he thrust inside me, hands squeezing my hips.

"Nod," he chokes. When I give my confirmation, he pulls out and pushed back into me. Hard. Over and over, he slams into me. With my legs a knee width apart, he feels so large inside me. He's so deep at this angle, I barely remember to bring in air. Despite the intense climax I had a moment ago, my body is revving up for more. His punishing pace allows for nothing less than more from me.

"Fuck, you really are perfect. I'm going to come soon," he croons. "I can feel you tightening around me, baby. Come with me. Come hard for me."

I gurgle unintelligible noises. I'm so fucking close. Every nerve in my body is on fire. Leaving one hand on my hip, Kent's other hand slips down to give my pussy a final slap. I erupt, coming harder than I ever imagined possible. With a final thrust, Kent stills inside me and moans my name through his release. I collapse and rest my head on the seat in front of me as he leans over my back.

When he finally comes down, he kisses my shoulder lightly. "You okay?"

"Yeah," I answer.

"Best damn fair I've ever been to," he mumbles against my skin. I laugh as he nuzzles into my neck.

Searching through the console, Kent finds some napkins to clean us up before discarding them with my tattered panties and ushering me into the front seat. The ride back to my place is quiet but content. A heartwarming moment of peace before everything falls apart.

I wake up the next morning with Kent's warm body wrapped around me. It's rare that he isn't already up, since he typically does a morning workout on non-game days. Taking advantage of the morning snuggle, I push back into him, sensing when he stirs.

"Good morning, Firefly," he says in his graveling morning voice. A voice I can never get enough of.

"Good morning, Big Shot. No workout today?"

His arms tighten around me as he rests his chin on my shoulder. "Miller and I are supposed to meet up after Lola's appointment. He said he'd call when they were done." Rolling over, he grabs his phone from the nightstand and scrolls through it.

"That's weird," he comments.

"What is?" Missing his warmth, I pull the covers under my chin.

"My PR rep, Molly, sent me a text asking for us to call her ASAP."

"Us? As in, you and me?"

"Yeah."

"I wonder what that's about. You don't think anyone saw us last night?" I ask in a panic. The windows in his SUV are tinted as dark as legally allowed, but there is still a chance someone caught us through the windshield or on the Ferris wheel. Thank God we did everything with our clothes on. I would die if my family had to deal with seeing naked pictures of me.

"I'm sure it's fine. I kept you hidden. Let's call her and see what's up," he soothes.

"Yeah, okay."

"Hey, Molls. What's with the cryptic text? Yes, Raven is here. Sure, I can put it on speakers."

"Hi, Molly," I greet. "What's going on?"

"You tell me, Mrs. Dela Cruz. Anything either of you want to share?"

"Um, no?" I reply, confusion lacing my tone.

"If this is about last night, there is no way anyone saw anything. And if they did, just pay them off," Kent states.

"This isn't about that. Wait, what happened last night?"

"Oh, uh, nothing. We had a nice date at the state fair. There were no shenanigans on the Ferris wheel or elsewhere."

"Kent," I hiss, hitting him with the pillow.

"Hey, I said there were no shenanigans!"

"Dela Cruzes!" Molly yells through the phone. "Can we focus, please? I'm trying to keep my cool and assume there is a reason you hid something this monumental from me, but my patience is razor thin."

"What are you talking about, Molly? The only thing we 'hid' was us hooking up. I didn't realize you cared that much about my sex life. You never asked about any of my other fuck buddies."

I grimace.

"Sorry, babe, you know what I mean," he apologizes.

"What's the big deal?" he directs at Molly.

"The big deal," she seethes. "Is that none of your other bed buddies were your fucking wife!"

I freeze. "Did she say—"

"Did you say 'wife?'" Kent bellows. "I know it's rare for me to get in a serious relationship, but we are jumping the gun, the knife, and about seventeen other objects by calling Raven my wife. You know my stance on marriage. Not until after I retire, if ever."

Ouch. I understand this relationship is new, but he doesn't have to sound that upset about someone calling me his wife. Also, what does he mean 'if ever?' I knew he was averse to commitment, but I didn't think it was a whole anti-marriage thing. I'm not trying to get married tomorrow, but I want to someday. He's close to the average retirement age. I could wait a few years if he wanted to, but only if I knew the option was on the table. This sounds as if it may not be.

"I'm not calling her your wife because she's the first serious girlfriend you've had," Molly says, clearly annoyed by this conversation.

"I'm calling her your wife because she's your wife. The two of you are married or did you somehow forget that?"

Eyes wide, Kent glances up from the phone and meets my gaze.

He must see my matching baffled expression. "We didn't get married, Molly. I think we'd remember that."

"Alright, what did you do after Miller and Lola's wedding in Vegas, then? Because I have pictures of the two of you at that same chapel exchanging rings."

Well, shit. Maybe we are married.

Chapter Forty

• KENT •

Raven and I quickly get dressed and head to the G&K office in relative silence. I was lost in thought, trying to pull out any memories of the night. Raven was alternating between fiddling with her bracelets and God knows what on her phone. I'll have to call Mom later and tell her about this before the story gets too out of control. Once I understand what the story is, at least.

When we arrive, we are met by Molly, her intern, and my agent. They immediately usher us into a sitting room, where a screen shows the face of my personal attorney, Eugene.

"Alright, someone tell me what the hell is going on here because there is no way we are married," I say as I settle in one of the armchairs. I probably should have sat on the sofa so Raven didn't have to sit alone, but all I can think about right now is figuring this out.

"As I said on the phone," Molly states, exasperated. "You and Raven got married in Las Vegas, several hours after Miller and Lola."

"How is that possible? We were both intoxicated enough that we don't remember anything. Where did these pictures come from?"

"I can answer that," the intern, I think her name is Leah, pipes in. "A magazine spread came out featuring the Miller nuptials last week. One of the chapel's employees saw it and noticed the earrings Raven was wearing. Apparently, they found one and wanted to reunite it with its owner."

Raven squeaks next to me, surprised and delighted that her missing earring is located, but we have bigger fish to fry at the moment.

"She's shipping it here," Molly interjects with a soft smile.

"Yes," Leah continues. "The woman reached out to the publication to see if they had identified the woman. One thing led to another, and the story of your marriage was revealed when they asked if the chapel had more pictures to 'get a better look.' There is a video, too, but they didn't release it. We're getting a copy. The magazine hasn't run the story yet, but by the weekend, it will be everywhere."

"Are we sure this is real? We're exchanging rings in the picture, but neither of us woke up wearing one." Raven asks as she ignores the chime of her phone on the coffee table. I nod my head. That detail escaped my attention, but she is right. We didn't have rings on in the morning – at least, I didn't.

"We're not sure about that. From the security video we were able to get from the hotel, you didn't return with them on. You did get to second base in the elevator, though, which I could have lived without seeing. The hotel agreed to delete all that footage, thankfully."

"I'm not worried about a video of me feeling up a girl leaking right now. No one will be shocked by that. I'm a little hung up on the marriage thing. We didn't even have a license. I don't know exactly what Miller had to do to get everything squared away, but it seemed like a lot," I note.

"I can help you there," Eugene chimes in. "You are legally married, but getting an annulment would be simple. At least that's what I thought when I was under the impression this was a one time hookup situation. If you are dating, that may complicate things. We may have to file for divorce instead."

"Why?" I ask. "We'd only fucked once at that point, and it was supposed to be a one-night stand. We didn't get together again for months." I know this is not my finest moment. Based on the intake of air beside me and the glare Molly is shooting my way, the rest of the room agrees. I don't have it in me to care, though.

"We'll say whatever to get it annulled," I assert.

"Hold on. Let's not do anything rash," Molly tuts, eyeing Raven sympathetically. "There are some PR implications to consider here. It's a lot harder to put it back in the bottle of public perception than it is legally."

"The public shouldn't be surprised at all that I had a drunken wedding," I assert.

"True, but you aren't the only person this affects. It could hurt Raven's career based on the image HRN is portraying. You're dating, there is no reason this wedding has to change anything. You can deal with it later if you break up."

"You think we should stay married?!" I snarl. "You're supposed to protect me, Molly. We don't even have a prenup."

"I protect your image," she quips back. "Being in a stable relationship wouldn't be the worst thing for it. Tossing aside a sweet up-and-coming media darling might be."

The walls are closing in on me – in this room, in this situation. The blood between my ears is rushing loudly in my brain, as is a 'danger' alarm playing on a loop. The only thing louder is the incessant dinging of Raven's phone.

"Do you mind?! Whoever is trying to reach you can fucking wait. We have a crisis on our hands right now. Silence it." I snap.

Raven flushes in embarrassment. "Sorry. It's the network. They want to talk about us being married and what it means for the show."

"You told them already?" I bellow.

"No, but they have eyes and ears everywhere. I'm not shocked they know before it hits the mainstream. They keep track of their assets. They want to know what is going on."

"What's going on is we're getting an annulment or divorce or whatever we have to do to end this sham. Tell them that.".

Molly stands and motions the others to do the same. "We're going to give you two the room to discuss. Let us know what you decide, and we can determine next steps, okay? Eugene, I'll call you when we know more."

As my team hightails it away from me as if I am an erupting volcano, I stand and pace in the space they vacated. This cannot be happening. It is too crazy. Even for me. When my gaze finds Raven again, she watches me pensively.

"It's not that big of a deal," she whispers.

"It's a huge deal!" I counter. "We're fucking married, Raven. As in what's mine is yours, sickness and health, all that bullshit."

"I can sign a postnup," she offers. "I don't mind protecting your assets. I don't want your money."

"Who needs my money when you can have my name?" I sneer. The meek expression she had processing the news hardens and becomes thunderous.

"What is that supposed to mean?"

"It's awfully convenient that we are not only married but that the news comes out around the same time your show is set to air. MLB star and sexy interior designer, we're a real power couple."

"Are you insinuating I did this on purpose?" she accuses.

"I'm just saying that it is a little suspicious."

"You know what, fuck you!" she shouts. "I was ready to work through this with you and figure out what needed to be done to contain this. But if the idea of being married to me is so terrible, have Eugene file the papers today. I'll have no problem telling them we weren't a couple. In fact, that's the truth. Because I sure as fuck don't want to be with a guy who would rather throw both our careers in the toilet than be accidentally married to me.

"When you calm down and realize what a complete jackass you've been about this whole thing, remember that YOU are the one who pursued me. Not the other way around. YOU were the one who asked to be my boyfriend after I tried to end it. Every step of progress we had was at your behest."

Raven stands as she continues to yell at me. "I may not remember what happened in Vegas, but this is not my fault. We were both there. We are both adults. When you eventually pull your head out of your ass, don't come for me. I have no interest in being in a relationship with no future or with a man who can't give even a shred of the benefit of the doubt.

"Mail me papers, divorce, annulment, I don't care. I'll sign whatever I need to. Otherwise, I don't want to hear from you. Better yet, have Eugene contact my attorney." With those parting words, Raven storms out of the room.

After watching her leave, I sink down into the chair and cradle my head in my hands. How the hell did I end up here? Six months ago, I was at the height of my career without a care in the world. Now, I'm about to divorce my first girlfriend and blow my friend group and life the fuck up.

"That went well," Molly's voice chimes from the doorway. I peer at her through my fingers and catch her worried expression. "It'll be okay, bud. We'll fix it."

I bark out a humorless laugh. "I don't know how much you heard, but it doesn't sound as if there is anything to fix."

She sits down beside me and pats my knee. "I wasn't made to be married, Molly. I'd make a shitty husband."

"I don't know about that," she tsks. "You're a great man, an amazing son, a wonderful friend. Sounds like before this, you were a pretty decent boyfriend. You are good at everything you put your mind to. You need to decide whether this is going to be one of those things.

"Speaking of being an amazing son, you should call your mom. The story will hit tomorrow, and it will be full steam ahead after that.

We'll come up with a plan to support whatever option you decide, but don't be rash in your decision.

"I've never seen you as happy and content as you have been in the last several weeks. Don't let fear and self-doubt fuck this up."

Chapter Forty-One

It only took twenty-four hours for the story of our quickie Vegas wedding to blow up everywhere. It even overshadowed the pictures of Lola and Miller's wedding, which is a good thing considering the struggles she has been having with her pregnancy.

Not wanting to pull focus, I haven't spoken much to the girls about my marriage – I cannot believe I'm even saying that word – or the state of my relationship. I know it will shake up the group dynamic when I tell them we broke up. The guys all play together. I'm simply Lola's friend from high school. It's pretty clear which of us will lift out, and I'm not ready to deal with that yet.

Thanks to advice from Molly and the HRN PR team, the press hasn't been too bad. I've been screening my calls and directing any DMs to contact the network. I've said 'no comment' more in the last few days than in my entire life.

The reaction from the public has been a mix of disbelief and support. It's hard for many people to believe Kent would settle down – which they aren't wrong about – especially since we don't have any solo pictures together besides the wedding. Those who do believe it are mostly happy for us. There are a few trolls, but I don't take them personally. And I have content filters that block most of the negativity.

I have stayed locked up at home since the story broke. If there were any paps outside my house, they're long gone by now. They probably assume I'm at Kent's since married couples usually live together. They'd have a field day if they knew the truth. Most outlets are reporting we kept it under wraps to keep his reputation from hurting my chances of landing my HRN show. Or that I married him for the MLB spousal benefits since I was fired. Charming. I'm not sure who at GHI spilled those beans since I had to sign an NDA.

Thankfully, I am not important enough to be truly hounded over this. With the sheer number of professional athletes, the general population doesn't have time to care who and when they marry. Kent is more high-profile than most, but the appetite for baseball isn't as big as other sports.

Screening my calls means I have also avoided talking to my family and friends about this. I gave the girls a brief rundown, but we were all so preoccupied with Lola that they didn't ask many questions. My family is another story. When my sister's name flashes across my screen for a video call, I know it is time to pay the piper.

"Hello?"

"If it isn't baseball's most popular WAG," she teases. "I didn't realize when I met your hunky boy toy earlier this summer that I was meeting your husband. Care to explain why you didn't share that detail?"

"I didn't know," I grumble, face pressed into my bed.

"Awesome. Can you tell me now that you've informed the pillow?"

"I didn't know," I confess. "We got plastered after Lola and Miller's wedding and apparently decided we should get married, too. Neither of us remembered it happening the next morning."

"You're kidding," she gapes. When I shake my head, she devolves into a fit of laughter so intense her husband comes in to check on her.

"She's fine, Brett," I call out. "Just reveling in my pain and suffering."

"The usual, got it," he deadpans, and she waves him off.

"I'm sorry. I never thought I'd hear my baby sister say she drank too much and married a multi-millionaire with a six-pack. If the Corn Queen judges could see you now."

"Ugh, don't remind me of my failed beauty pageant career. Aren't I suffering enough?" I lament.

"Okay, okay. Tell me what happened, Ray Ray, because you don't sound thrilled about this turn of events."

Reminiscent of when we were kids, I sit in my room and spill my guts to my big sister. She let me get through the ordeal at G&K and the brief history of my relationship with Kent – now a former relationship – before she chimes in.

"I'm proud of you," she announces.

"What?" I ask incredulously. "You're proud that I can't handle my liquor and drunkenly married a near stranger who I then got into a friends-with-benefits relationship with, only to end it after he accused me of using him to boost my career?"

"When you put it that way, it sounds silly. But yes, I'm proud of you. Proud of you for standing up for yourself and knowing your worth. Not everyone could do that. Not everyone would demand what they deserve and not settle for the crumbs others were willing to give them. That takes balls."

"Thank you," I stutter, full of emotion. Hearing that small praise is a balm to my fragile psyche after everything that has happened.

"I hate to pick at a wound, but what has HRN said about all this?"

"They aren't happy," I admit. "Since I haven't talked to Kent, I don't know what to tell them about the dissolution of the marriage. I'll have to face him eventually, but I haven't been up to it yet. Plus, I put the ball firmly in his court. He's the one who has to make the next move. A part of me expected divorce papers to arrive at my house that night."

"Maybe he doesn't want a divorce?" she suggests, hopefully.

I bite my lip as I consider the idea, but push it away quickly. "You should have heard him, Em. You would have thought he'd had a slew of ex-wives or stepdads with how against it he was. Marriage is not something he was even considering, which, as his girlfriend, does not bode well for the permanency of our relationship. I thought it was going somewhere. He knew when we made it official that I wanted something serious."

"Plenty of people are in permanent relationships without marriage. Being official is serious for a guy who has never done that before," she notes. "But I know what you mean. That is something you should have discussed. What happens now?"

I blow a raspberry, causing a napping Cappy to shoot me a dirty look for disturbing him. He's been extra cuddly through the ordeal, but even he is over my wallowing and dramatics.

"I live my life, I guess. I can't make any moves until he does. The Songbirds are nearing the end of their season. Maybe he wants to wait until after the playoffs. I have several projects to wrap up for the show. That is where my attention needs to go right now. I'll deal with the rest of it when it comes up."

"That's a solid plan. Call me if you need me. I can blow off work and stick Brett with the kids for a few days," she offers. "Don't worry about Mom and Dad. I'll call them and explain the situation. I'll leave out the fun, sexy bits, though, and tell them it was a bet or something."

"Oh God!" I exclaim, burying my head in my hands.

She's laughing hysterically again. "Bye, sis. Keep your head up. Everything will work out. Don't let this derail you. Good things are happening for you, and they will continue to as long as you keep moving forward."

Taking my sister's advice, I don't let the situation with Kent stop my momentum. In the next two weeks, I have two projects wrapping up. I have one more to go before filming is complete on my test season, and we enter editing and promo mode.

Today is an extra special filming day as it is the reveal of my friend Ellie's boutique. Ellie lived with Macy in college. While we were acquaintances back then, we've become closer through the design process of her new store. Even though I have to finish the bakery and insurance office projects, Ellie's project is the season finale. Mostly due to the star power of her dating one-third of the country trio, the Ryder Brothers.

Ellie and I hang out in the shop while there is a lull in filming. She is one of those people with an infectious energy you can't help but match. I know she's had her struggles, but you never see her down.

"Are you getting excited to open?" I ask.

"Yes," she replies. "But also nervous. It's one thing to have a good sense of style; it's another to run a business selling clothes you pick out to others. Mia is the stylist, not me. She promised to use pieces I have stocked in the store when she can."

Mia is Ellie's BFF and boyfriend's sister. Not only is she living her best rock star romance life, but she also lived through a best friend's brother saga. I don't know much about her relationship, but she and Jack have been together for about a year.

Speak of the devil. It's as if my thoughts conjured Jack Ryder to life. The wavy-haired musician pops his head in the front door and smiles brightly when he spots Ellie. "I'm not interrupting, am I? I brought my girl some lunch. She skipped breakfast." He shoots Ellie a meaningful expression, which she answers with a sheepish one.

"Thank you, babe. I don't know what I'd do without you," she replies.

"Starve, probably," he grumbles. Stretching out his arms, he wraps her up in a tight hug and kisses the top of her head.

"You two are so cute you're going to give me a toothache," I joke.

Ellie beams up at Jack like he hung the moon; I think he would for her. Breaking their eye contact, he addresses me. "I hear congratulations are in order. I hope Kent knows how lucky he is to land you as a wife."

I still at the mention of my 'husband' but tamp down my emotions, hoping they can't read the apprehension on my face.

"Oh my gosh, I didn't know you got married!" Ellie squeals.

"Yeah, it was one of those quickie Vegas weddings. Are your brothers going to make the grand opening, Jack?" I ask, changing the subject. Thankfully, they take the bait.

"Bryce will be here for sure. Gray is filming a reality show in LA but said he will be here. Declan doesn't know if he can get away since his mini tour will be in full swing. But it's a women's boutique anyway; if we don't have him, it'll be okay. All the Heron Heroines will be here. That's all that matters. My PR team is vetting some other high-profile attendees."

"I told you that you didn't need to do that." Ellie admonished.

"And I told you that this is your dream, Clover. I'm going to do whatever it takes to make it a success. What's the point of dating the most lovable Ryder Brother if you can't enjoy the perks?"

"I thought Declan was the most lovable Ryder," she teases.

"He wishes," he scoffs. "Does my girl have a few minutes to eat?" I glance over and see the director arguing with the lighting team.

"I think we are good for a while longer. Go enjoy some time with Jack. I will check in on my other projects," I instruct Ellie.

The pair heads into the back room and I pull up my phone to double-check that the salt blocks were delivered to the spa on time. We have a tight turnaround to get them installed before sealing the concrete.

While replying to some DMs, I make the mistake of clicking on a notification for a tagged post. I am greeted with a picture of Kent out on the town with Derrick and Leo. I don't know what city they're in, but they are having a good ole time, surrounded by bottles and women.

I guess Kent gets back the bachelor life he was worried about giving up. Exiting the app before seeing more pictures of their night, I decide my time is better spent talking to the producers about what we have left to film.

Chapter Forty-Two

"Time to go home, buddy," a gruff voice says.

"Sorry, man, you're not my type," I slur.

"Thank God for that," the voice laughs. "I wouldn't touch you with a ten-foot pole, Dela Cruz. I don't know how you got that girl to put up with you for so long."

"She's not anymore," I singsong.

"Yeah, I figured that's what all the drinking was about. Your boy, Leo, had to leave for an emergency, but I told him I'd get you home."

"That's nice of you, Mr. Deep Voice."

"Mr. Deep Voice? Holy hell. Kent, it's Big Ron. You're at Holler's, but we already had last call. Am I sending you to your condo, or is there somewhere else you'd rather go?"

"Big Ron! How are you?"

"Better than you."

"That's probably true. You're a happily married man. The missus is mad at me."

"I figured. Chin up. You're rich and pretty. She'll forgive you. I hear you can be rather convincing. But for now, you need to go home."

"Lake house," I murmur.

"You know the address?" he asks. I rattle it off for him. "That's going to be an expensive ride."

I shrug.

Ron guides me into a dark sedan. "You good, ma'am?" he asks the driver, who is vaguely familiar. It hits me that she was the one who drove me to Raven's house after the gala. Oh, how times have changed.

"Shirley!" I cheer.

"Hello, dear," she says before addressing Ron. "I've got this big fella. Kent and I go way back." I nod in agreement.

"Okay," he replies. "Try to hold it together, man. You'll bounce back."

"Thanks, Big Ron. You're good people."

"You too, bud," he says as he closes the door.

Rolling over in my bed, it takes a second to register that I'm at the lake house. I vaguely recall Big Ron putting me in the car last night and Shirley driving me here. I told her all about my breakup, and she consoled me as only a mother could. She agreed I would sleep better without all the reminders of Raven at my condo. The couch where I made her come during the movie, her favorite cookies in my pantry, and worst of all, her scent that lingers on every surface haunt me.

Staring out the window, I think about how glad I am I never brought her here. It would have been adorable watching her redesign it in her mind the way she did every time we went to a new place. But I at least have an escape without her mark. Although untainted, the house has a sense emptiness. No life is led here. It simply exists, like me.

Even though I know deep down that Raven didn't do any of the things I accused her of, I can't shake the sense of betrayal. Not that I blame her after the way I talked to her. But she wouldn't have blown up on me if she were innocent, right? She left me high and dry to deal with this mess. Not that I am.

Molly and Eugene are both pressing me for answers. In the short term, we released a statement asking for privacy during this transition. The press isn't buying it, though. My constant nights out don't scream 'happy newlywed.'

I wish I could remember the night we got married. I have so many unanswered questions. What did we do after the club? Whose idea was it to get married? How did we get to the chapel? What the hell happened to our rings? How did we get back to the hotel?

My muscles radiate with tension as I stretch before getting out of bed. I forgot how hard partying every night is on your body. I am not as young as I once was, and I am paying for every shot of tequila this morning. Not that Coach will go easy on me because of it at my training session later. I hope there is some food in the freezer I can use to make breakfast. Otherwise, I'll have to grab something fast and greasy on the way to the stadium. Time to start another fucked up day.

"You look like shit," Zach comments from where he stands in our underground training facility.

"Thanks, man," I reply sardonically. "It's my new skincare regime. Scrub until you no longer feel shame from the night before."

"And you're a ray of sunshine, too. Nice."

Letting out a groan, I drop my bag in the waiting area. "Can we get this over with?"

"What's going on?" Zach asked, voice laced with concern. "You usually love tune-up sessions. It's not like you to show up hungover."

"I'm not hungover, just tired. I had a late night." Grabbing a resistance band, I sink to the floor and stretch out my hamstrings.

"Been having a lot of those lately?"

"A few," I retort.

He laughs when I flop onto my back after working my quads.

"I'm glad my pain is funny to you."

"It's not funny, but it is predictable. I figured you'd get in your head and mess it up with Raven. I'd hoped you wouldn't, but I see a lot of myself in you, and I made the same mistakes."

"You drunkenly married a girl and then dated her, only to freak out when you found out you were married?"

"I didn't do that. But I did find a reason not to get serious with a woman who deserved it. It was different since I had a daughter to consider, but I had girlfriends who would have made great partners if I let them in. I am guessing you are doing the same thing."

"What's so great about being married? My mom and dad were married. It didn't make him stay. People divorce every day."

"If that is what you think, what's the big deal? Get married. Get divorced. Who cares? Why fight against it?"

Stopping mid hip stretch, I ponder those words. Why do I care so much if that's my logic? Plenty of guys I know are divorced and move on from it.

I think back to my parents' marriage. My mom tried hard to be a good wife, but nothing was ever good enough for my dad. He left when I was young, and we never heard from him again. I thought he might reach out when I made it to the big leagues, but he's a proud man, and I imagine he's embarrassed he never supported us. It must irk him that I made it this far without him.

Still, I remember the shame and sadness on Mom's face when she was served divorce papers. It's the day I vowed never to be the cause of that expression. Somehow, that morphed into strict rules and then never getting married. As if you can't disappoint someone without a ring. But I saw that expression on Raven's face when I accused her of using me to further her career before it transitioned into righteous anger.

"Can I give you some advice?" Zach asks, interrupting my thoughts.

I nod because, at this point, it can't hurt.

"Whatever you did, whatever you think she did, forget about it."

"Forget about it? That's your advice?"

"Yeah, forget about it," he repeats. "There are few things love can't overcome. I am confident that is the case here. You guys did things a little backward with the marriage before the dating, but who cares?"

"You love her, right? You want to spend the rest of your life with this woman?"

"I—" I pause, because, do I? I loved what we had. I loved waking up beside her and listening to her talk about her hopes and dreams. I loved knowing that she had my back, no matter what. Does that mean I loved her?

I've never been one to envision a future further than a season ahead. Things can change in an instant in this game. But as my friend group has expanded and the guys are starting families, I want to be a part of that.

I don't want to be the sad uncle who gets pity invites. I definitely don't want to be the bitter uncle who watches the girl he could have had fall in love with someone else.

The idea of that makes me feral. Raven is mine. The only one who is going to rub her shoulders after a long day of hanging decor is me. The only one she's going to read their horoscope to over breakfast is me. The only one who is going to give her whatever future she wants is me.

"Turn those wheels while you take out your aggression on the ball machine. I noticed you've got a kink in your swing, and I want to work it out before the New England series," Zach states.

After forty-five minutes of hitting balls in the cage, I have a sense of clarity. I know what I want, who I want. Now I need to figure out how to show her I can be the man she wants and deserves.

"Good luck. Hope you get whatever went wrong sorted out soon. She's good for you," Zach comments as I pack up to leave.

"Thanks, man. You're pretty wise for a washed-up baseball player. I bet if you showed off that caring side, you could find someone, too."

He laughs. "Nah, when you get to my age, women don't care that you can still bench two-hundred fifty pounds. They want to know why you haven't settled down yet."

"I'm sure they'll understand once they get to know your winning personality," I joke.

"Oh, piss off before I make a move on your girl!" he retorts. "Get some rest before we head out on the road, okay?"

With a one-finger salute, I bid him farewell.

Chapter Forty-Three

• KENT •

After a grueling session with Zach – both physically and mentally – I shower in the locker room. I could go back to my condo, but my mind is still a jumbled mess. I'm not ready to face a bathroom full of Raven's products – an idea courtesy of Lola, who was not pleased about being left out of the group chat.

While drying off, I check my chat with Robby, Miller, Leo, and Georgie. It's mostly filled with Georgie and Robby fighting over who will be the Godfather of Lola and Miller's baby. I should chime in and tell them it's Miller's brother, but watching them duke it out is entertaining.

I reluctantly open my thread with Molly. I'm sure it's filled with pleas to call her back. The latest text does instruct me to call her, but it also includes a video with the caption, 'You need to see this.'

The camera POV is a live feed of a wedding chapel, showing the tail end of two strangers leaving hand in hand. I'm about to click out of it when two new figures enter the frame.

I instantly recognize Raven and me. We walk down the aisle in front of the officiant. We must be mic'd up because our voices are loud and clear.

"Did you text the stream link to your friends?" the man asks.

"Nah, it's going to be a surprise," I state.

"Are you sure we should do this? I'm pretty sure we can lie and tell people we're newlyweds to get the newlywed special at the diner," Raven insists.

"No way. Being married will be way more fun."

"But to each other?" she asks.

"Why not? You're hot. I'm hot. And I've thought about you every day since I met you. If we spend the days together, I won't have to think about you anymore because you'll be right there. And we can repeat last night every night."

"I don't think that's a good enough reason. You might stop wanting me once you have me. I don't want you to regret me."

"I'd never regret you, Firefly. You're perfect! You know you want to marry me. I'll buy you a house, and you can decorate it however you want. I'll give you everything you ever wanted."

"Including unlimited Diet Coke," she negotiates.

"Including unlimited Diet Coke," I agree.

"And you have to pinky promise you won't be mad at me when we wake up married." Raven sticks out her pinky for me to link. I do, kissing our joined hands for good measure.

"Alright preach, let's do this! I came to Vegas, and all I'm leaving with is a wife!" I shout.

The rest of the ceremony is fairly standard, aside from DIY vows that are too much to process right now. I witness the exchanging of rings we saw in the pictures and me giving Raven a filthy kiss that makes the organist blushes.

I'm about to click out of the video when our voices sound again. We aren't in the frame, but we are still mic'd.

"Do you think we'll be happy? After you freak out, I mean," she asks.

"I'm not going to freak out! I'll make you the happiest wife in the world, Firefly. But we can wish for a good marriage in the fountain if you want."

"We don't have any coins. You left your wallet in the room. That's why we need the free newlywed breakfast, remember?"

"Right," I reply, as if that makes perfect sense. "What if we toss the rings in? They're coins with holes in them. I'm sure it will work."

"Okay! Let's go. I'm thirsty and want to cash in on my wedding present now."

"Whatever the wifey wants, the wifey gets."

When the video stops, I sit in stunned silence. Fuck. Not only was getting married my idea, but I did it because I was too drunk to go back to the room and get my wallet or order room service. And I decided we should throw our rings in the fountain. I am such a dumb-ass. Raven gave me plenty of chances to stop it. Even in her drunken state, she was worried I'd regret it. Regret her.

Hindsight being twenty-twenty, she wasn't wrong. I did freak out. I was an absolute jerk to her over something that was my idea. Drunk me wasn't afraid of being married; maybe sober me shouldn't be either. There is no one I'd rather be married to than Raven. At this point, I'd take being her errand boy. I know I have major groveling in my future. This video gave me the perfect idea of how to show Raven how sorry I am and how serious I am about us. Now, I just need help to pull it off.

There is only one person who can help me make this plan work. Pulling up our thread, I send her a message.

2:34 PM

ME

Hi.

TIFFY

I'm mad at you. How am I supposed to believe there are nice guys in the world when the best one I know acts like a colossal douche nozzle?

ME

I know. I'm sorry. I was a jerk.

TIFFY

A douche nozzle.

ME

Fine, a douche nozzle.

But I've seen the error of my ways and want to fix it. Will you help me?

TIFFY

Why should I?

ME

Because you love me? And because I can help you with your problem.

TIFFY

Who says I have a problem?

ME

Sure, we won't admit it's a problem. But I can help you get revenge on the Puerto Rican Papi who is definitely not causing you any problems.

TIFFY

How?

ME

Meet me at the coffee place to talk? I'll buy you one of those scones you like.

TIFFY

And a large latte?

ME

The largest.

TIFFY

Be there in twenty.

Chapter Forty-Four

• RAVEN •

September

Labor Day Weekend has come and gone, which means tonight is the premiere of my show on HRN! Everyone stayed in town this weekend instead of going to Miami. Between my show airing and Baby Miller's early entrance into the world, it has been a whirlwind of activity.

I tried to tell everyone I was fine to watch the show at my place or even Carina's, but they demanded we go all out. I think that's what they're doing. They haven't told me all the details. All Tiffany said was that she would be by my house at four to help me finish getting ready, and then we were going to the screening they planned.

At 4:07, because being on time isn't her strong suit, Tiffany is knocking on my door.

"Ray!" she shouts when I let her inside, smothering me with a hug. "It's premiere day!"

"Hi, Tiff. Yes, it is!"

"Are you nervous?"

"Considering, I want to throw up, and I've barely been able to eat, you could say that."

"It's going to be amazing. I know it. I've told everyone I know to tune in, and you know that's a lot of people."

"Thank you," I say.

"Are your parents going to watch?"

"Yep, they have the whole extended family coming over to watch together. Their party may be bigger than whatever you have planned."

"Please," she scoffs. "Don't underestimate Carina and I. We are event planning queens. You should have seen the apartment parties we had in college. You'd be surprised what we could pull off."

"Nothing you two do surprises me," I deadpan.

"Smart girl," she snorts. "Okay, let's accentuate the beauty that is your face. I've brought the perfect lip color for you."

Once Tiffany is pleased with the state of my makeup and hair, she ushers me into her car, and we are out the door.

"Do I get to know what we're doing yet?"

"Nope. Stop worrying, you're going to break your bracelets, and then I'll have crystals everywhere, interfering with my energy. Take a breath. We're almost there."

True to her word, we arrive minutes later. Tiffany pulls up to a house in East Nashville that is decked out with a red carpet, back-drop, and balloon arch. I see several familiar people mulling around in the front yard.

"Tiffany!" I say, shocked. "This is too much."

"It is not. This is your premiere, and it should be treated as one."

"How did you pull all this off?"

"We had some help." The gleam in her eyes makes me too nervous to ask who or what. Since I have enough to deal with today without her schemes, I let it go for now.

Walking through the front door, I barely have time to admire the architecture before I am nearly bowled over by Carina. She tells me how excited she is for me and how she knows it is going to be the most successful renovation show of all time. Robby, who popped up behind her, congratulates me and gives me a sad smile. The exact smile you would expect to get from your ex's friend. Thanks to my promotional schedule, I haven't had any time to spend with the group but I'm sure by now everyone knows.

Now that the dust has settled on the whole marriage thing, I expected to hear from Kent. I know I broke up with him, but I thought he might fight for me. Or at least tell me if he wants an annulment or divorce. But instead, he's said nothing. With goodbye screaming in the silence, I am letting his actions speak and leaving him be.

A month ago, I wanted nothing more than to have him here by my side. He spent countless nights listening to me debate over design choices. He talked me down from the ledge more than once over paint colors and even let me cry on his shoulder when I had a PMS-fueled meltdown over delayed cabinetry. I thought he would be here.

He isn't, though. Because we want different things and as I said many months ago, I'm not the girl who gets the guy to commit when he doesn't want to. I was never destined to have my 'you are my exception' moment. And that's fine. I don't need him here to celebrate all my hard work.

Surveying the room, it is filled to the brim with friends and clients who are all happy for me. I spot Marc talking to Charlie in the corner and the McMahans chatting with Ellie and Jack. Dr. Michaels, the dentist whose office I renovated, is flirting up a storm with Melanie, whose bakery I redid. That's an interesting match. All these people came to support me. And that is enough. It has to be.

After mingling and munching on food from my favorite local restaurants and pastries from the bakery I renovated, everyone settles onto the velvet couches around the house. I don't know how Tiffany found this place, but it is gorgeous. It needs some TLC for sure, but the bones are great. I'm guessing it is an event space of some kind since it is empty aside from the rented furniture brought in for my viewing party.

After everyone is seated, Tiffany stands in the front and makes a speech. "It is almost that time, ladies and gentlemen! Before the show begins, I want to give the woman of the hour the chance to say a few words."

Walking to the front, I give Tiff a big hug before she walks to her spot between Carina and Georgie.

"I am not usually one to make speeches," I confess. "But I have a lot of people to thank. I want to say how grateful I am that all of you are here. It means the world to me that you want to help me celebrate the launch of *Music City Revitalized*.

"Though the show itself was a recent dream, helping local small businesses thrive has been in my heart for a long time. To my clients, both on the show and not, thank you for allowing me to renovate your space. It isn't lost on me that you trusted a relative newbie in commercial renovations with your businesses.

"To my friends who were with me on this journey, your unwavering support means more to me than you can ever know. Without you, this show, and my career wouldn't be possible.

"Even if we're the only people who tune in, I consider this experience a success. It brought so many wonderful people to my life and started me on a path to making my career dreams come true! Thank you again for coming. I hope you enjoy it!"

With my message relayed, I take my seat and watch the premiere with everyone else. I have seen glimpses of the edits, but I haven't viewed the finished product in its entirety. My heart fills with joy as I watch the McMahan's studio transform on screen. The time and attention to detail put into editing the weeks-long renovation process into forty-four minutes is incredible.

The room erupts in claps and cheers when the episode ends. Choked with emotion, I bow my head and soak in the praise. I make a point to reiterate my thanks to everyone who attended tonight's party, especially those featured on the show.

When the last person leaves, I plop down on one of the couches, only to be joined by Tiffany. "I'm proud of you, Ray. The show was amazing."

"You think? You can be honest. You won't hurt my feelings... much."

She laughs at my candor. "I mean it. Your designs are obviously incredible, but you come off as knowledgeable and fun. While I was watching, I kept thinking, 'damn, I want to be friends with that girl,' only to remember that I already am!"

"You're the best, Tiff. Thank you for tonight. It went beyond my expectations. You made it a truly memorable evening."

"Don't thank me yet. It isn't over. There is one more thing for you to watch. I'll leave you to it, but call me if you need me."

"Call you? Are you going somewh—" My question hangs in the air as the screen lights up and Taylor Swift's "Timeless" plays.

My eyes widen when I realize what I'm watching. It's Kent and I. Dozens of videos and pictures of us before and after we got together. Spliced in are clips from what I have to assume is our wedding. The music fades, and the sound of Kent's voice fills the room as he recites his vows.

"Firefly, since the moment I saw you, I wanted you. I know my reputation is shit, but sometimes when I look into your eyes, I pretend you're mine. You see through all the playboy bullshit to the guy underneath. I don't fully know who that guy is, but I know I want to be him so you'll keep looking at me as you are now.

"I've never been a husband before, and I'll probably be bad at it, but I promise to stick around no matter what. I promise to hold your hand on flights and befriend your grumpy cat. I promise to make you laugh and roll your eyes. I promise to make your dreams come true and to let you fill our house with pretty things.

"I've never wanted anyone the way I want you. If we're going to get married one day, it might as well be today when the dude's already here. Since I only want to do this once, I promise to make being my wife so incredible you'll never want to leave. You are the best prize I've ever won."

When it's over, the screen freezes on a still of us leaving the chapel. I'm smiling beaming, Kent is staring at me with an expression of awe, reverence, and, if I didn't know better, love.

I press my hand to my mouth to keep in the bubbling laugh at how ridiculous and sincere those vows were. I can only imagine what I said in my inebriated state.

"He may be drunk, but he's right. We were inevitable," a voice says from behind me. Turning, I see Kent staring at the screen before his gaze travels down to me. "Hey, Firefly."

Chapter Forty-Five

I spend all night watching Raven flit through the party that Tiffany helped me plan from one of the side rooms. I'm a little worried it's giving me a stalker kink. Seeing her smile and laugh is exhilarating. I didn't realize how much I missed that sound until met with it again.

Once I accepted I was an idiot, I went into full grovel mode. Sure, I could have gone to Raven on day one and begged her to take me back. But after what a jerk I was, I wouldn't take me back. That day in Molly's office, Raven said that every move forward in our relationship was made by me. And thinking back, that's true. She always respected my boundaries, and yet I still met her with suspicion and doubt.

I spent the last several weeks meticulously planning a grand gesture worthy of Raven. I watched *He's Just Not That Into You* four times to make sure I got rid of all my red flags. I'm ready to be the Alex to her Gigi.

As she watches the video I made, my nerves skyrocket. I have a lot to say, but first, she needs to hear from this version of me. The version that was ready to jump into a relationship with feet first, no fear. When the clip is over, I make my presence known. "He may be drunk, but he's right. We were inevitable."

Raven whips around so fast I'm afraid she might fall over.

"Hi, Firefly." I greet. I take a moment to soak in her presence. Having her eyes on me is that first gulp of air after surfacing from the water. It's a cool breeze during a sweltering game or that sip of Gatorade after an intense run. It's invigorating and grounding all at once.

"What are you doing here?" she asks.

"You didn't think I'd miss your big night, did you?" Her apprehensive expression says that is exactly what she thought and I don't blame her.

"What kind of husband would I be if I didn't celebrate with you?" I walk until I am standing directly in front of her. Being this close and not touching her is pure torture, but I need to get through what I have to say first. If I touch her, I'm not sure I'll be able to stop.

I can tell she has a snarky response to my question, so I move on to my speech before she can say anything. "Raven, I've done a lot of stupid things in my life, but none as dumb as letting my fears and baggage overshadow the incredible relationship we were building. Not letting you know the place I wanted in your life is one of my greatest mistakes.

"You were right when you broke up with me. You deserve someone who sees a future with you. You deserve drunk Kent. He knew how to treat you before sober me did. You've never given me a reason to doubt your devotion, and it's time I strive to do the same."

"Kent," she sighs.

"Hear me out. I know I ran away at the first sign of trouble, but that was a lapse in judgment I won't make again. Everything came at me so fast that my fight or flight kicked in. Turns out I fight and fly."

Flexing my hands, I make my confession. "I want you. I want to be with you. Now and forever."

"If you feel that way, why did you wait until everyone left to make your declaration? Why not do it in front of everyone or better yet, before tonight? You left me stewing for weeks?"

"Tonight was about you," I say. "I didn't want to overshadow your premiere by hijacking it with my issues. You deserved all the attention to be on you. I wanted to prove to you I could be invested in this and I was afraid you wouldn't come to the party if you knew I helped with it."

"You did?" she asks, spinning around as if she will be able to tell what aspects I had a hand in.

"I did. I provided the venue."

"You provided—what? This isn't your house. We aren't near the lake. Isn't that where your other house is?"

"It is. Or it was. I put the deed into Mom's name now that I finally convinced her to move down here."

"I thought she wouldn't come until you settled down."

I nod, waiting for her to understand the meaning behind that. Some things are clicking in her mind, but I can tell not everything is sinking in.

"*This* is my new house. Technically it's your new house, but I'm hoping you'll let me move in with you."

"This is... mine? You rented this house for me?"

"Not rented, baby. Bought."

Her eyes widen. "You bought this house?"

Shit. Panic creeps in as I wonder if I did something wrong. "Is this not the kind you wanted? You said a Victorian in Historic Edgefield you could fix up. I know it's not a total disaster, but there is plenty that needs to be done.

"Robby and Miller bought places a few blocks away so you girls could be close, but if we need to find a different house, they can get over it. Ooof!"

All the air leaves my lungs as she slams her body into mine and wraps her arms around me. "I can't believe you remembered that."

Leaning back, I give in to my urge to touch her and sweep a lock of hair out of her face, tucking it behind her ear. "Of course, I remember. I don't know if you heard those vows, but I promised to make your dreams come true. Plus, I didn't play you the part where I offered to buy you a house if you agreed to marry me."

"Geez, I'm a pricey bride."

"You have no idea. Still the best prize I ever won, though."

I kiss her forehead before revealing the other part of her dowry demand. "You also required unlimited Diet Coke."

"That sounds about right," she says with a smile.

Turning the tone back to serious for a second, I make a final vow. "I know I messed up. I know I broke my promises. But now that I remember or at least was reminded, I swear to spend every day upholding those vows and to prove I am worth loving."

"You already have," she blubbers with watery eyes.

"Oh, baby, don't cry," I croon.

"I can't help it. You bought me a house! And you love me."

"I did. And I do," I say with a grin.

"I love you, too."

Her confession pulls at my last thread of self-control. Gripping the back of her neck, I pull her face up to mine and smash my lips into hers. The kiss is filled with love and longing and all the pent-up emotions we've been holding onto for the last month. When my lungs demand air, I pull back and stare down at her lust-filled gaze.

"Want a tour?" I pant between pecks.

"Yes," she quickly agrees.

Raven lets out a squeak when I hoist her up my body, forcing her legs to wrap around my waist.

"I can walk," she giggles, and God, it's good to be the reason for that sound again.

"And I can carry you. Wouldn't want you to get lost."

"We can't have that," she sasses.

I swat her ass. "Don't get smart with me, babe. At least not until we get to the bedroom."

"Is that next on the tour?" she questions hopefully.

"Not yet, I want you to see the house. There weren't a ton of options on the market, but this one had a lot of features similar to the houses on your Pinterest."

"You stalked my Pinterest? Sneaky man."

With her in my arms, I walk through the first floor discussing the various rooms and answering her questions as best I can.

"What's that?" she asks when we're upstairs. Following her gaze, I see it on the structure outside.

"That's the carriage house, They were using it as a workshop, but it is run with electrical and plumbing. I thought you could turn it into an office and you can meet with clients there without having to bring them in the house."

"You thought of everything, didn't you?"

"I tried to." I can feel the tips of my ears turning red.

"Did you think of where we were going to christen our new home?"

Walking past several guest rooms and an alcove that would make a perfect reading nook, I stop in front of a door at the end of the hall. Kicking it open, we are immediately basked in warm light from the salt lamp I plugged in for ambiance. I wasn't going to risk unattended candles burning down my wedding/grovel present.

"Considering the floors are original and need a solid pass from a sander, I thought a bed would be the smartest choice." Her body bounces when I drop her on the mattress I set up earlier today. I didn't bring it here for this, but I thought we might want to spend the night in our new house if she forgave me. Not that I'm complaining about the direction this evening has taken.

Ripping my shirt over my head, I ask, "Do you want to know my favorite thing about the house?"

"What?" she replies, chest heaving as she tries to work her dress up her body. I force her backward when I place an arm on either side of her. I let my head drop until my mouth is level with her ear and my nose can graze her cheek.

"My favorite part is that no matter how loud you scream, none of the neighbors will hear. Care to test that?"

Biting her lip, she nods. As my hands drift to remove her dress, she teases me.

"You know, husband, you've only lived up to half of your side of the bargain."

"Oh yeah? What did I forget?"

"Where's my Diet Coke?"

"I'll put in a soda machine in the basement. Say it again."

"Diet Coke?"

"No. Husband."

"You like hearing me call you husband?"

"Fuck yes, I do, wife. It's time I show you one of the many benefits of being Mrs. Dela Cruz."

Epilogue

• RAVEN •

November

After the first night in our house, I offered to go through with the divorce so we could remarry when he was ready, but Kent refused. He said he got it right the first time, and there was no reason to go through the legal process twice. But we did agree to have a renewal for family and friends. I'm not sure if you can call it a renewal when you don't remember the first wedding, but we keep that detail mostly to ourselves.

The last few months have been a whirlwind. While Kent and the rest of the Songbirds hammered away for the end of the season and the playoffs, I worked on renovating our East Nashville house. Kent decided to keep his condo and rent it out to Leo and any other players who are called up and don't have their "big boy" salaries yet.

The house Kent bought us has been utter perfection. It has all the amazing Victorian charm I could dream of, but with an MLB player budget to buy the best fixtures and furniture. The appliances are a chef's dream. Kent was so appreciative when he came home and saw the fancy kitchen appliances that he thanked me right on top of the new butcher block island. Who knew a six-burner stove would earn a girl multiple orgasms?

I have been rushing around all day getting ready for tonight's festivities: a housewarming party. Since the boys were busy winning the World Series. Tonight, we are throwing a party to celebrate the win, finally having a single home base, and my show getting picked up in a three-season deal.

I told Kent we could make it a birthday celebration for me as well since they were deep in the postseason, but he wouldn't allow it. We were in Austin on my birthday, and despite having a game the next day, he played tourist with me as we traipsed around the city. It's a cool place. If I wasn't settled in Nashville, I might consider a move.

Our housewarming party is Halloween-themed since we didn't get to celebrate that either. As I put the finishing touches on the mantel and check the dip in the Crock-Pot, the doorbell rings, signaling Tiffany's arrival. While she sets up in the bathroom, I seek out Kent. It's impossible to hold in my laughter when I find him on the screened-in porch hanging fairy lights with Cappy sitting directly beside him on the cat shelves he installed. It appears as if my cat is overseeing the process, and I have to snap a pic to memorialize the best buddies working.

Hearing my snicker, Kent peers over his shoulder to greet me. "Hey, wifey. See something you like?"

"Yeah, two of the most ridiculous men I have ever met."

He mock gasps. "Did you hear how she talked about us, Captain? And while we're out here doing her bidding? Unbelievable."

I can't help but roll my eyes. "Tiff is here. We'll be in the bathroom getting ready. Your costume is laid out on the guest bed."

"And is this your costume?" he questions as he waltzes over to me and plants his hands on my hips.

I wouldn't tell Kent what I plan to be for Halloween, and it has been driving him crazy. He, honest to God, pouted all last weekend when I announced it arrived, but he wasn't allowed to peek.

As excited as I am for Kent to see my costume, I am most excited to see little Leona's. Due to some complications, Lola had her baby a few weeks early. Leona, named after her grandmother, is the cutest baby I have ever seen, aside from my niece and nephew. The newborn smell has given us all baby fever, but no one more than Carina. I doubt it will be long before Leona has a cousin.

While she already had a proper Halloween, Lola and Miller are going to bring her to the party to show her off. Miller's mom will take her home, giving them their first night out. I know Lola is nervous, but their new house is only a five-minute walk away. She can sneak out to check on her if she needs to.

"Ray!" I hear Tiffany yell from inside right as Kent presses his lips to mine and wraps his hands around my ass cheeks. "Let's get this show on the road. I need to touch up my hair before everyone arrives."

"I've been summoned," I say as he hangs his head and groans against my shoulder.

"Buck up, Big Shot. You're that much closer to finally seeing me in my costume."

"Fine," he grouses. "It better be worth it."

I shoot him a wink as I saunter inside.

• KENT •

Our house slowly fills with my friends and teammates as I fiddle with the headband displaying my cat ears. I may not know Raven's costume, but she doesn't know mine, either. I was hoping she'd want to do a couple's costume, but she insisted she and the girls already had something planned and promised we could match next year. I was grumbly about it at first, but she quickly turned my frown upside down by going upside down on me while she sat on my face. All-in-all, a productive conversation.

This is the first time I have seen most of my teammates since the parade after we won the series. Though rewarding, the postseason was grueling for us all, and after the initial celebrations, hunkering down with our loved ones was what we all needed. Moving wasn't the most peaceful break, but having all our stuff in one place has been amazing.

I still can't believe Raven and I are married. I obviously saw the tape, but not remembering something that monumental sucks. I know she's bummed her family wasn't there. Now that it's the off-season, we're planning a renewal ceremony and reception to honor the commitment – and to party – as we should.

As I wonder where Raven is, I am distracted by voices behind me. "What the hell are you supposed to be?" Leo asks. I turn to face him, giving him the full effect of my attire. The behemoth of a catcher laughs so hard he bowls over. "Holy shit. Has Robby seen you?"

"I don't think he's here yet," I respond.

"They got here a few minutes ago," Macy snickers beside him. "I saw Carina run upstairs to come down in costume with Tiff and Ray."

"Please, please, please, let me be here when he finds you," Leo says.

"What are you two supposed to be?" I ask as we wait.

"She's Marty McFly, and I'm Doc Brown, duh," he responded. I shift my gaze to Macy, who shakes her head.

"He insisted we do a couple's costume and fighting him was useless. Since I didn't care, I let him pick."

"Rookie mistake," I mumble.

She sighs. "He and his brother always fought over who got to be Doc Brown. Here we are."

"What's going on over here? Nice party, Ke—what exactly are you supposed to be?" Robby bellows.

"I think you know," I taunt, picking up my cat tail and swishing it at him.

"You better say fucking Cappy," he snarls.

"Is that any way to talk to your Kitten?" I ask innocently.

"Oh my God!" A feminine voice laughs from behind me. "This is incredible," Carina exclaims. Robby snorts in derision.

"I'm glad someone appreciates it," I mock pout. "You make a gorgeous Belle, Care."

"Thank you! Tiffany is Cinderella, and Lola is Snow White."

"What does that make Raven?" I ask.

"See for yourself, Big Shot," my wife whispers in my ear.

When I turn around my jaw hit the floor. Raven has on a hip-hugging sequin skirt with a slit high up the thigh. Her top is a shiny, purple halter wrap showcasing her ample cleavage. Long red hair falls in waves down her front and is accentuated by a starfish pinned to one side. She is the sexiest Ariel I have ever seen. If thirteen-year-old me could see where I am now – hours away from fulfilling our biggest fantasy – he would be fist pumping.

Instead of commenting on how gorgeous she is, I remain frozen like a dumbass choking on my tongue.

"Speechless isn't the reaction I expected, but I'm not disappointed," she teases.

My eyes shoot up to meet hers after scanning every inch of her again. "Firefly, you look... wow. You're a goddess."

"Princess, actually, but thanks. We're going to grab a drink. Meet you on the dance floor later."

I watch her saunter away, eyes glued to her ass. Fuck it's a great ass. That outfit is incredible. Finally shaking myself out of my admiration, I get a glimpse of Robby smirking at me. "What?" I demand.

"Nothing," he says over his beer, taking a swig. "I think Raven got my payback for me and your stupid costume."

"How do you figure?"

"You have to spend the rest of the night with every single man's eyes on your girl. Even some guys who came with dates can't look away."

"Psshh. Unlike you, I am not a caveman. I don't care if every man in the world is staring at Raven. I know who she's going home with. And this Prince Eric can't wait to show her a whole new world."

"That isn't even the right movie," Robby jeers.

"Yeah, but *A Part of Your World* didn't make as funny of a pun."

"I think this conversation is making me dumber," he mutters. "Let's catch up with the girls. This beast wants his babe."

When we find them, all four girls are huddled around baby Leona. Miller watches his wife and child like the proud Papa Bear we've always joked he was. Fatherhood suits him and almost makes me wonder if it would agree with me, too. I know my mom would be thrilled.

The thoughts swirling in my head would send Kent from a year ago into a panic. But I realize now nothing is too scary to face with Raven by my side. I watch her coo at Leona. Yeah, I'm putting a baby in that girl. And until she's ready, I'm going to enjoy practicing.

• The End •

Want more Kent and Raven? Visit katsummerwrites.com to access to Songbirds' bonus scenes. You'll also see Kent again in Zealous Intentions which you can preorder now and get a preview of in the Once Upon a Valentine's Anthology.

If you enjoyed this book, please leave a rating or review. They help more than you know!

Acknowledgements

I cannot believe this is my third book! Kent and Raven really tested me but at the end of the day, I am happy their story made it out in the world. Somedays I wasn't sure it would.

Which leads to a special thanks to Maria and Bobbi for helping me craft Kent into a man I could love despite being a Miller girlie for life. And Maria's reminder that annoying problems like finding a place to park still exist even in romance novels.

Working on this story with encouragement of my baddie brothers made this experience so much more than past processes. Thank you, Addey, Ana, Bobbi, Dany, Hailey, Karley, Maria, Mollie, and Sarah!

Big thanks to my beta readers for helping me polish this story and loving my characters as much (sometimes more than) me. Elle, Emily, Jesse, Kristy, and Regan, y'all are real ones.

As always, I couldn't have done this without my wonderful editor, Emma, from EJL Editing. She not only cleans up my work but also engages in philosophical discussions about cum vs come on Wednesday afternoons.

Thank you @BookedForeverShop for creating a cover that matched my vision yet somehow managed to blow me away.

Shout out to Elsie Silver's Daddy Cade for inspiring me to rev up the spice content in this book.

Last but not least, thank YOU for reading this book. Without readers, I would just be yelling stories into the forest.

– Kat

Also by Kat Summers

Want more Nashville Songbirds?

Check out the other books in the series: Behind in the Count and Stepping Up to the Plate .

Read bonus scenes from your favorite Songbirds couples by visiting bit.ly/ katsummersbonus and signing up for my newsletter!

Along with more Songbirds novels, Kat has a few surprise releases and a new series planned for this year. Country rockstars, anybody?Get updates on upcoming projects through my newsletter, by following me on social media (@katsummerswrites), or on my Amazon author page.

About the Author

Kat Summers is a millennial spicy, contemporary romance author living in Tennessee. Her books are filled with just enough angst to hurt your feelings, witty banter to make you laugh, and steamy, swoon-worthy men to make you blush. She creates stories with strong, sassy heroines who can hold their own but love being called a "good girl."

Kat has had a love for reading and writing her entire life. After consuming what some would call way too many romance books, she decided to take the stories she told herself to fall asleep and put them on paper.

When she isn't writing, she can be found reading (duh) and spending time with her family and furbaby or gossiping over Mexican food. Fueled by Diet Dr Pepper and a dream, Kat is excited to bring the couples that live in her mind to the rest of the world. Follow her for sneak peeks of future projects.

Find her at @katsummerswrites on all the things.